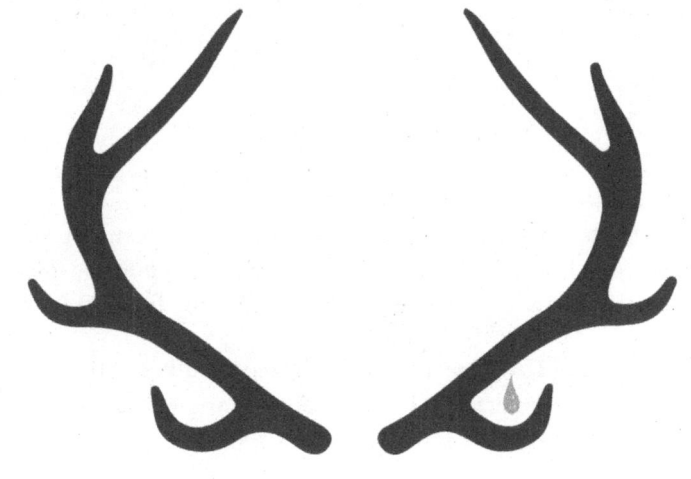

S.T.A.G.S.

M. A. BENNETT

HOT
KEY
BOOKS

First published in Great Britain in 2017 by
HOT KEY BOOKS
80–81 Wimpole St, London W1G 9RE
www.hotkeybooks.com

A CIP catalogue record for this book is available from the British Library.

ISBN: 978-1-4714-0676-8
also available as an ebook

6

This book is typeset using Atomik ePublisher
Printed and bound in Great Britain by Clays Ltd, Elcograf S.p.A.

Hot Key Books is an imprint of Bonnier Books UK
www.bonnierbooks.co.uk

*To Conrad and Ruby, who are Medieval
and Savage in the right places*

'Trace the deer to its lair'
Master of Game – Edward of Norwich, 1373

S.T.A.G.S.

(I)

chapter one

I think I might be a murderer.

Although, as I didn't mean to kill, I suppose it was manslaughter, so technically I would be a 'manslaughterer', although I don't think that's a word. When I got my scholarship to STAGS, my old headmistress told me, 'You'll be the cleverest student in that school, Greer MacDonald.' I might be, I might not. But I'm clever enough to know that manslaughterer is not a word.

I should make it clear here, before you lose all sympathy for me, that I didn't kill with my own hands. There were a few of us. I helped to *cause* a death, but not alone. I'm a murderer in the way that foxhunters are murderers – they are each responsible for the fox's death, even though they hunt in a pack. No one ever knows which dog tore the fox apart, but all the dogs, and all those riders in their smart red coats, are part of it.

I just gave myself away. Did you spot it? Those coats – the coats that posh people wear out foxhunting – they are pink, not red; hunting pink. And the dogs are not dogs, they are hounds.

Every time I open my mouth I give myself away; Greer MacDonald, the Girl Who Doesn't Fit In. It's my northern accent, you see. I was born and raised in Manchester and went to Bewley Park Comprehensive School until this summer. In both those places I fitted in just fine. When I won my scholarship to STAGS I stopped fitting in.

I ought to tell you a bit about STAGS, because I now realise how connected the school is to the murder. STAGS stands for St Aidan the Great School and it is *literally* the oldest school in England. Not a single building in my comprehensive school, Bewley Park, was built before 1980. The earliest bit of STAGS, the chapel, was built back in 683, and it is covered in frescoes. *Frescoes*. Bewley Park was covered in graffiti.

STAGS was founded in the seventh century by the man himself: St Aidan the Great, I mean. Before the Church decided he was Great, he was just a plain old monk, and wandered around northern England telling anyone who would listen about Christianity. Then, presumably so he could stop wandering, he founded a school, where he told his pupils all about Christianity instead. You might assume that he'd been made a saint for all that telling people about Christianity, but apparently that's not how it works. In order to become a saint, you have to perform a miracle. Aidan's miracle was that he saved a stag from the hunt by turning him invisible. So the stag became Aidan's emblem, and the school's too. When I got my letter calling me for interview, the stag's antlers were the first thing I noticed, right at the top of the letter, like two little jagged black tears in the paper.

The first time I saw St Aidan the Great School was when I went for my interview. It was one of those sunny midwinter days, all glittering frosty fields and long, low shadows. Dad drove

4

me through the gates and up this long driveway through lush green grounds in his ten-year-old Mini Cooper. At the end of the drive we got out and just stared and stared. We'd seen some pretty amazing scenery on the long trip from Manchester to Northumberland, but this was the best of all. It was a beautiful, vast medieval manor house, with a sort of moat and a little bridge to the entrance. It didn't look at all like the headquarters of a disturbing cult, which is what it actually is. The only clue, if I'd been looking for it, might have been the pair of antlers over the great door.

'*Another Country*,' I said shakily.

Dad didn't nod, or murmur, 'You can say that again.' He said, '*If.*'

My dad is a wildlife cameraman, and he loves films of all kinds, not just the nature documentaries that he mostly works on. We watch loads of films together, from obscure subtitled films to the stupidest brand-new blockbusters. I'm even named after Greer Garson, a film star from the black-and-white days. When Dad's travelling, or on night shoots, I watch films on my own, just to make up for the thirty-year head start he has on me. We have this game that we play; when something we see reminds us of a film, we say it out loud, and the other person has to name another film on the same theme. Now we were doing films featuring private schools. 'And,' he said, '*Zéro de Conduite.*'

'*Oh là là*' I said, 'a *French* film. The gloves are off.' I thought hard. '*Harry Potter*, films one to eight,' I said, a bit shakily. 'That's eight points.'

Dad could obviously hear the nerves in my voice. He knows

so many films he could have beaten me easily, but he must have decided that today wasn't the day. 'All right,' he said, giving me his lopsided grin. 'You win.' He looked up at the grand entrance, and the antlers over the door. 'Let's get this over with.'

And we did. I had the interview, I did the exam, I got in. And eight months later, at the beginning of autumn term, I was walking through the entrance of the school, under the antlers, as a sixth-form student.

I was soon to learn that antlers are, appropriately, a big thing at STAGS. Antlers bristle from every wall. There is also a stag on the school emblem, with the words *'Festina Lente'* embroidered underneath. (No, I didn't know either; it's Latin and it means 'Make Haste Slowly'.) In the chapel those frescoes that I mentioned show scenes from the 'miraculous' stag hunt, when St Aidan turned the stag invisible. There is also a really old stained-glass window in the chapel, of him holding one finger up in front of the face of a nervous-looking stag, as if he is trying to shush it. I've stared at those frescoes and that window a lot, because we have to go to chapel every morning, which is pretty boring.

As well as being boring, chapel is freezing cold. It's the only time I am glad to be wearing the STAGS uniform. The uniform consists of a long black Tudor coat of thick felt, all the way down to your knees, with gilt buttons down the front. At the neck we wear a white clerical tie, and at the waist a slim deer-leather belt which has to be knotted in a particular way. Under the coat we wear bright red stockings, the colour of arterial blood. It is pretty dumb as outfits go, but at least it keeps you warm on the borders of Northumberland.

STAGS, as you might imagine, is pretty religious. Me and my dad are not religious at all, but we kind of left that fact off the application form. In fact, we may have given the distinct impression that we were churchgoers. That was back when I actually *wanted* to go to the school. Dad was going to be mostly abroad for two years, making a wildlife documentary for the BBC, and if I hadn't come to STAGS I would have had to go to live with my Aunty Karen, and *believe* me, I didn't want to do that. My headmistress at Bewley thought I had the brains to get a scholarship to STAGS and it turned out she was right. I also happen to have a photographic memory, which didn't hurt either. I can't tell you how useful it was when I was sitting that entrance exam. But if I'd known what was going to happen that autumn half-term, I wouldn't have been such a try-hard. I would have gone to my Aunty Karen's without a word.

Apart from the incessant chapel-going there are loads of other differences between STAGS and a normal school. For one thing, they call autumn term 'Michaelmas', spring term 'Hilary' and summer term 'Trinity'. For another, the teachers are called Friars, not 'Miss' or 'Sir'. So our form master, Mr Whiteread, is Friar Whiteread; and, even stranger, our housemistress (Miss Petrie) is Friar Petrie. The headmaster, a really friendly Santa Claus-looking bloke who I met at interview, is called the Abbot. If that wasn't odd enough, the Friars wear a weird gown like a monk's habit over their suits, with knotted ropes at the waist. A lot of the Friars are ex-pupils and keep going on about when they were at STAGS in their day (which, by the sounds of it, was *exactly* the same – STAGS is so antiquated I'd be surprised if a single thing had changed). The Friars are practically antiques themselves – I'd have to guess they're all in their sixties. There's no doubt that this gives them loads of teaching experience, but I've also got a sneaking suspicion that oldies were employed so that no one would ever, *ever* fancy any of them. There's absolutely no danger of any of those teacher–pupil relationships you read about online.

The sports are strange at STAGS as well; we don't play ordinary games like netball and hockey and football but things like fives and real tennis, in Tudor wooden courts out beyond the playing fields. Those playing fields, known as Bede's Piece, are immense, but are not used for anything standard like athletics, only for sports like rugby ('rugger') and lacrosse. STAGS has its own theatre, but it doesn't have any fancy lighting or sets; it's a faithful Jacobean replica playhouse lit by candles. *Candles*. Instead of German and French we study Latin and Greek. The food too is different from normal school food, in that it is really nice. Actually it's amazing – it's the sort you would get in a really good restaurant, not at all like the slop we used to get at Bewley Park. Meals are served by women from the local village, who seem perfectly nice but are rewarded with the nickname 'dinnerbags'. But the major difference between STAGS and a normal school is, as you might have guessed, that it costs an absolute fortune. The STAGS parents pay the fees willingly, and it didn't take me long to figure out what they are paying for. They are not paying for their little darlings to benefit from the Jacobean theatre, or the Olympic-sized swimming pool, or for the incredible, knock-your-eyes-out beauty of the place. What they are paying for is for their children to be different too.

For the first thousand years or so there were just four houses at STAGS: Honorius, Bede, Oswald and Paulinus. Then a few decades ago they started to admit girls, so they founded a new girls' house called Lightfoot. I was told in my admissions letter that the Lightfoot dormitories were in one of the more 'modern' buildings, and I arrived expecting lots of pine and glass and central heating. It turned out that the Lightfoot building was built in 1550, and was all diamond-paned windows and crazy spiral chimneys. At STAGS 1550 was evidently considered 'modern'.

My room was on the third floor at the end of a panelled Tudor passageway. Through an immense oak door, the room itself was modern. It had chipboard furniture, office-blue carpets and a girl already in it. The habit of thinking in films was a hard one to break. If my first encounter with my roommate was in a film script, it would look like this:

GREER (smiling): I'm Greer. What's your name?

Greer's roommate looks her up and down in a snotty way.

ROOMMATE (rolling her eyes): *Jesus.*

After that first encounter I always called her 'Jesus' to myself, because it made me smile, and there was little enough for me to smile about at STAGS. I found out later that her name was actually Becca. She was a horse-mad girl, who had pictures of her ponies on her wall like I had pictures of my dad. Maybe she missed them as much as I missed him. I didn't see how.

That's pretty much it for dialogue in this part of the story. There will be lots later, but the sad truth was no one talked to me much in that first half-term. Teachers asked me questions in lessons; the dinnerbags would say things like, 'Chips or mash, hinny?' (Their accents would make me homesick.) And Shafeen, this kid in my learning set, would occasionally murmur things at me like, 'The thermal stability of the nitrates follows the same trend as that of the carbonates.'

Despite sharing a room with me, Jesus did not talk to me until it was nearly half-term, and that was only because I got The Invitation. I now think that if I'd had more friends – or *any* friends – in that first half-term, I never would have accepted The Invitation. Maybe I accepted it because I was lonely. Or maybe, if I'm being honest, I accepted it because it came from the best-looking boy in the school.

chapter two

I mean, of course, Henry de Warlencourt.

You might have read about him online by now, on that creepy Facebook page they set up for him, or seen his picture on the news. But back then he wasn't famous – or infamous – outside of his own circle. They say you shouldn't speak ill of the dead so I'll just say you would never have known by looking at him what a terrible person he was.

I have to really struggle, now, to remember him as I first saw him; to be fair to that first impression, and try to forget what I know now. He was, quite simply, the most gorgeous boy I'd ever seen. Tall for seventeen, all blond hair, blue eyes and tanned skin. When people were around Henry de Warlencourt they watched him all the time, even though they pretended they weren't. Even the Friars seemed to be in awe of Henry. He never got punished for anything – and that's not because he didn't do anything wrong; it's because he got away with it. He was like one of those really cool frying pans that everything slides off. He thought he was invincible. But he wasn't.

Henry de Warlencourt was as British as they come, despite his foreign-sounding name. Apparently some distant ancestor had fought in the Frankish army on the Crusades, and had settled in England afterwards, conveniently marrying some noblewoman who owned half of northern England. The de Warlencourts had been fabulously rich ever since. Their house, Longcross Hall, is a beautiful manor house in the Lake District. I know it better than I ever would have wanted to, because Longcross was the scene of the crime.

Because I was in the top set for all my subjects I saw Henry de Warlencourt a lot; him and his five closest friends. The six of them were known as the Medievals. Everyone knew the Medievals, because it was the Medievals – not the Friars – who really ran STAGS.

The Medievals were the unofficial prefects of the school. You'd see them walking in the quad in their immaculate uniforms, long black coats fluttering in the autumn breeze. The Medievals were allowed to wear any colour stockings they wanted under their Tudor coats, and they emphasised this privilege by choosing crazy patterns like leopard print, or tartan, or chessboard checks. But it wasn't just the stockings that marked them out; it was a particular kind of confidence they had about them. They lolled about like expensive cats. That confidence, that comfort in their surroundings, told you that their houses were probably not that different to STAGS; that they probably had grounds too, rather than gardens, and houses with wings, instead of neighbours. And antlers too, houses with lots of antlers on the walls.

The Medievals were all tall, beautiful and clever, as if they were especially bred for the job. They held court in the Paulinus quad – a beautiful square of perfectly manicured grass, surrounded by four walkways of elegant arched cloisters, at the heart of Paulinus house.

Henry de Warlencourt was always at the centre of the group, his blond head visible, as if he was that king at Versailles, whichever one it was, one of those millions of Louis. Henry was the sun, and the rest revolved around him. They would hang out there in all weathers, talking, reading and, after dark, secretly smoking. There was a sort of ancient stone well in the middle of the quad, and if you ever got close enough to look down it, you could see that about a foot down a circle of chicken wire had been fixed for safety, and the chicken wire was stuffed with cigarette butts. I once dropped a coin through the holes, to see how deep it was. I listened for ages, but couldn't hear the splash of the coin hitting the water. I assumed that the bottom of the well was so full of fag butts that they were cushioning the coin's fall. The Paulinus well was just like the Medievals themselves. It looked pretty, but in its depths it was gross.

If Henry was the Medievals' leader, Cookson was his second-in command. Cookson was actually called Henry Cookson, but he was always known by his second name, as there could only be one Henry in the group. Cookson was good-looking too, as they all were, but he still looked like a bad photocopy of Henry. He was slightly smaller, slightly chubbier and his hair was a dirtier blond. His features were blunter, his skin paler, his voice more braying. But the two were inseparable, as close as the brothers they resembled.

The third boy in the group was Piers. Piers was elegant, and dark, and he had a monobrow that made him look like he was constantly annoyed. Piers added little details to his uniform, like a pocket watch, and a tooled leather belt instead of the regulation slim tan, and handmade shoes from his London bootmaker. Piers had been Henry's friend since they'd been shipped off to the junior bit of STAGS – the prep school – at the age of eight.

The three girls were pretty similar in appearance, all blonde-haired and blue-eyed. We'd been studying Homer in Greek that term and they reminded me of the Sirens: beautiful mermaids who looked gorgeous but would actually lure sailors to their deaths. Their names were Esme, Charlotte and Lara. They were all pretty, and slim, and they managed to make the strange ecclesiastical uniform look like something from the catwalks of Milan. Charlotte was some distant cousin of Henry's, Esme was minor royalty, and Lara, seemingly as British as the rest of them, was from a Russian family with an Oligarch-level fortune. They all had that hair that lifts at the hairline and falls over one eye, and they constantly flicked it from one side to the other as they talked. My hair (bobbed, black, heavy fringe) doesn't behave like that, but all the other girls at STAGS (including, tragically, my roommate Jesus) tried to copy their style. To begin with I made the mistake of mixing the Medieval girls up, dismissing them as all the same. If Dad was here to play our film game we'd be saying *Heathers* or *Mean Girls*, but those movies don't really do justice to the evil that lived behind the white smiles. They weren't dumb blondes, those girls, they were highly intelligent; you underestimated them at your peril, and that's exactly what I did.

All of the Medievals were incredibly rich – Henry's family had been coming here for centuries, and the school theatre was even called the De Warlencourt Playhouse. Lara's family, it was rumoured, paid for the pool. This made them behave as if they owned the place; because they kind of did.

There were only ever six Medievals, three boys and three girls from Six Two – the second year of sixth form. But beyond this hard core there were a whole bunch of hangers-on who idolised them, and did exactly what they wanted in the hope that in Six Two they would become Medievals themselves. Every year, six Medievals leave and a new pack is forged, so there are plenty of wannabes hanging around. Jesus is definitely one – she would die to be a Medieval.

All of the Medievals were OK individually; I was in a lot of their classes and they could be quite human. But when they were in a pack, like hounds, that's when you wanted to be invisible, like Aidan's stag. They mostly left me alone; occasionally the three girls would mimic my accent and snigger behind their hands once I'd walked past them in the quad. I'd feel like there was a cold stone of unhappiness lodged just below my ribs, and the feeling wouldn't subside until I'd gotten out of their eyeline. But I had it easy. Some people seemed to be in their crosshairs all the time. People like Shafeen.

The Medievals called Shafeen the Punjabi Playboy. He was tall and quiet, with a handsome, serious face and unreadable dark eyes. The nickname they had given him was wilfully inaccurate. For one thing, he was not from the Punjab at all. For another, he was painfully shy around girls, quite the opposite of a playboy. But that, of course, was what they found so funny. From the Medievals' perspective, if a nickname sounded good, and it made them laugh, it stuck. Shafeen was one of the only people who talked to me; we'd chosen the same subjects for A level, and we were in the top set, so we talked about our classes a bit. You could say he was the nearest thing I had to a friend that first term, but as he was in Honorius and I was in Lightfoot, he wasn't much comfort. I didn't know much about Shafeen at the beginning – of course, I know him now. (Guilt is quite a bond, I've discovered, and since Shafeen is a murderer too, we now have a very particular connection.) People said Shafeen was some sort of prince back in India, so you might have thought the Medievals would welcome him into their group. But they teased him mercilessly, and, as I found out later, their dislike of Shafeen came from some old quarrel that took place at STAGS about a million years ago, between Shafeen's father and Henry's. Shafeen too had been at STAGS since he was eight. He'd been all the way through the prep bit and the main school to the sixth form, as his parents were in India. But although Shafeen knew all the rules, and even spoke like the Medievals did, he somehow managed to be an outsider too.

I've asked myself many times why Shafeen accepted The Invitation when he knew what the Medievals thought about him. He can't *not* have known what they thought about him; they made it so public. Even in lessons Shafeen wasn't safe.

I heard one exchange in history that made me a bit scared for him.

We were in the Bede library, seated at our single desks in rows, with the weak autumn sun streaming through the stained-glass windows and brightening our black coats with multicoloured patches. We were studying the Crusades, a tussle between the Christians and the Muslims over the city of Jerusalem that started in 1095, when STAGS, unbelievably, was already four centuries old.

'Who can tell me about the Battle of Hattin?' asked Friar Skelton, our round and cheerful history professor. 'Mr de Warlencourt, one of your family was actually there, wasn't he?'

Henry smiled; the Medievals always took the trouble to be charming to the Friars. 'Yes, he was, Friar. Conrad de Warlencourt.'

Friar Skelton tossed a piece of chalk in one hand. 'Perhaps you could give us the family perspective.'

'Certainly,' said Henry. He sat a little straighter in his chair and I couldn't help thinking that in the black Tudor coat, with the sun striking his blond hair, he looked a bit like a young Crusader himself. ('Henry V,' said Dad in my head, *or maybe* Kingdom of Heaven.') 'The forces of Guy of Lusignan met the Sultan Saladin's forces at Hattin. The Christian army was already starving, and dying of thirst. Desperate for water, they were lured to Lake Tiberius, where they found their way blocked by the sultan's army. It was a trap.'

I could see, looking at the shuttered expression on his face, that it hurt him. Crazily, Henry de Warlencourt still minded what had happened to his ancestor all those years ago.

Friar Skelton hadn't seen it. 'Then what?' he asked cheerily, chalk poised in mid-air.

'They made a mess of us, Friar. The Crusader army was completely destroyed. The defeat led directly to the Third Crusade. The sultan took the True Cross and the city of Jerusalem too.'

I registered that 'us'. Henry really was taking this personally. 'The survivors were captured, but Saladin didn't want to be burdened with prisoners. His men begged to be allowed to kill the Christians. They were lining up to do it. With their sleeves already rolled up.' He jabbed his pen viciously on his writing pad. 'They only let my ancestor go on condition that he told Richard the Lionheart what had happened. And he did. It was a war crime, an atrocity.' His voice rang out around the old library.

Shafeen, sitting just beyond Henry, made a tiny sound. He shook his head and smiled ever so slightly. I was well placed to see it, because I was sitting just behind them all.

Henry shot him a look, his eyes suddenly very blue. But Friar Skelton beamed; he loved a debate. 'Got something to add, Mr Jadeja?'

Shafeen looked up. He cleared his throat. 'Yes, Hattin was an atrocity. But there were atrocities on *both* sides. The "Lionheart", as you call him, murdered three thousand Muslim prisoners at Acre in cold blood. *That* wasn't even in battle. *They* were unarmed, and tied up.'

'Good point,' said Friar Skelton, pointing his chalk at Shafeen. 'More of the events at Acre later. But for now –' he knocked on the blackboard, his gold signet ring making a sharp metallic sound – 'we must return to Hattin. I would like you to write a short essay about, and form some understanding of, how the topography of the area contributed to the Crusaders' rout. And please watch your punctuation, or I will be obliged to remind you, once again, that the sentence "Hannibal waged war, with elephants" does not convey the same meaning as the sentence "Hannibal waged war with elephants." He wrote both examples on the blackboard (there were no whiteboards at STAGS), making a huge deal of chalking in the comma. 'The former means that elephants were his war machines. The latter means that a great Carthaginian general was fighting a bunch of big-eared mastodons.' Normally we might have laughed – we all liked Friar Skelton – but today the atmosphere was too strained.

Friar Skelton turned away to rub his sentences off the board and replace them with a drawing of the horns of Hattin. Cookson saw his opportunity and leaned forward in his chair towards Shafeen. 'I suppose one of your ancestors was at Hattin too, eh, Punjabi?' he said out of the side of his mouth. 'On the camel-jockey side?'

Now, I knew nothing about Shafeen's religion, if he even had one, but what Cookson had done was to look at the colour of Shafeen's skin and place him firmly with Saladin and the 'infidels'. The message was clear: the Christian white boys against the Muslim brown.

Shafeen did not look at Cookson. He was doodling a black Crusader cross on his pad of lined paper, filling it in so firmly that his knuckles paled. I thought, irrelevantly, how long his eyelashes were in the stained-glass sunlight. He said, quite clearly, 'Perhaps you should pay as much attention in geography as you do in history. The Punjab is nowhere near Jerusalem. Neither is Rajasthan, which is where I'm *actually from*.'

I was amazed. I had never heard Shafeen speak so many words at once, and with such confidence and command. He didn't sound afraid of them at all.

Friar Skelton turned back to the class and Cookson subsided into his seat. He'd just been owned, and I could see he didn't like it. 'Little shit,' he hissed, under his breath.

'Not little,' murmured Piers. 'He's a long, brown shit.'

'Like the ones you do after a vindaloo,' agreed Cookson. 'Long and brown and smelling of curry.'

Piers sniggered. 'We'll settle him.'

Cookson rocked back on his chair and stretched extravagantly. 'Not long now,' he agreed.

There was such venom in their voices that I felt sorry for Shafeen. I tried to smile at him, but he didn't catch my eye, staring instead, unseeing, at Friar Skelton's chalk stickman rendering of long-dead Crusaders. I knew Shafeen had heard every word. I glanced at Henry. Blond head bent, he was painstakingly copying the diagram onto his pad. As ever, Henry had not taken part in any name-calling; he had done nothing but look at Shafeen, but his attack-dogs had sprung to his defence. Back then I still thought Henry the best of them, before I realised he was the worst.

chapter three

The Medievals were not straightforward racists; nothing so simple.

I suppose you'd have to say that they were pretty even-handed really, in that they were quite happy to make fun of anything that didn't fit. Their other major target, besides Shafeen, was 'Carphone Chanel'.

Like me, Chanel was new to STAGS that autumn term. I tried to make friends with her then, but she was too afraid of getting things wrong to make friends with the likes of me. She was too weak to ally herself to another outsider. Of course we are friends now: Nel, Shafeen and me, we three murderers. (I wonder what the collective name for murderers is. It can't be a 'murder', since the crows took that one. Maybe a 'conspiracy'.

Nel has French-polished nails; ten perfect half-moons of white. She has caramel-coloured hair extensions and a perfect coffee-coloured tan. But underneath all the varnish she's really nice. Her father dropped her off in a gold Rolls-Royce on her first day, and I found out later she was more bothered by that than I was by my dad's ancient Mini. You see, we haven't got money. But what I've learned from Nel is that when you're at STAGS there's only one thing worse than no money, and that's the wrong kind of money. 'My mum called me Chanel because she thought it had class,' she told me once in her carefully trained voice, betraying no trace of her Cheshire origins. 'She's got no idea.'

I knew what she meant by that. Class; it wasn't on the syllabus at STAGS, because there was no need. It was something everyone else seemed to know, bred into their bones over hundreds of years. Where to go on holiday. What wellies to wear. How to tip your soup plate (not bowl) at dinner. None of this meant having things that were brand new. That was Chanel's problem – she was brand new. Your shirt could have a frayed collar and buttons missing, as long as it came from the right maker in a little shop in London's St James's. Chanel could buy the same shirt, brand new, and still get it wrong. The Medievals called her a 'try-hard'. But that didn't stop her trying.

Chanel's father had made his money from his phone empire. He had nothing whatsoever to do with the Carphone Warehouse, but this didn't matter to the Medievals any more than it mattered to them that the Punjabi Playboy wasn't from the Punjab. They liked a bit of alliteration and Carphone went well with Chanel so it stuck, even though about two days into her time at STAGS Chanel began to call herself Nel. In actual fact Chanel's father had developed a phone called the Saros 7S – sort of half-tablet, half-phone – and the whole world had bought one. Chanel possibly had more money than the Medievals, and had a palatial house in Cheshire with a pool and a cinema room, but because of where the money came from she was even more of an outsider. Because one of the major differences between STAGS and The Rest Of The World was that at STAGS there were no mobile phones.

I don't mean the school banned phones; it didn't. The lower years used them as much as they were allowed, which was weekends and evenings. But in Six One and Six Two it became a weird point of honour to be phone-free. The Medievals were a six-person social-media backlash. YouTube, Snapchat and Instagram were looked down on as 'Savage'. Selfies were Savage. Twitter was Savage. Facebook was Savage. Video games were Savage. For the Medievals, the tech revolution had sent evolution into reverse. They went round ostentatiously reading books. (Books were Medieval. Kindles were Savage.) The Internet was acceptable only in the library and computer room, to be used for research, not social media. (I heard that one of the Six One boys had been expelled for sneaking into the library at night and looking at porn. Poor thing; I guess he was desperate.) *Very* occasionally the Medievals would watch TV in the Six Two TV room, but when I passed they were always watching *University Challenge*, competing with each other to get the most answers.

You'd think the kids would rebel, but they didn't. Everyone was fine with the phone-free universe, and that was because the Medievals embraced it. Such was the power of their personalities, of their little cult. Everyone wanted to be like the Medievals. Even I, in the face of such social pressure, put my phone in a drawer and let it run out of charge. I had no wish to stand out more than I already did. With no contact with my old friends I was even more isolated. I spoke to my dad at weekends, on the landline that all my floor in Lightfoot had to share, but there was always a queue of Jesus and her friends, waiting and tutting, so I could never tell him half of what I wanted to say. Plus Dad was so excited about his documentary, and filming caves full of batshit in Chile, that I couldn't tell him how unhappy I was. If I had, he would have come home. He loves me, you see.

Apart from my dad, films were what I missed the most. I'd told myself that, even if I hated STAGS, I could just do the lessons and then shut myself away at night watching films on my phone. But I couldn't even do that; that is, I could've done, but in some weird way I wanted to comply – I didn't want anyone to think I was Savage.

Of course, I knew in my heart that the phones thing was a massive pose, as was the whole 'Medievals' cult. But for Henry and his cronies it was just another way of demonstrating that they ruled the school, that they could bend everything to their will. They could have imposed anything they wanted – like having to hop on one leg on Wednesdays – and everyone would have followed them. But what was clever about the phone thing is that it went with the whole ethos of the school, the virtue of being different. Maybe that's why the Friars kissed their arses so much. Instead of spending hours on screens, kids were reading, playing sport and doing drama and music and choir and stuff. Plus everyone wrote loads, using actual pens and paper. Texts were Savage; letters and notes were Medieval. At STAGS, handwritten notes flew around like autumn leaves, written in fountain pen with real ink, from folded notes on family-crested notepaper to creamy white invitations as thick as bathroom tiles. And that's how this all began, with The Invitation.

It was nearly half-term when the envelope came. Of course, being STAGS, they didn't call it half-term, but Justitium. Jesus and I were in our room, getting ready for bed. And now we come to about the only time my roommate ever voluntarily talked to me. She was there when The Invitation slid silently under the door. I didn't even notice, but she pounced on it excitedly, as if she had been waiting for it. I was brushing my hair at the time, and in the mirror I saw her read the front and droop. 'It's for you,' she said, as if she couldn't quite believe it. She reluctantly handed it over.

It was completely square, a kind of thick ivory envelope folded over on four sides, and sealed – I kid you not – with a blob of wax, the red of our school stockings. On the wax was impressed a little pair of antlers. *Robin Hood, Prince of Thieves*, I thought.

Jesus hovered. I broke the seal, just like I'd seen in the movies. Inside was a thick square card. There were just three words on it, right in the middle of the creamy card, embossed in black ink. The letters were slightly shiny and raised to the touch.

huntin' shootin' fishin'

I looked up. 'What does it mean?'

'Turn it over,' Jesus urged.

I did. On the back, in neat italics, was printed:

You are invited to spend Justitium
at Longcross Hall, Cumberland.

Coaches departing STAGS at 5 p.m. Friday.

RSVP

I turned the card over. 'RSVP to who?' I said. 'There's no name on it.'

'That's because everybody knows who sends them,' Jesus said, with just a hint of her former scorn. 'It's from Henry.'

There was, as I've said, only one Henry at STAGS. The black embossed type jiggled in front of my eyes. I should have known. Huntin' shootin' fishin'. It sounded like some sort of joke; the 'g' was missing from all three words. But the Medievals didn't make mistakes; if they made errors – the Punjab, the Carphone Warehouse – they were deliberate. Henry had written the blood sports like that for a reason, exactly as he said them. 'Are you sure?'

'Yes. Longcross is his house. You lucky beast,' she said. 'You've got the chance to be a Medieval.'

I sat on the bed heavily and squinted up at her.

'What are you talking about?'

Jesus was so excited that she forgot herself so far as to actually sit bedside me. 'Henry de Warlencourt always asks people from Six One to his house for the weekend at Michaelmas Justitium – hunting season. If you do well in the blood sports, and they like you as a person, then next year when you go into Six Two you could be a Medieval.'

Despite the novelty of actually having a conversation with my roommate, I was silent, processing it all.

'You are going, right?' prompted Jesus. 'Longcross is supposed to be amazing. The absolute lap of luxury.'

I had the power for once, and I just shrugged. I wasn't willing to share any confidences. If Jesus wanted to know about my stuff, she'd have to be a bit nicer to me. All the same, I did need information, so I thawed. 'Coaches?' I said aloud. Knowing the Medievals, I wondered if it meant *actual* coaches, with eight horses for each, snorting and pawing on the drive.

'Henry sends for the estate cars,' Jesus said. 'You get driven to Longcross by his gamekeepers.'

I looked from The Invitation to Jesus's jealous expression. If I'd been heading home at half-term, to see Dad, I would never have even thought of going to Longcross. But I wasn't. Dad would still be in South America, and I was due to go to my Aunty Karen's in Leeds. Now, I have nothing against my Aunty Karen, or indeed Leeds, but she has twin toddlers who are a total pain. That's why I didn't want to live with her and ended up coming to STAGS.

So, although I had never hunted, shot or fished, I seriously considered going.

I might have been academically smart, but I was monumentally stupid not to realise sooner what was going on. It's not as if I wasn't warned. I was, in very clear terms. The warning came from Gemma Delaney. Gemma Delaney was a girl who had got into STAGS three years ago, also from Bewley Park, my old school. She was always held up as a shining example to the rest of us – she had her picture in the Bewley Park reception next to the sparsely filled cabinet of achievements (so different from the medieval atrium of STAGS, where you can hardly see the oak panels for silverware). Gemma came to talk in assembly at our school a year ago, to encourage us to try for a scholarship at STAGS, and I'd hardly recognised her. Gemma used to have dip-dyed hair with dark roots and straw ends, and a strong Manchester accent. In assembly that day she had long honey-blonde hair, a spotless STAGS uniform and clipped vowels. I know now that she'd looked like a Medieval.

She looked very different now, outside the chapel at STAGS, clutching at my arm as we were all filing out of morning Mass. I turned to look at her. Her face was as pale as bone, her hair lank, her eyes haunted. 'Don't go,' she said. The 'o' of 'go' was flat; in her urgency, her northern accent had returned.

I knew exactly what she meant at once. She meant The Invitation. She meant don't go huntin' shootin' fishin'. I wondered how she knew. 'Why not?'

'Just *don't*,' she said, more forcefully than I'd ever heard anyone utter anything. She pushed past me, to be carried along with the crowd. I stood for a moment while students flowed around me, weighing up what she had said. But I hadn't really absorbed it. As she disappeared into the crowd the feeling of unease faded with her.

The truth was, after weeks of being ignored and belittled and excluded, I was flattered to be wanted, to be invited by the Medievals. The night before, I'd met Henry himself crossing the Great Hall in Honorius. He too had touched my arm, and spoken to me, actually spoken to me, for the first time ever.

'You are coming this weekend, aren't you?' he'd said urgently. 'It will be *such* a laugh.' He pronounced it *larf*.

'What kind of laugh?' I said *laff*.

He smiled again, and my insides did a little flip. 'You'll see.' He squeezed my arm and I looked down at his hand where it lay on my sleeve – long fingers, square nails, and a gold signet ring on the little finger. A signet ring with a design of two tiny antlers.

So as I stood that morning outside chapel, with the pupils all flowing around me, thinking about what Henry had said, and what Gemma had said, I wasn't really deciding anything. In my mind I was already packing. It was like that moment when you flip a coin but you already know, before the coin comes down, what you're going to do.

chapter four

Once I'd decided I was going huntin' shootin' fishin', it seemed like blood sports were all anyone at STAGS could talk about.

We only had half a day of lessons on the Friday we broke up for Justitium, and every single one of them seemed to be about hunting.

In Latin we were doing a translation of Ovid about Diana, the goddess of . . . wait for it . . . hunting. Apparently she was bathing one day and was seen naked by a guy called Actaeon. She was pretty angry, and to stop him boasting about what he'd seen she told him if he ever spoke again she would turn him into a stag. The hunt happened to be riding past and, since Actaeon was clearly as stupid as most people are in myths, he called out for help. Sure enough, he was instantly transformed into a stag.

'What happened next, Miss Ashford?' Friar Mowbray asked Chanel. Friar Mowbray had a gift for knowing when people weren't listening, and Chanel, like myself, was clearly having trouble concentrating that morning. She'd spent the last twenty minutes staring out the window at the dripping playing fields. She gave a little start and looked down at her copy of Ovid.

She placed one of her perfect white crescents of nail under the words. '*The hunter became the hunted*,' she translated haltingly. '*The hounds were struck with a wolf's frenzy and tore him to pieces as they would a stag.*'

'That's right,' said Friar Mowbray. She had arched black eyebrows, despite her greying bun, and they wiggled when she was excited. They were wiggling now. 'Fifty hounds *tore Actaeon to pieces as they would a stag.*' She practically licked her lips. 'There is some dispute among classical writers about the names of the hounds,' she droned on. 'But these, of course, are details. Ovid has it that they were called Arcas, Ladon, Tigris . . .' But I'd switched off by this point. If Friar Mowbray was going to name all fifty hounds, I was going to go back to daydreaming about Longcross.

In history, Friar Styles too seemed to have got the blood-sports memo. She told us about Gian Maria Visconti, a useless Renaissance prince, whose sole mission in life seemed to be to ruin the ducal empire his forefathers had built up. Even this lesson came back to hunting.

'Of course, Gian Maria was most famous for his singular hobby,' said the Friar. 'He was a great huntsman; but he did not select his prey from the animal kingdom.' She looked down her long nose at the textbook in her hand. '*For sport he set his hunting hounds to course and dismember men*,' she quoted. 'Mr Jadeja, assist us with the meaning of the verb "to course".'

Shafeen cleared his throat. 'To course means to chase, or to hunt.'

'Precisely,' said Friar Styles. 'It means to *hunt*.' Her eyes shone with a weird light. 'Gian Maria's servants became his prey; he would set his hounds upon them for his own enjoyment – and if they were slow enough to get their throats torn out he would simply hire more. Little wonder, you might think, that Gian Maria earned himself the name "Gian the Cruel".' But there was no judgement in the Friar's voice; more . . . *admiration*. It was creepy.

Then it was off to Justitium Mass, the service that marked the end of the half-term. We sang, as we always did, Psalm 42; *As the running deer seeks the flowing brook, even so my soul longs for you*, O God. Then the Abbot got to his feet. As well as the usual bullshit about how great we'd all been so far this term, and who had got what marks, and which teams had won which sports, the Abbot also chose – yes, you've guessed it – hunting as the theme for his sermon. Once again we were treated to the story of our founder, Aidan, and the stag.

Mind wandering, I turned to look at the stained-glass window of the saint, but somehow my gaze never reached it. It was caught instead by the back of six perfect heads. The Medievals were sitting together a few rows in front of me. They all sat in the same way – with one leg crossed over the other so you could see their coloured stockings, emphasising their elevated status. Piers, Cookson, Esme, Charlotte, Lara. And, next to Lara, Henry de Warlencourt. I found myself staring at the back of his head: the scroll of his ear, the way the close-cropped blond hair glittered at the nape of his neck and disappeared into the black collar of his Tudor gown, the lighter, longer wavy hair growing in a swirl at the crown of his head. I shivered, but I wasn't cold. It was hard to believe I'd be spending the weekend at his house.

I registered a sudden silence. The Abbot was staring down from the pulpit right at me, an amused look on his pleasant face.

'Have we lost your attention, Miss MacDonald?'

My cheeks burned as the whole school turned to look at me, even the Medievals. They all looked pretty haughty, except Henry, who looked at me with a quizzical smile that set my heart thumping. 'As I was *saying . . .*' intoned the Abbot exaggeratedly, gently poking fun at me. He pushed his glasses higher up his nose and read from *The Life of St Aidan*, where it balanced on the eagle lectern. I gave him my full attention, although I could have recited the lesson by heart: '*The blessed saint, when the hounds were running close, held up his hand to the stag and rendered him invisible. In such wise the hounds did pass him by, and their tooth did not touch him; whereupon Aidan restored the stag to the sight of men, and his pelt and antler could again be seen, and the stag did go upon his way in peace.*'

As we filed out of chapel I was left with the strong impression that even the Abbot knew what I'd be doing that weekend, and particularly wanted me to hear his lesson.

When I clattered back up to my room after Mass, my stomach was doing weird somersaults. From the landing window I could see shiny, expensive cars already coming and going in the STAGS drive; parents collecting their little darlings, watched jealously from the windows by those poor saps who had to stay at school for the weekend. They were the ones whose parents lived overseas (lots), were in the armed forces (some) or were the children of foreign royalty (a few). I was one of the lucky ones; I had a luxury weekend ahead of me and there was nothing to do now but pack for Longcross. I'd packed once, of course, for Aunty Karen's, but I'd since unpacked again, having a feeling that the stuff I'd packed for Leeds wouldn't quite cut it at Longcross. Frankly, I wasn't sure what kind of stuff *would* cut it at Longcross. Happily, help was at hand.

chapter five

As I got to the top of my staircase in Lightfoot, I saw that Esme Dawson was sitting in the window seat.

The leaded diamond panes threw shadows that criss-crossed her as if she was in a net. She gazed prettily out at the grounds, looking self-consciously posed, as if she was modelling for a photo shoot in some posh magazine. She'd arranged herself, I was sure, so I'd find her like that.

She uncurled herself gracefully when I approached my door. 'Hello,' she said. 'We haven't formally met. I'm Esme.'

'Greer,' I said guardedly.

She actually shook my hand. I noticed she wore a gold signet ring, just like Henry. 'How d'you do?' she said.

Now, I have literally never been asked this question before. I know it's how people used to greet each other in Ealing Comedies and stuff. But I'd never heard it In Real Life. I suppose this was how the Medievals rolled. *How do you do?* A number of answers popped into my head. *To be honest, Esme, I'm not really sure how I do. One minute you and your fellow sirens are sniggering at me and making jokes about me sounding like I'm from* Coronation Street, *and the next, you're nice as pie* ... But of course I didn't say any of this. I was just happy that someone was talking to me. 'Fine, thanks.'

'Ready for the weekend?'

'Not remotely.'

She smiled, segueing neatly from *Country Life* spread to toothpaste ad. 'Henry asked me to come and help you pack, and also answer any questions you may have.'

'Well, I have a whole bunch of those.'

She gestured to the heavy oak door, with my name and Jesus's (real) name on it, and a message board with lots of scrawled messages, all for Jesus. 'Shall we?'

I opened the door. Jesus was already there, lolling on her bed – she must have made a quicker getaway than I from chapel. At the sight of Esme she got up at once and stood to attention. 'Would you excuse us?' Esme asked sweetly.

Jesus went bright red, shot me a jealous look and scuttled from the room.

I unhooked my chapel cape from my shoulders and threw it across my chair. My wheelie suitcase gaped empty on the bed, and my clothes were all over the place. Esme eyed the mess, and me.

I was busted. I like to think of myself as a Strong Feminist Girl, but since Henry had invited me to Longcross, I'd been letting the sisterhood down a bit by obsessing about what I would wear. I'd ignored the Friars in every lesson, while having mini-daydreams about walking in Longcross's grounds in elegant tweeds, or boating on a lake in a white tea dress. In each scenario I was accompanied by Henry de Warlencourt, chatting and laughing at my side. Thing is, I didn't have tweeds, or a white tea dress. And even though Henry's grounds probably didn't, like my daydreams, come straight out of some Merchant Ivory film from the eighties, they probably weren't far off. My skinny jeans and beanie hats and the ironic film T-shirts that my dad liked to buy me certainly wouldn't fit in.

'The first thing to say is, don't worry about clothes,' said Esme, reassuringly. 'Anything you don't have, they'll provide at Longcross. Just take the basics – underwear, lots of socks, nightclothes. As for the rest, keep it classic.'

She rifled through my wardrobe, and my 'floordrobe'. 'Here we go. White shirt. Jeans. A couple of warm jumpers.' She flung them in the case. 'T-shirts . . . hmmm.' She picked one up. It had a picture of Nosferatu on it, saying, *'Mornings Suck'*. 'No . . .' she said, as if I wasn't there, and selected a plain white one. 'Yes.' She went on picking through my stuff, rejecting the Savage, putting anything she found vaguely Medieval in the case. There seemed frighteningly few things in there. At last she turned to me. 'Have you got a formal dress?'

That was another for the list of questions I'd never been asked, but I actually had an answer to this one. A posh dress was the one thing I *did* have. My mum, who is a costume designer for movies, made me one before she left. And here's the weird thing. She didn't leave recently. She left my dad and me when I was sixteen months old.

I've seen the last pictures of me with Mum (they didn't make it onto my wall at STAGS); I was just a little toddling thing with a swirl of black hair and big grey eyes. I've looked at those pictures a *lot*, trying to see what was so bad about me that she had to go. I look pretty cute. I certainly wasn't a monster. But apparently, after getting through the worst bits of shitty nappies and night feeds and teething, she decided she wasn't the mothering type. My dad – and this tells you what a good guy he is – has never, *ever* said a bad word about her to me. He says dads leave their kids all the time and no one makes a fuss about it, so why should it be any different for a mum? I see his point. But, somehow, it *is* different.

The one thing Mum ever gave me (OK, OK, except for *life*) was The Dress. Mum and Dad met when they were both working on this film at Elstree Studios. Before you go thinking it was some kind of classic, it wasn't. It was like *The Princess Diaries* but even worse, if that's possible. I try not to remember the name of it. It was about some girl who doesn't know she's a princess till the end, and my mum had to make all the clothes for the princess actress, this horrible Disney brat. Anyway there was a bunch of nice material and beads left over and by the end of the shoot Mum was pregnant with me, and she knew I was going to be a girl, so she made this dress for the adult me. Sweet, right? Well, it would have been, except for the fact that she barely stuck around for sixteen months, never mind sixteen years. Now you know why my dad turned down all the foreign jobs for sixteen years, and only went away this year because I got into STAGS. When she left, Mum said that Dad should keep The Dress safe and I should wear it for my prom. And he did. And I did. And guess what? It fitted me perfectly. Spooky.

I'm not usually vain (well, not *very*), but I have to say I looked pretty nice in that dress on my prom night. Dad sent

Mum a picture of me wearing it, to Russia or wherever the hell she was filming. That was back in the summer, and still no reply. I'm not holding my breath.

That same photo was on my wall in Lightfoot, and I looked at it now. It was the only photo on my wall that wasn't of me and Dad. It was of me and my class at Year 11 prom at Bewley, just before I left the school. There were about ten of us, arms around each other, eyes wide and mouths smiling, all jumping in the air at the same time. I always got a pang when I looked at it. I missed, *so* much, not just those friends in particular, but friends in general.

I turned back to Esme – she was the nearest thing I had. I held up The Dress over my Tudor coat. It was beautiful. This, I knew, would be suitable, even for the Medievals, even for Longcross. You see, I didn't wear it to the prom out of loyalty, or yearning for my mum or any of that sentimental horseshit. I don't actually care about my mum. I wore it because it is a gorgeous dress. And you can tell it was made for me; it is a silvery grey which picks out the silver in my eyes, and there are tiny black beads, sewn in a kind of swirl on the front, the kind of swirl you see flocks of starlings doing at dusk on an autumn night. Well, you do at STAGS anyway.

Esme looked at The Dress as if she smelled something bad. '*God*, no,' she said. 'That won't do.' My face must have fallen, cos she said hurriedly, 'Don't worry. They'll have something for you at Longcross.'

I laid The Dress tenderly on the bed. 'Even dresses?'

'Oh yes.'

I felt I needed to make a joke. 'Are they Henry's?'

She laughed. Not the bitchy laugh I'd heard so many times behind my back, but a nice, open sound. 'So,' she said, arranging herself cosily on the bed, one long leg under her, the other dangling to the floor. 'That's clothes sorted. What d'you want to ask?'

I sat on the other side of the rejected clothes mountain and spread my hands wide. 'What happens? What happens at the weekend?'

'It's *such* a larf,' she said, just as Henry had. 'The gamekeepers pick us up at five sharp from the entrance. It's not a long drive; Longcross is in the Lake District, about an hour south. Good hunting country, you see. You'll have time to wash and dress when we get there and then there's a formal dinner in the Great Hall. Then on Saturday it's the stag hunt, Sunday is the pheasant shoot, and on the holiday Monday it's trout fishing on the lake.'

Jeee-sus. For the first time it was occurring to me that as well as all the fancy-pants country-house weekend stuff, I was actually going to be required to shoot things, and I wasn't at all sure how I felt about that. I know this makes me a total hypocrite, as I'll happily eat meat and wear leather, but I wasn't sure I wanted to end the life of a beautiful creature just for fun. A stag, I mean; fish are pretty ugly, so I wouldn't exactly cry if I caught one of them. 'Do I have to . . . you know . . . *kill* stuff?'

Her perfect eyebrows shot up. 'Well, of course you should *try*. No point hunting if there's no kill.' She laid a hand on my arm. 'But in point of fact, novices rarely make a kill on their first weekend. So don't worry too much.'

'Thing is,' I said, 'I've never even *held* a gun, or even a fishing rod. I won't know what to do.' If I was honest, the one thing worse than killing a beautiful animal would be looking like a total fool.

'Don't worry,' she said. 'There are dozens of gamekeepers on the estate, not to mention loaders and beaters and pickers-up. Masses of people to tell you what to do.'

I had no idea what most of those were, but I listened politely. 'At every step there will be someone experienced on hand to help you. And if blood sports aren't your thing, well –' she smiled again – 'there's the social side, isn't there? There's a formal dinner every night, and marvellous shooting lunches, and cocktails and tea. It's *enormous* fun.'

My stomach back-flipped again, but I nodded readily.

Esme's eyebrows knitted with concern and she leaned forward. Her hand was, somehow, still on my arm. 'Has that been helpful?'

It had been actually. 'Yes,' I said. 'Thanks.'

'The cars come at five. The headkeeper's driving you. He's a perfect poppet.' She got up from my bed in one fluid movement and flipped her hair from one parting to another. It fell perfectly. 'See you tonight. Dinner's at eight. Travel safe.' At my door she did this neat little wave, flapping just the finger part of her hand.

'You too,' I said.

Of course, I look back now and think exactly what you are thinking. What a sap I was to let that witch paw through my clothes and tell me what to wear. But you have to remember that those few moments in my room with Esme was the most conversation I'd had all term. I was starved of friendship. And, back then, it seemed as if that was what Esme was offering.

Still, I did have a little seed of rebellion within me, even then. When the door shut behind her I put The Dress in my case.

chapter six

The chapel clock chiming five told me that I was a little bit late getting downstairs.

I'd been tonging my hair so that it fell really straight and shiny, and then dragged my case downstairs to find that a mean, mizzling rain was falling, just enough to have made it absolutely pointless me tonging my hair at all.

I could see a convoy of racing-green Land Rovers already moving off slowly down the drive. For a moment I panicked; I thought I'd missed my ride. (So ironic. Of course, now I wish I *had* missed my ride.) I'd presumed from what Jesus had said when I'd received The Invitation that I wouldn't be the only newbie going from STAGS – surely I'd be travelling with the other unknown guests, or even the Medievals? But it was OK – there was one Land Rover still standing in front of the steps. A massive stocky man stood leaning on the bumper. It was impossible to tell his age from his weather-beaten face – he looked like that guy from *Guardians of the Galaxy*, the one who is basically a tree. I couldn't really see his hair as he was wearing a flat tweed cap. He had on a checked shirt and a sort of quilted green waistcoat. He was smoking discreetly, his cigarette curled in the palm of his hand like a sixth-former hiding it from the Friars.

'I'm Greer,' I said, much more breezily than I felt.

He touched his cap, unsmiling. 'Howdo,' he said, a northern, contracted version of the greeting Esme had given me upstairs. Usually a northern accent comforts me, but not this time. He was about as unfriendly as he could be. Unhurriedly he took a final drag on his cigarette, squinting his eyes at me and against the smoke, then ground it out on the sole of his heavy walking boot. He tucked the stub neatly in the pocket of his waistcoat.

He put out his huge nicotine-stained hand. I nearly shook it, the way I'd shaken Esme's, before I realised he was offering, in his curt way, to take my wheelie case. I rolled it to him and he slung it in the back of the car, slamming the boot loudly. I considered making a joke about riding shotgun, thinking it would be witty to say this to a gamekeeper, but he didn't seem like a jokey kind of guy; plus he opened the back door for me. Then he got in the front and started the engine. As we drove away I turned for a last look at the school. And this I particularly remember: every single window in the place had a face in it. The whole school was watching the chosen ones go. Even the Friars.

As we headed down the drive, only the fact that we were following the other estate cars reassured me that I wasn't, in fact, being kidnapped. The headkeeper drove in absolute silence, concentrating on the road ahead. Once we got out into the real dark of the country, we would, at times, fall behind the others on the winding roads. Then it was as if my silent driver and I were the only people in the world. When I was a kid and my dad used to let me sit in the front seat of his camera truck – I guess we were both lonely – I used to think that tail lights were creepy red eyes watching me in the dark. Tonight whenever I caught sight of those red eyes, I felt ridiculously relieved. I watched the back of the gamekeeper's head. He drove easily, one big hand on the wheel, cap still firmly on his head, saying nothing. I assume the Land Rover had a radio, but he didn't put it on. I could have done with some stupid cheerful tunes. I didn't know any of the new releases since the phone ban, but the silence was really starting to freak me out. I tried desperately to think of something to say to start a conversation, and fell back on the old British fail-safe. 'D'you think we'll have nice weather this weekend?' I asked.

''Appen,' he grunted. There didn't seem to be any point in probing him further. So I gave up and tried to see out of the window, wiping the misted glass with my sleeve. Being late October, it was already night. I knew from Esme that Longcross was somewhere in the Lake District. 'Good hunting country,' she'd said. And in fact as I peered out I could see, between the massive dark hunched mountains, glassy moonlit lakes, which would appear for an instant and disappear again like hide-and-seek. I don't know how long we drove for. (There was no clock on the dashboard, I don't wear a watch and, of course, no phone.) It can't have been much more than an hour, but it felt like ages. The silence seemed to get louder and louder, becoming so oppressive it almost made me want to scream. My nerves were stretched to breaking point. But just as I felt I couldn't bear it any more and I was going to have to ask him to pull over, I saw a shining beacon in the darkness. There, in the distance, was a constellation of lights, like a huge ocean liner in the black sea of hills.

If I'd had a chatty car journey, in company, with the radio on, the sight of Longcross would have reminded me to be afraid. As it was, after an hour in the dark with the taciturn gamekeeper, I saw the approaching lights with nothing but relief.

It didn't occur to me at the time that that might have been part of the plan.

HUNTIN'

chapter seven

Henry was waiting in this kind of panelled hall, standing with his back to a roaring fire.

He was alone except for a couple of lazy Labradors, who were dozing on the hearthrug.

I was quite relieved that clearly I wasn't expected to meet his parents straight away, and relaxed a bit. Everything about my host and the room was welcoming, his smile as warm as the fire, his gold hair glinting. Henry was wearing a long-sleeved rugby top and these sort of red-coloured jeans. He was not exactly *more* handsome than he was at school – he was probably the only pupil at STAGS who actually looked good in the black Tudor coat – but different. More . . . grown-up. He suited the room though, just as he suited STAGS.

The room wasn't half as forbidding as I'd expected Longcross to be. There were rows of wellies and walking sticks and fishing rods and an old wetsuit propped around the walls – it was quite cluttered really. There were yellowing sporting prints of old-fashioned people doing old-fashioned sports hanging from the panelling, including huntin' shootin' fishin' of course. And above Henry's head, the inevitable stags' heads gazed down with their glassy eyes.

Henry saw me. 'Greer!' he said. He came halfway to meet me, and kissed me once on each cheek; not those stupid air-kisses that posh people usually do, but proper kisses, lips to skin. The greeting threw me a bit, since he'd never before made any contact with me beyond that touch on the arm.

'Where are the others?' I asked.

'Changing. Come and get warm. Sorry it's so beastly cold.' He rubbed his hands together briskly. 'Good for the huntin' though.' He turned to his headkeeper, who was looming respectfully behind me.

'Ah, Perfect. I see you conveyed Miss MacDonald safely.'

Perfect – for that, unbelievably, was his name – took off the tweed cap, which was apparently *not* glued to his head, and curtly nodded his balding, greying dome.

Henry smiled at me. 'Did he talk your head off, Greer?'

I wasn't quite sure what to say to this, but thankfully I wasn't required to give an answer; Henry then turned to the gamekeeper himself. 'Perfect, did you talk Miss MacDonald's head off?'

The headkeeper scratched his chin. ''Appen.'

Henry threw back his head and laughed, showing all his white teeth, and even Perfect looked like he might, for his master, almost have broken into a smile. It was obviously an acknowledged joke between them.

'All right. Check the gun room for tomorrow, would you, Perfect?'

Perfect nodded again and disappeared. Henry turned to me. 'Listen, you'd better go straight up if you're not to be late. I hope you don't mind dressing for dinner.'

I wasn't quite sure what the alternative was. To come down to dinner naked? So I just said, 'Not at all.'

'Good. We gather for drinks in the drawing room at seven thirty, and dinner is in the Great Hall at eight.'

I turned around on the spot. 'Isn't *this* the Great Hall?'

'*God*, no,' he said. 'This is the Boot Room.'

As I was processing the fact that the boots at Longcross enjoyed better accommodation than my dad and I did in Manchester, he touched a bell, *Gosford Park* style, and a middle-aged woman appeared.

'Betty, show Miss MacDonald to her room. Where did you put her?'

'Lowther, sir.' The maid had the same accent as Perfect.

'Lowther. Is the fire lit?'

'Oh yes, sir. Is that everyone now, sir?'

'That's everyone. Would you like a cup of tea, Greer?'

'I could *murder* one,' I said thankfully.

His smile stiffened a little, and I wondered if I hadn't been quite genteel enough. 'Tea up to the room, Betty.' I noticed that he didn't say please or thank you.

But the maid didn't seem to mind. 'Very good, sir.' She sort of stood back and put her hand out to show the way – apparently I was to go first, even though I didn't know the way; some sort of pecking order, I suppose.

I went to pick up my case, but Henry put out *his* hand. 'Leave that,' he said. 'I'll have someone bring it up.'

Apparently posh people don't carry their own stuff. I began to enjoy myself, especially when Henry took my hand and squeezed it. 'Welcome,' he said. 'Sincerely. I'm *so* glad you're here.'

My room – I suppose I should call it Lowther – was gorgeous. And massive. It was like the best hotel suite in the best hotel you could possibly imagine. I walked all the way around it, which took some time.

There was an enormous dark wood four-poster bed, with heavy rose-coloured curtains and bedclothes. On the walls there seemed to be material instead of wallpaper, with very faint gold leaves sort of stencilled on it. There were rugs out of *Aladdin* on the floor. The windows had clear panes at the bottom, stained glass at the top. There was one of those fireplaces which is so old it has a date on it. (This one said 1590.) And, get this: it had a roaring little fire already burning in it. There was no TV in the room, as there would have been in a hotel; in fact I never saw a telly the whole time I was at Longcross.

Actually nothing in the room was new, when you looked closely. The rugs were a bit threadbare and the gold leaves on the walls had thinned and faded, and one of the panes in the window had a silvery crack right across it. But the room screamed heritage and class and quality, and as such it had the inevitable hallmark of all those things – a stag's head on the wall above the fireplace, his dark glass eyes flickering in the firelight as if he still lived. And here's something you wouldn't get in a hotel room. On the bed, almost camouflaged, lay a dress. It was the same colour as the rest of the room, a dark rose.

As I picked it up it sort of slithered, and it was heavy. Quality again. I wondered, irrelevantly, what Henry's room was like.

The maid left me to get the tea, which she brought in, just as I'd imagined, on a silver tray. A young bloke about my age followed her with my suitcase, which he deposited in the middle of the rug. And then a third person entered the room: tall, blonde and beautiful. It was Charlotte Lachlan-Young, the second siren.

Charlotte was wearing a beautiful frock – no, you couldn't really call it a frock; it was definitely a gown. She skipped forward and kissed me on both cheeks. 'Greer, isn't it.' It was a statement, not a question, as if she was telling me my name. I took a step back when she released me. If Henry's kisses were surprising, hers were definitely an over-the-top greeting since she'd never directly spoken to me before. 'It's *so* great you could come. *Welcome* to Longcross.' She said it as if it was her house, and then I remembered that I'd heard at STAGS that she was some sort of cousin of Henry's. I suppose she thought that gave her the right to act as hostess. It was weird though – I would've thought it was for his mum to greet me this way. But I supposed I would meet her at dinner. Charlotte went on. 'Lowther is the *sweetest* room; you'll get *such* a view in the morning.'

And that first sentence told me exactly how Charlotte differed from the other Medieval girls. She spoke as if everything she said was in italics. She was perpetually enthusiastic and gave everything a special emphasis. I could see how it would quickly get on your nerves. The maid poured the tea into little pointless china cups, through this tiny little silver sieve, a world away from the big hand-warmer mugs my dad and I used, filled with dark reddish builder's tea. While she poured, Charlotte sat cosily on the bed, flipping her hair from one parting to the other as Esme had done. It too fell perfectly. 'Oh, is this your dress for tonight? *Gosh*. It's *perfect*. That *colour* with your dark hair. *Yum*.'

I noted that the maid handed Charlotte her cup of tea first, and me second. 'Betty, you are a *darling*. Tea!' She turned to me, wide-eyed, as if the drink had just, that moment, been invented especially for her. '*Just* what I needed. *How* was the journey? *Who* drove you?'

The tea tasted weird and weak, like washing-up water, and the cup was really thin. I felt that if I closed my teeth on it suddenly, I would take a bite out of it. 'Perfect picked me up.'

'Oh, the *headkeeper*. He's an absolute *poppet*.'

That was exactly what Esme had said. I could only imagine that poppet was Medieval-speak for miserable bastard. 'Yes, he was a prince,' I said ironically. 'Really put me at my ease. You know *Taxi Driver*? Well, he was like Robert De Niro in that. Except a bit less chatty.'

Charlotte widened her eyes at me and jerked her head towards the maid, who was pressing her thin lips together. I wasn't sure what she was signalling, so just kept quiet. At that moment, though, the clock on the mantel – Cogsworth from *Beauty and the Beast* – chimed and Charlotte screeched. '*God*, look at the *time*!' Now you've had your tea –' I'd had one sip – 'you should *think* about getting *changed*. Drinks at *seven thirty* in the *Drawing Room*.'

Regretfully I set down my china cup.

Charlotte held up the dress and shook it, as if she was a matador and I was a bull. '*Cinderella* time.'

Neither she nor Betty showed any sign of leaving, so I had no option but to strip down to my undies with them standing there. Perhaps this was how rich people rolled. Perhaps it was Savage to mind undressing in front of others. I wriggled into the dress with their help – at that point I had to admit I was grateful they were there. That was when I remembered seeing the film *Elizabeth* and watching Cate Blanchett as the queen just standing there with her arms out and letting her ladies dress her, frock, rings, everything. That was why rich people didn't get dressed alone. The clothes were so tricky they needed help.

Once I was dressed, my helpers sat me down in front of the mirror to do my hair. On a good day, my black hair falls straight and shiny as a bell, heavy fringe tickling my eyelashes, blunt edges grazing my shoulders. Today was not a particularly good day, because the rain had made it a bit crinkly, but it seemed I didn't need to worry about that. Charlotte had quite different ideas for me. 'Betty does hair *beautifully*.' And over the next twenty minutes I have to admit that Betty did work some magic. She tonged my hair into ringlets, swept my fringe to one side, twisted the sidepieces back and secured them with tiny sprays of rosebuds the same colour as the dress.

I did wonder if Betty was going to do my make-up too, but apparently that was all me. The maid left, no doubt to tend to someone else, and Charlotte wandered to the window to look out at the night, and started fiddling with the catch. 'By the *way*, you should *know* that Betty's *married* to *Perfect*. It's *really* worth *remembering* that you should *never gossip* in front of the *servants*.'

That was not, I felt, a rule I was ever going to need to observe outside of this house. I felt a bit bad about what I'd said, but if that poor cow was married to the headkeeper, I wasn't telling her anything she didn't already know. Trying to style it out I said, 'Well, all I can say is, she's one lucky, lucky lady.'

I picked up my usual black eyeliner, then paused with it hovering in the air. Somehow it didn't seem right for this dress.

Charlotte walked over, laid a cool hand over mine and made me set the pencil down. '*Less*,' she said. She held up a nude creamy colour. 'How about this?'

So I sat back and let her do it all for me. Ten minutes later, when I looked in the mirror, I didn't recognise myself.

Charlotte had been right about the old-rose colour of the dress – it made my cheeks glow. My grey eyes were accentuated by the creamy shimmer on the lids, and my lips shone with a little coral gloss.

I'd been transformed.

Emo to prom queen.

Savage to Medieval.

Charlotte clasped her hands to her chest. 'Oh My *God*,' she said. (She'd never OMG; she was a Medieval.) 'You look *divine*.'

It was the fricking *Princess Diaries*.

chapter eight

I was glad I'd made an effort.

We swept down this ridiculous marble staircase, with huge paintings all around it, straight out of Wayne Manor in *The Dark Knight*. Then when Charlotte and I entered the drawing room (we didn't even have to touch the doors; two footman types opened them as we approached) I could see that everyone was mega-formal – all the boys were in black jackets with long tails, and white shirts and bow ties. For a minute I just saw a blur of smart people, but then I began to recognise the faces above those unfamiliar clothes. I knew, of course, that this was the moment I'd have to meet Henry's parents, and possibly other adult guests who'd come for a country-house weekend, but the only people I could see to begin with were Medievals. Henry with his blond head, standing, inevitably, with Lara, who was dressed in deep blue. Piers and Cookson talking to a tall dark man with his back to me, and, by the fireplace, Esme in ivy green talking to Chanel.
Chanel.
A waiter guy in a black waistcoat and bow tie held out a tray to me – something fizzy in tall glasses – and I was so

shocked I took one automatically. *Carphone Chanel*. What was *she* doing here?

No wonder she'd been staring out of the window in Latin; she was obviously as anxious-slash-excited as I'd been, and for the same reason. I couldn't quite believe it. Chanel, I knew, had had it much tougher than me all term. I sipped at the glass in my hand just for something to do while I processed her presence here, and the drink, which I suppose must have been champagne, was so bitter tasting and fizzy it made my eyes water.

Then I got the second shock of the night. The dark guy who was talking to Piers and Cookson turned round, and it was *Shafeen*. I watched him talking easily, standing elegantly and looking completely at home. Then he looked up mid-sentence and caught sight of me. His eyes flared a little, widening with surprise. I couldn't quite figure out the look. It's kind of hard to explain, but I don't think he was surprised to see me there; I think he was surprised at how I *looked*. I suppose I must've looked OK, and it was a good job I did: the sirens – Charlotte and Esme, and, the most beautiful of all, Lara – looked amazing in their jewel-coloured couture gowns. Chanel too looked really pretty in her white dress, even though I was damned sure that the Medievals would think her fake tan was a bit too dark, and her dress a bit too pale. I felt I could hold my own beside all of them – or even if Greer MacDonald couldn't, the princess I'd seen in the mirror could. I lifted my chin a little.

I have to admit Shafeen also looked amazing in the white tie and tails. He was taller than the rest of the boys, and his dark skin made a lovely contrast to the crisp white shirt and bow tie. Tonight his longish black hair was slicked back from his forehead, and his face looked really handsome and sort of *noble*. *Prince Caspian*, I thought. He certainly seemed to fit, but why the hell was he *here*? He'd had a worse time from the Medievals than any of us. Then I watched him a bit more; his stance, his manner, the way he held his glass. His sheer *ease*. My lip curled a little. He was one of them. I'd felt sorry for him all term, thinking he was being bullied with all that Punjabi Playboy stuff. But it was obviously just joshing, the Medieval version of humour. After all, everyone said Shafeen was some sort of Indian prince. I'd been a sucker. He'd obviously been friends with them all along. I couldn't help feeling a bit let down. I don't know why – Shafeen had been at the school since the prep bit, so he'd grown up with the Medievals. Still it was a bit of a disappointment to me, somehow, that he was one of them. He smiled at me, but I didn't smile back.

At eight we went through to the Great Hall for dinner. The Great Hall was a vast room, with ceilings so high that the frescoes on them receded into the dark, beyond the reach of the candlelight. The inevitable stags' heads stared down, their antlers making crazy shadows on the walls. The long table was covered with a snowy-white cloth, and crowded with silver candelabras, crystal glasses and sort of silver cake stands piled high with pyramids of fruit instead of cake.

As I found my place, marked by a little cream card saying '*Miss Greer MacDonald*' in handwritten calligraphy, one of the footman dudes sprang forward to snatch up my napkin and pull back my chair. I sat down in front of more silver cutlery than Dad and I had at home in our entire cutlery drawer. Did you ever see *The Remains of the Day*? You know the bit where the under-butlers are all measuring the placement of cutlery on the table? I'll bet these place settings were all measured to the millimetre by one of the many servant types who were standing all around the edges of the room.

I looked in trepidation at the cards next to mine; no Henry (bad), no Shafeen (good), but Charlotte on one side and Piers on the other (OK, I *guess*). Weirdly, though, before everyone was even seated, I counted only nine places in total: for the six Medievals and the three guests. At least this gave me a conversation starter with Piers, whom I'd never, ever talked to before. I asked him the question that had been bothering me since my arrival. 'Where are Henry's parents?'

Piers picked up his wine glass almost before the servant guy had finished filling it. 'In London,' he said. 'They have a house in Cumberland Place; just by Regent's Park, you know.' He gave a little shout of laughter. 'Rather good that: Longcross is in Cumberland, and their London house is in Cumberland Place.'

Servant-guy came round again, putting himself between Piers and me, placing a perfectly round bread roll on my littlest plate with some silver tongs. This action gave me time to process this information. 'So there are no . . .' I didn't want to use the word adults, or grown-ups – that would make me sound about five. 'There are no other guests at all this weekend?'

Piers, his mouth crammed with bread, shook his head. 'More fun,' he said. He attempted a wink, didn't quite manage it, and clinked my glass. But I put down the wine glass and took a gulp of water instead, trying to swallow down a sudden strong sense of foreboding. The servants were adults, of course, but they were completely bossed by Henry. It made me feel a bit funny that there was no one . . . in *charge*.

No parents.

Just nine teenagers in a massive house.

Dinner was not exactly a relaxing start. We were sitting roughly boy–girl, with Henry (of course) at the head of the table. Shafeen, sitting right at the other end, chatted easily with Esme, his dark eyes sparkling, a lock of the slicked-back black hair falling over his brow. I'd never seen him like that before, talkative and sociable; quite different from the aloof, awkward loner I'd thought him. I felt, again, like I'd been fooled. Esme was showing every sign of being utterly charmed by him, her chin on her hand, laughing up into his eyes. Chanel was on Henry's right, and he in turn was doing a great job of charming her, while his consort, Lara, talked low-voiced to Cookson. I saw Chanel's face as she talked to Henry, and felt a pang – she was loving it, really loving the whole thing: the dinner, the company, the setting. You could see she was lapping it up. My odd feeling of foreboding returned.

I had the pleasure of Charlotte italicising on one side ('So you're from *Manchester*. How *amazing*. I've never *been*. What's it *like*?') and Piers on the other who seemed fascinated by what my 'father' did; it seemed in the Medieval world that this was some sort of standard by which you could judge people. Maybe this was part of the whole screening process for prospective Medievals. You see, I still believed then what Jesus had told me, that the huntin' shootin' fishin' weekend was some sort of job interview for Medievalhood. How wrong can you be?

Piers was perfectly friendly, but seemed weirdly old. In the absence of Henry's parents, it was almost as if Piers had taken on the role of Henry's dad, just as, earlier, Charlotte had greeted me like she was Henry's mum. There was no way Piers, with his monobrow and his pocket watch, seemed eighteen. He was a fifty-year-old trapped in a teenager's body. 'And what exactly *is* a wildlife cameraman?'

I threw out the idea of stating sarcastically that a wildlife cameraman was someone who points his camera at wildlife. 'He operates the camera on those wildlife documentaries you see on the TV – David Attenborough stuff, *Planet Earth*, *Autumnwatch*, that kind of thing.'

Even though the reality of my dad's filming life is that he can wait three days for a gecko to come out of a hole, for just three seconds of amazing footage of a racer snake trying to eat it, most people are reasonably impressed when I tell them what he does. From Piers I got nothing.

'Know a lot about wildlife, does he?'

'Yes. He comes back from shooting with all these facts. He's in Chile at the moment. Shooting bat caves.' I was reminded of Wayne Manor again. 'Did you know that bat poo used to be a valuable commodity in the nineteenth century? It was called guano – people used it for fertiliser, and merchants sailed shiploads of it all around the world.'

That tickled old Piers. He laughed again in that weird way he had, like a little shout. He shook his head. 'Batshit,' he said. 'Really?'

'Yup,' I said. 'And here's another one: if you put the smallest amount of alcohol on a scorpion, it will go crazy and sting itself to death.'

'I'll bear that in mind.'

'And stags . . .' I said. 'My dad told me that when they're being chased they always look for water, and they stand in it to try to lose the hounds. It's some instinct they have.'

Piers raised his monobrow at me. 'Now that one I did know,' he said, heavy with irony. I kicked myself under the table. Of *course* he knew that. Stags were staring down at us from the walls and we'd be chasing one tomorrow; Piers must've grown up with this stuff.

In between the Piers conversation I could hear Chanel chatting to Henry in her perfectly trained posh accent. She was getting excited and waving her hands, her flawless white nails flashing in front of her face as she became more animated. Her cheeks were a little flushed, her eyes shone and she couldn't have been prettier as she rabbited on and on about her father, his house in Cheshire, the pool, the cinema room, the fleet of cars. Then she started to talk about the Saros 7S, and how her dad had invented the half-phone, half-tablet, and how much money it had made. My stomach shrivelled within me. Henry was looking all polite and engaged, but something in me wanted to warn Chanel, tell her to stop.

Esme and Shafeen, as far as I could tell, were talking about some wedding she'd been to in the summer, and how he knew all the same people that'd been there. Shafeen was giving nothing away. But then again, I reminded myself, if he'd actually been friends with the Medievals all along, they'd know everything there was to know about him anyway. If the Medievals *were* shopping for new members, Shafeen certainly had the right pedigree.

The one consolation at dinner was the food, which was delicious. A sort of white soup, creamy and savoury, a flat white fish in a green sauce, a slab of red meat with roasted vegetables. The meat had an interesting tang to it. 'What's this?' I asked Piers.

'Venison,' he said.

Mouth full, I glanced guiltily up at the stag heads on the wall. They looked down at me accusingly.

Gradually I began to notice that Piers was not only acting like a middle-aged man but drinking like one too. He was getting steadily drunk. I was on the water, because just that one glass of champagne in the drawing room had made me feel quite lightheaded, but he worked his way through all the wines on offer, cycling through the colours as the courses went by; white wine for the soup and fish, red for the meat, yellow wine in little glasses after the pudding. And it was with the arrival of the port, dark as blood, that things began to get nasty.

Before then we'd had little pockets of conversation – turning to one neighbour, then the other – but after the food was cleared away and the servants had disappeared, the conversation became more general, including all of us, and that's when the bloodletting began.

'That's enough about fathers,' Piers said as the port came round. 'What about your mother?'

Suddenly everyone was quiet. Everyone was listening.

I took a breath. 'My mother left when I was sixteen months old.'

Piers leaned towards me, his eyes glassy, his speech slurred. 'Why?'

I saw Shafeen shoot him a quick, angry look.

I straightened my cheese knife on my plate. 'I don't know.' I hoped Piers would drop it now. But he didn't.

'Didn't Mummy wuv you?' he said in a hideous baby-talk voice.

I shrugged. 'Guess not,' I said lightly, but I was praying he wouldn't ask me anything else. I didn't feel I could speak. There seemed to be a strange lump in my throat.

Luckily Piers turned away from me and shouted across the table. 'What about you, Carphone? Your mother a bitch too?'

'I never said –' I protested.

'Shhh,' said Piers, swinging back to me and inaccurately placing his forefinger on his thick lips. 'I am asking. Carphone. A question.' He turned back to Chanel, who had turned as white as her dress. 'Well, *Chanel*? What's Mama like? She must be a bitch to have saddled you with a name like that.'

Shafeen dropped his knife on his side plate like a gunshot. Everyone jumped, but all eyes remained firmly on Chanel. Suddenly her answer seemed really important. I looked at Henry; couldn't he stop this? But he was looking at Chanel too.

Chanel sat a little straighter in her chair. She looked Piers right in the eye and said, quite clearly, 'My mum is luvly.'

I heard it at once.

She'd said *luvly*, not *lovely*.

Under all her layers of careful elocution lessons, the Cheshire accent was still there, and, in a moment of stress, it had come back. She spoke like I did. Like they did on *Coronation Street*. I could see, then, the hazards of pretending to be what you are not, and was glad I'd never bothered. How much worse it was to pretend to be one of them and slip, instead of speaking like me all the time.

The Medievals, of course, spotted it at once. The girls snickered bitchily. Cookson pretended to be all concerned. 'What's happened to your accent, Chanel?' he said, as if she'd lost something. Piers, of course, was the worst. He hooted with laughter and suddenly regressed from middle-aged man to primary-school kid. 'Luvly!' he crowed in his best northern accent. 'Ay oop! Where's me flat cap? Where's me whippet? Ma mum's *luvly.*' He got up and suddenly jumped onto the table, his great feet sending china and glasses flying. 'Luvly, luvly, luvly,' he sang, to the oompah-oompah tune of a northern brass band. He waved his hands around, as if conducting an orchestra. And then, unbelievably, they all started singing it, all the Medievals in a chorus, everyone but Henry. *Luvly, luvly, luvly.* It was nightmarish.

I looked at Chanel, who had slumped in her chair, eyes fixed on her cheese plate, and I knew that in another moment she would cry.

Then, urgently and loudly, Shafeen spoke. '*My* mother,' he said harshly, cutting across the row, 'is a wild animal.'

Well, that got our attention. Everyone shut the hell up, their heads snapping around to look at Shafeen at the foot of the table. Piers clambered down and slid back into his chair. Shafeen placed his hands out either side of him on the polished wood and held the room's total attention.

'My father's palace,' he said slowly and deliberately, projecting like an actor, 'lies in the Aravalli mountains of

Rajasthan, above the hill station at Guru Shikhar. My mother tells a story of when I was a baby and had just begun to crawl. It was the hottest part of the summer and I was a thirsty little thing, so she was breastfeeding me almost constantly.'

We were all listening intently, Chanel's slip forgotten. Shafeen the shy, the awkward around girls, was transformed; he was quite the storyteller. His voice somehow made you see what he was saying as if you were watching a film. I found I was imagining mini-Shafeen as the haughty little maharajah from *Indiana Jones and the Temple of Doom*, breastfeeding in a nappy, a silken turban and a jewel between his eyebrows.

'We were on the veranda, my mother reclining on a couch. The white curtains of the palace, fine as cobwebs, were stirring around us in the warm air, the parakeets calling from the acacia trees. Well, my mother was exhausted, as I'd kept her up all night, and she fell asleep right in the middle of feeding me. When she awoke, hours later, the curtains were still stirring, the parakeets still calling, but I was gone.'

We were absolutely still, listening. Piers had actually frozen with his port glass halfway to his lips, as if he was under a spell. Shafeen's place at the table had been transformed; he was not at the lowest place any more, but the highest. He was the maharajah among us. 'My mother jumped up and called my father and the servants. My father called the palace guards. They searched a hundred rooms, the water gardens, the stables, but I was nowhere to be seen. In the end they left the grounds altogether and went into the forest – where they stopped and could go no further. For under a canopy of acacia trees was a tiger.'

No one moved.

'It's famous tiger country up there. But this was the biggest one any of them had ever seen. It was a she-tiger, lying in the shade with her cubs. And they are the most dangerous. Tiger mothers will do anything to protect their young. My mother fell to her knees and started wailing; for she had spotted me crouching in the middle of the cubs, right by the tiger's belly. She was sure I was dead and the cubs were gathering to devour me. My father told her to be quiet – tigers don't like noise.'

They would have liked the Great Hall at that moment – no one even breathed.

'My father's guards had guns, but they could not shoot for fear of hitting me. In the end my mother walked forward alone. She looked in the she-tiger's eyes as she went to claim her son. My mother says it was the longest walk of her life – green eyes meeting dark eyes, man and beast, mother and mother. When she got closer, she fell to her knees again, this time to give thanks for the miracle she saw. I was alive; not only that, but I was in no danger at all; I was snuggled in between the tiger cubs, fighting for my place, feeding from the tiger's nipple.'

Now there were gasps, and a little nervous laughter. Shafeen remained deadly serious. There was still clearly a punchline to come, and he fixed his eyes directly on Henry. 'Ever since then they've called me *baagh ka beta*. The tiger's son. Because I was suckled at a tiger's *tit*.'

He uttered the last word like a challenge. I'd never heard him use even the mildest swear word before, because swear words, as we all know, are Savage. But he'd judged his audience perfectly. The word itself, edgy, but not a curse, was a gauntlet in his host's face.

Henry leaned back in his chair. He looked at Shafeen speculatively, as if they were in some sort of poker game. The moment was tense, dangerous. Then Henry smiled. 'Amazing,' he said.

This was the cue for approval; the Medievals started yakking like hyenas. I think I actually breathed a sigh of relief, and I could see Chanel doing the same. Piers gave his little shout of laughter, and repeated 'Tiger's tit! Tiger's tit!' over and over again. Cookson, who was clearly as drunk as Piers, jumped up and started wrestling with the tiger-skin rug that lay before the great fireplace, kissing the whiskery cheeks and saying, 'Mummy! Mummy!'

Shafeen sat still, his eyes on Henry. Then he lifted his glass in a salute to his host. Throwing his head back, he drained it in one go.

Henry clapped his hands and rubbed them together, brisk and businesslike, but also as if anticipating something delicious. 'Ladies –' he nodded to Charlotte – 'would you excuse us?' And all the Medieval girls got up, as if they all knew exactly what to do. I'd seen this in *Maurice*, the men and women splitting into different rooms after dinner. This meant I would not get a chance to talk to Shafeen, and I really wanted to. I had a weird feeling that I had to thank him on behalf of – well, *women*, I guess – for jumping in to save Chanel. The men stood too, while we left the room, and as we filed through the door to the drawing room I was the last, so I took my chance and grabbed his sleeve. He turned with an odd expression – pent up, excited and impatient all at once. I opened my mouth to thank him on behalf of the world's women, realised how dumb that sounded and just couldn't do it. Instead I whispered, 'Was that true? The tiger-mother thing?'

He frowned. 'Of *course* not,' he said. 'My father runs a bank in Jaipur. You're as bad as they are.' And then I had to leave.

So now I knew. He wasn't their friend after all. He had woven a tale to turn the guns on himself, to make himself the focus and the target, instead of Chanel. And, more than that, he was locked in some strange rivalry with Henry de Warlencourt, fought from their two ends of the table. But, I had to keep reminding myself, just as in the history lesson, Henry had done nothing. Cookson and Piers were his attack dogs. Henry was that Renaissance prince who had trained his hounds to hunt men. He didn't do the ripping apart himself, but he held the leash.

The girls made polite, soothing conversation. They reassured Chanel that they'd only been teasing and it was all in good fun. I wondered if it was always the girls' job to calm things down and put the brakes on when the boys had gone too far. I didn't believe any of their bullshit.

All I could think about was Henry watching the carnage at dinner, his eyes glittering like the Friars'.

The hunting had already started.

chapter nine

The first thing I saw when I woke up in the morning was the stag's head staring down at me from above the fireplace.

Of course I was used to these kinds of trophies on the walls of STAGS, but even so, a disembodied head seemed an odd thing to have in a bedroom. It's quite creepy, really, if you think about it. Now it was daylight outside I could see the stubby lashes above the glass eyes, and the moth-eaten fur, but that didn't make it any better. I sat up in the four-poster bed, and the eyes followed me. It unsettled me a little bit, so I decided to give the stag a name – a real doofus name that couldn't scare anyone. 'Hello, Jeffrey,' I said. The stag stared at me, but he already seemed a little bit less scary. He seemed like he was listening. 'So, Jeffrey,' I said, 'what do you suppose today will bring?' Glassy stare. 'No. I'm really asking. I'm really wondering.'

And I was. After the dinner last night, and the roasting of Chanel, and Shafeen's crazy *Jungle Book* bullshit story to put an end to it, the girls had all gone to bed pretty early. We were all aware that we'd need to be up at the crack of sparrows today for the stag hunt. I pointed two fingers at Jeffrey's head, cocked my thumb and pulled the trigger. 'Bang, bang,' I said.

I got out of the bed and went to the window. The stag head watched me. I opened the heavy curtains and blinked at the view. Practically as far as I could see there were grounds and parklands, including walled rose gardens and a sort of vegetably kitchen garden. Beyond that was a formal woodland area, dotted with statues, temples, lakes and fountains, where the hedges were cut into shapes like peacocks. Further still there was a kind of fenced paddock with, of course, horses in it. And far in the distance was a little frill of forest, and, rising up beyond the trees, the purple hills of the Lake District. It was stunning, and about as far from our terraced house in Arkwright Road, Manchester, as you could possibly get. 'We're not in Kansas any more, Jeffrey,' I said.

I shivered a bit – the fire was out and it was pretty cold, but that wasn't what was making me shiver. The drive was a whole bunch of activity already. Land Rovers and jeeps were already pulling up, and there was a horse there too. Not loads, like you see on those films with hunt scenes in them, like *A Handful of Dust*, but just one, saddled up and skittering about on the drive. I swallowed. Surely I wasn't going to be expected to ride?

There was also a bunch of hounds, smart-looking black-and-tan ones, swarming around the horse's legs, yipping and tail-wagging. Then I saw something that really made my stomach turn over. Loads of these guys in flat caps – including man-mountain and chatterbox Perfect – were loading guns into the back of the jeeps. The guns had smooth pewter-grey barrels and glossy stocks of caramel-coloured wood. They were being packed into these sort of racks, rows and rows of them. They looked harmless and dangerous all at once. I suddenly felt a bit sick. 'Well, Jeffrey,' I said, trying to style it out, 'shit just got real.'

Perfect finished his scary packing and suddenly turned and looked up at my window, as if he knew I was watching him. Our eyes met for a long, long minute before I sidestepped behind the curtains as if I'd been caught doing something wrong.

Just at that moment someone knocked at the door, and then opened it without waiting for a reply. It was Betty, with an enormous tray – silver, of course. It had loads of stuff on it – glasses and cups and a kind of silver dome, and a little crystal vase with a flower in it.

I went to help her, but she said coldly, 'That's all right, miss,' and placed it on the bed. She stood back, clasped her hands and pursed her lips. She obviously hadn't forgiven me for that crack about her freaky husband. Looking at the floor the whole time, she said, 'There are fresh towels in the bathroom, miss; if you'd like to take your bath after breakfast, I'll get the fire lit and lay out your clothes.'

She just stood there. 'Sure,' I said. 'Thank you.'

I wasn't sure that I could eat anything, but once she'd gone and I clambered back into bed I found that I was ravenous. There was toast wrapped in a crisp white napkin, orange juice, coffee in a little silver pot, a basket of pastries and, under the silver dome, a full English breakfast: bacon, eggs, sausages and black pudding. It was the best breakfast I'd ever tasted, and I was willing to bet that was because every animal on the plate had very recently been walking around the Longcross estate. I even ate the black pudding, which I don't usually do because I'm always a bit freaked out that it's made from blood. Today it was delicious; perhaps because it was just the right thing to eat on a huntin' day. *Blood for breakfast*, I thought.

Full up, I went to have a bath (no showers at Longcross – I guessed they were Savage) and when I came out, all wrapped in this big white dressing gown, the bed was made and the fire had magically been lit; Jeffrey's eyes were shining again and his fur was all orange under his chin. You know that bit in the Disney *Cinderella* when she's chopping all the vegetables in the kitchen, and the fairy godmother comes, and when she looks back all the vegetables are chopped and the fires lit and the pots and pans are sparkling? That. On the bed was a neat array of clothes, beautifully laid out. Esme had been right; I hadn't needed to bring any more than underwear. There was a shirt with a discreet green check, a sludge-coloured cashmere jumper, a kind of silk scarf (I wasn't sure where to wear that – on my head like the Queen?) and a waxed jacket. For my bottom half there were khaki trousers made of this kind of tough material and the inevitable green wellies. There was a hat too – a brown, brimmed Indiana Jones thing. As ever, nothing looked brand new. All the clothes had really good labels from the really posh outfitters that the Medievals favoured, names like Turnbull and Asser and Harvie and Hudson. They were great quality, but a little . . . second hand. I wondered who had worn them before.

I looked in the mirror. I looked like one of *them*. I took the hat off again and threw it, Indy style, on the bed. It felt like a step too far.

Then I just kind of sat about, getting more and more nervous. I kept going to the window and watching the increased activity on the drive. Now I could see Henry and Piers and Cookson, all in tweed jackets and flat caps, laughing and smoking by the Land Rovers, completely at their ease. I wasn't sure what to do, but soon there was another knock at the door. 'His lordship's compliments, miss,' said my grumpy fairy godmother, 'and would you join him and the other guests downstairs on the drive?'

chapter ten

It was only when I went out onto the driveway that I realised how truly beautiful the house was.

And how massive. Ever seen *Brideshead Revisited*? Remember that fricking huge house with the fountain and the dome and the massive servants' wings and stable blocks and the thousands of windows and dozens of pillars? It was just like that. It was so huge, and so stunning, that it was hard to believe that it belonged to one family. Then I remembered that the de Warlencourts didn't just own this house, they had a London house too. And probably a ton of other houses. I was definitely in the Land of Oz.

I walked towards where the cars and the boys were, my wellies crunching on the gravel. Servants in long black coats went about with silver trays, handing out some small strong drink. I took one and downed it, as that seemed to be the thing to do. I thought it was a mistake to start with as it mingled vomitously with my black pudding. But after a while it began to warm my stomach, giving me the courage to stride up to the boys.

Henry said, 'Greer! Good morning. Did you sleep well?'

I smiled at him sweetly. 'Yes, thanks,' I said. I wasn't sure what I thought about him now – I thought I had seen, last night, some sort of relish in his eyes, a keen enjoyment of what had happened to me, to Chanel. But today it was hard to believe. He was friendly, very normal and very, very handsome.

Piers and Cookson, taking as ever their master's lead, smiled too, the cracks about my mum and Chanel's apparently forgotten. In the cold light of day it seemed hard to believe that that nasty little scene at dinner had really happened. They looked completely at home in their hunting clothes, and that was saying something, because Piers, I'm not kidding, had on a deerstalker, exactly like you see Sherlock Holmes wearing in films. But he didn't even look ridiculous, I guess because we were about to go, well, deer-stalking. I didn't really know what to say to any of them; their very ease was intimidating. But the hounds came to my rescue; they circled around me, jumping up and licking, and thumping my wellies with their tails, until Henry and I both collapsed with laughter. 'Sorry,' he said, and shoved them off. 'Arcas, behave! Get down, Ladon! Down, Tigris!'

'Cute names,' I said, and fell to my knees to pet them while they slobbered all over me.

'How lovely,' he said, looking down fondly, hands in pockets. 'I didn't imagine you would like animals.'

'I've grown up with wildlife,' I said.

'Ah yes,' he said. 'Your father and his filming.'

I was a bit surprised – I didn't know he'd heard my conversation with Piers at dinner. Maybe the boys all compared notes last night after the girls had left. I was still pissed off about what had happened at dinner, and I didn't want to let him off the hook so easily. 'Do *you* like animals?' I asked. 'Or just killing them?'

'Both,' he said, and as if to prove his point his groom walked the horse up to him, and he stroked its velvety neck. Despite my wildlife boast I backed off a bit from the massive creature, the hounds yipped and Henry, like the Crusader of whose blood he was born, vaulted onto the horse and gathered the reins. It was an impressive move, and I had to fight hard to be all wry and sardonic and all the other things I prided myself on being in the face of Henry's charms. Henry called down, from horseback, 'If you'll forgive me, I'm going to ride ahead; I'm the harbourer today.'

Still brave with the fiery little drink, I said, 'I don't know what that is.'

The perfect smile widened. He leaned down to place a warm glove on my shoulder, but didn't explain. 'See you up there. You're coming with the girls in the shooting brake. Have fun.' He turned the horse's head with the reins and kicked its glossy sides. The horse took off in a whirl of hoofs and Henry rode it easily, thundering down the drive with the hounds running in his wake.

I watched him, feeling a bit like Guinevere in *First Knight* watching Lancelot ride away. I'm not going to lie; Henry riding down the drive of that palace of a house, on a black horse, with the hounds at his heels, was one of the most exciting things I've ever seen. I decided in that moment that while Piers and Cookson were clearly tossers, Henry was really OK.

A dry voice spoke at my back. 'The harbourer rides ahead of the rest of the hunt party on horseback.' I turned to see Shafeen standing behind me. Once again he looked absolutely right. He suited the muted autumnal colours as much as he'd suited the white tie last night. At the same time he looked somehow different from the others, without looking out of place. He had decided against the hat, as I had, but it had been the right choice – his dark hair, no longer slicked back, blew softly around his face. But he still looked stern, and he sounded it too. 'The harbourer's job is to single out a stag from the herd to be hunted by the rest of the party.'

'OK,' I said. I didn't really know what to say to him either – last night he'd jumped in to save us with his tiger-mother tale, but then he'd told me I was just like the Medievals. Having imparted his lesson, he didn't seem inclined to go on chatting, so I looked around for other company. I could see the Medieval girls walking up the drive, and I did a double take.

There were *four* of them.

As they came closer I could see that there were the three sirens, and Chanel. They were all talking and laughing, their blonde hair bouncing as they walked. They looked like an advert, and actually appeared to be walking in slow motion. There were tiny variations in their costume, the colour of their hats, the cut of the waxed jackets, the knot of the silk scarves at the throat. Charlotte was wrapped in one of those massive tartan shawls that are so big they look like a blanket. But from a distance they looked completely interchangeable.

As they got nearer I could actually see there was a difference, and the odd one out was Chanel. I knew immediately that all the clothes she was wearing were her own – they hadn't been put out on her bed by a sulky servant. She'd bought them all, brand new. As she got close I could see that her wellies were box fresh – with a little red-and-white tab saying 'Hunter' on the front. Her jumper was too bright, her trousers too tight, her waxed jacket not weathered and seasoned like mine but pristine. Whichever one of the Medieval girls had been sent to dress Chanel before she left STAGS must have struck out – Chanel obviously already had all the right gear, probably ordered the best of the best the minute she'd got The Invitation. And, man, did she look excited. Her eyes were shining and her cheeks as pink as they had been last night at dinner – before, you know, the *incident*.

I greeted the girls as soon as they came close, and they all smiled nicely enough, but they ended the conversation they'd been having as they walked, and didn't start it again, as if they didn't want to talk about whatever it was in front of me. I moved next to Chanel and grinned conspiratorially. I'd really felt for her last night, and wanted to let her know she had an ally. 'Bit weird this, isn't it?'

She looked down her nose at me. 'I think it's perfectly divine,' she said coldly, shutting me down. She sounded just like them. Then she did this freaky thing: she lifted her hair with her hand and flipped it to the opposite parting. It fell perfectly. It was their move, the tic of the sirens; they tossed their hair around 24/7 and now Chanel was doing it too. In fact, she performed it perfectly. God, I thought, she'd make a perfect Medieval. She had bounced back, it seemed, from the ridicule of last night's dinner and embedded herself right at the heart of the sirens. Very clearly she thought she was their friend, and not mine.

I see, I thought. Four against one.

'Come on, girls!' trilled Charlotte in her role as fake-hostess. 'We're going in the shooting brake.' Apparently this was a long car with wooden panels down the side, the most Medieval car you've ever seen. We could all sit easily, if not comfortably, in the back. We set off bumpily up the hill, following Henry's path.

The huntin' had begun.

chapter eleven

I'm not going to lie; the start of the day was pretty boring. (Of course it got pretty exciting later, but not in a good way.)

Once the cars had dropped us at the top of this massive hill, we just walked – the three (four) Medieval girls in front, me behind.

Don't get me wrong; it was really beautiful country. In the weak autumn sunlight the hills looked as if they'd been buttered like my breakfast toast, and the purple, heather-covered valleys gave way in the far distance to the glimpse of a glassy lake. Longcross, far behind us, looked beautiful, like some advert for the British Empire. If I'd been told I was going on a walk, I'd probably have enjoyed it. But for a hunt it was pretty – well – pedestrian. No one really talked to me except to ask from time to time if I was 'all right' (the Medievals never said 'OK'), to which I would reply, over-enthusiastically, 'Great, thanks!'– and then move on. The truth is, I didn't want to admit I wasn't having a great time. It seemed like a weakness. This weekend had had such a build-up that to say I wasn't enjoying it would have felt like I'd failed in some way. And it was OK really. No one was nasty to me; it was just as if I wasn't really there. The Medieval girls were chatting up Chanel like mad – I mean really kissing her arse. Maybe last night had been some crazy sort of initiation ceremony, and Chanel had passed the test. Or maybe the girls felt bad about how the boys had behaved and were making it up to her. Either way, I was pretty sure they'd already decided she was going to be a Medieval and I wasn't. I might as well not have come.

After a bit we all stopped, on this hillside, and sort of hung around for ages. People were just chatting and drinking from hip flasks. The hunt servants caught up with us with the gear and another pack of hounds. Chanel was obviously very nervous of the dogs; either she was scared of them, or she was afraid of them jumping up and putting their muddy paws on her immaculate khaki jodhpurs. I could see her eyeing them apprehensively and skirting around them carefully as if they smelled. Which they sort of did.

I'd have liked to chat to the hunt servants, maybe ask a bit about the guns, and the stag hunt, but I was pretty sure it wasn't the done thing to talk to them. In the end I caught up with Shafeen, who was standing confidently with his gun sort of dangling over his arm. He'd obviously brought his own, but it didn't look in a very good state – the stock looked separated from the barrel. 'Is your gun broken?'

He *almost* smiled. Almost. 'No. That's how you carry them. Empty, open and over the arm. Stops you accidentally shooting someone's head off if you trip.'

'Oh.' As he didn't sound exactly unfriendly I asked, 'What's going on?'

'Our esteemed host – the harbourer – has ridden ahead with his chosen hounds. They're the "tufters" and they're selected because they are steady and won't "riot", as it's called, at the scent of a deer. He'll have separated his chosen stag from the rest of the herd and driven him to another part of the hillside known as a "couch". Once the stag is harboured in the couch, he'll stay all day unless he's disturbed.'

'And we're about to disturb him?'

'Correct.' He pointed to a tall man in the inevitable waxed jacket. It was human basilisk and headkeeper Perfect. You couldn't see his feet for hounds. 'See that fellow there? He's the whipper-in. Henry will have arranged with him to bring the hunt party to this spot, hoping that the stag will break cover here.'

I felt pretty sorry for the stag at this point, but at the same time I really wanted to see him. I'd only ever seen heads of stags, once they were dried and desiccated and stuffed and mounted. Jeffrey and all his body-less cousins.

'Is Henry coming back?' I asked casually. I remembered his farewell: *See you up there.*

'Yes, don't worry,' Shafeen said drily. 'He'll come back once the stag breaks cover, to change hounds. The whipper-in will take the tufters, and Henry will take the rest of the pack. Essentially he swaps the calm dogs for the crazy ones. The killers.' I looked at the black-and-tan hounds that were milling around Perfect, wagging their tails. They looked pretty harmless.

'For most of the day the stag will stay ahead of the hounds, outrunning them easily. But it has to run across moor and woodland – hard terrain – and leap walls and streams and fences. Eventually it gets tired.'

I felt tired already. 'Do we follow it all day?'

He nodded. 'The hounds follow its scent, and we follow its "slot" – that's his track. Hoof-prints in mud, splashed rocks . . . those kinds of things give it away. The beat keepers –' he pointed to Perfect's flat-capped underlings – 'stop him getting too far off track. And of course there'll be a lunch somewhere. The upper classes never kill without eating.' That was the strange thing about Shafeen; he obviously *was* the upper classes – he clearly knew every single thing about stag hunting, for example – but he spoke of his people quite scornfully, as if he was outside of their world. I couldn't figure him out.

'Then what?'

'Well, when it can't run any more, it will turn and face the hounds. That's called the stag at bay.'

'My dad's told me about that. They find water, and stand in it, to try to lose the hounds.'

'Except it doesn't work. They've been known to swim for their lives, with the hounds swimming after them with their teeth in the stag's hind parts.'

I swallowed. 'And then?'

'Then,' he said, 'it's all over; one of the guns, the "dispatcher", shoots it dead at close range. And the stag is rewarded for having provided a good day's sport by having its belly cut open and its guts thrown to the hounds.'

I must've made a face.

'Don't worry,' he said, more gently. 'Most hunt followers won't actually get to see the kill.'

'But it will have *happened*,' I said. 'It doesn't matter if I'm there to witness it or not.'

He looked at me in an interested way and opened his mouth to say something, when suddenly, and without warning, a fricking great deer shot past me, leaping through our company, so close to me I could feel the disturbance of the air.

I staggered back, hand on my chest. 'Jeee-sus.'

Shafeen steadied me. 'Are you OK?'

'Yes.' I watched as the deer bounded away across the heather. It was a beautiful sight, but sort of unexpected. In my mind's eye I'd pictured some sort of cartoon *Bambi* deer, all cute and big-eyed and wobbly-legged. But this was a lithe, gristly beast; all greasy dark fur and hard horn. He was fast; he'd put a fair distance between him and us before I'd even regained my balance. To my surprise, no one moved. The hounds yipped sharply, but their handlers held them back.

'Why don't we go after that one?'

'That's not the designated deer,' said Shafeen. 'Henry will have picked out a "warrantable" stag, one that's over five years old. That one's too young. They choose their victims carefully,' he said sardonically. 'If they murder that one now, what will they kill next year?'

Again, he'd used the word 'they', as if he wasn't of their number. He was really hard to read, especially as he'd turned away from me and was scanning the hillside.

'Look.' He pointed. 'There he is. He's a wily old one – he sent the other deer running and then lay down in the heather.'

I looked, but all I could see were the tops of antlers, just peeping above the tussocks like a gorse bush.

Then the hounds started baying and the stag rose up from the gorse. Back legs first, then front legs, in a graceful, rocking motion. He was absolutely enormous, much bigger than the decoy deer. This was a noble-looking beast, his head almost as big as a cow's, his antlers towering above. He looked directly at us for a split second, then turned his head to the hills and started to run.

Just then there was this big kerfuffle and Henry rode into sight, his hounds at his heels. He tumbled from the horse and exchanged his pack for Perfect's. The hounds were let go, and the hunt was on. My heart gave a leap as I watched, but it was the stag, not the hounds, that I was urging on. *Go on, go on, go on*, I said under my breath, using the force, willing him to outpace them. I was Obi-Wan Kenobi from *Star Wars*. *This isn't the deer you're looking for.* And, as if my Jedi mind trick had worked, the stag outran the hounds easily.

'Look at him go!' crowed Piers as everyone moved off to follow the bounding deer. 'He *loves* it! Let's get him.' I hated him at that moment.

'Show time,' said Shafeen, shouldering his gun.

He looked as if he knew what he was doing. 'Have you shot before?'

'Just tigers,' he said, and moved off ahead of me.

I couldn't tell if he was being funny or not.

chapter twelve

At some points through the hours that followed, as we stalked the stag through coppice, stream, hill and valley, I pulled myself up short and thought about what a weird ritual this was: all the servants, all the Land Rovers, all the expense, just so a handful of rich kids could kill a stag.

At other moments, when we caught sight of our noble quarry, I even found myself agreeing with Piers. The stag, at times, seemed to get some sort of enjoyment from outwitting the baying hounds. And if it could have stayed that way, with us following and him always getting away, it would have been fine. But, of course, it didn't.

We stopped for lunch, the stag safely 'harboured' and apparently happy to hang around for an hour or two for our chase to resume. We all trooped into a little building on the hillside called 'the bothy'. It was a cheerful place – just a single room with stone walls and roof beams and wooden floors, like a mini-barn, but it had a fireplace with a cheerful fire in it and a long table set for lunch. Over the fireplace hung – you've guessed it – a pair of antlers. No head this time, just the antlers.

Lunch was lovely, and even after my massive breakfast I was starving from all that walking. I was sitting opposite Henry and next to Shafeen, so I felt a bit like a small satellite state between two warring superpowers. I mostly kept my head down and ate. We had shepherd's pie made with venison, Brussels sprouts (which I've never had on any day but Christmas before) and carrots, followed by apple-and-blackcurrant crumble. Then there was Stilton cheese served, bizarrely, with ginger cake. The lunch was served by an entirely different set of servants, obviously driven up here just for this bit. Just as at dinner, there were no normal things to drink like juice or Coke, but just wine. I learned that posh wines are not called red and white but have their own names. This red wine was called claret and the white wine Sancerre. At the end of the meal there was no port this time, but a choice of damson gin or whisky. Basically, if you didn't want to drink alcohol you had to drink water. I noticed again that the Medievals drank like adults. (I know they were mostly eighteen, but you know what I mean.) The girls weren't too bad, and if Henry was he didn't show it, but Piers and Cookson drank heavily. And they couldn't take it.

I thought, as we ate and drank, about the stag outside, panting in the heather. No food, no drink, maybe mouthing at the bitter grass. Did he allow himself to lie down in the gorse and rest his weary legs? Did he think he'd got away with it? That the baying hounds and braying humans had gone away? That he was safe for another day? Or did he know how this went, and that if he ventured too far he'd be turned back by the beat keepers stationed about the hillside to keep him pinned?

My strong sympathies for the stag, who seemed destined for fireplace decoration, made it hard to listen to all the guff I heard at lunch about sustainability, and culling, and animal control, and how it was good for the deer population. Mostly this came from the girls and Piers and Cookson, talking over each other in their upper-class voices. Henry didn't join in. 'Is that all true?' I asked him. He shrugged and took a sip from his wine glass. Above the crystal rim of it, a familiar light shone in his eyes. 'I just like to hunt,' he said, and I had to respect his honesty, even if I didn't agree with him. 'In all seriousness though,' he said, and the whole table went quiet and everyone turned to look at him, 'nature is all a question of order and balance. If an inferior species begins to get too robust, or threatens to grow beyond the boundaries of what is natural, then it must be culled.'

'It's true,' agreed Cookson, Henry's echo. 'Deer, for instance; if they become too numerous, they can be a menace for farmers – they can damage the habitats of wildlife but also interfere with cultivated herds like cattle.'

'Dashed nuisance,' agreed Piers, slurring slightly.

'In order for the higher orders of species to thrive,' Henry went on in a measured, reasonable tone, 'the lower orders must be curbed.'

There was a weird energy at the table, a hungry attentiveness.

'So, what you're *saying*,' said Shafeen slowly, 'is that *some* species must not be allowed to get above themselves.'

'Got it in one.'

'You're speaking, of course, exclusively of the animal kingdom?' asked Shafeen.

Henry turned cool blue eyes on him. 'What else?'

After lunch, we prepared to go back out. Chanel had gone to the toilet and the Medievals went into some sort of huddle. There was a lot of sideways glancing and nodding, and a weird air of anticipation and eagerness. Shafeen, at my shoulder, narrowed his eyes at the little group.

'Wonder what that's all about.'

I shrugged my jacket on. 'Got me.'

Chanel came back, and we all headed out again. I hadn't been wrong – there was a real sense of excitement among the Medievals. They were fairly buzzing with it, and I assumed that they were jazzed by the prospect of the approaching kill. In contrast to this, Shafeen, whom I'd hoped was becoming an ally, became more and more withdrawn and silent as the afternoon drew on, and the chase approached its end.

And end it inevitably did. There was a growing sense of urgency, as the sun was dipping to the horizon and the dusk beginning to fall. As the light dimmed it grew colder, and even the jumper and the waxed jacket couldn't keep the chill from my bones. Chanel was shivering too, and, as we made our way down the valley I saw Henry catch up with her, take off his tweed jacket and drape it over her shoulders. It was a move I've seen in films a million times, particularly old black-and-white ones, but when Henry did it, it didn't seem cringy, but gentlemanly and considerate. Chanel kind of snuggled down into it, hugging it to herself and thanking him prettily. I felt, just for an instant, a little jag of jealousy. Did Henry like Chanel? The thought somehow made me even colder.

We made our way down the hill to the lake that lay at the bottom of the valley like a dropped mirror. I knew, everyone seemed to know, that we would find the stag there. And we did. The deer was cornered as my dad had said, as Piers had said, as Shafeen had said, in water. He stood nobly at the edge of the lake, his legs disappearing below the surface, his reflection, on this clear autumn day, perfectly replicated in the water.

A beautiful day to die.

The hounds crowded on the foreshore, staying out of the water for now, if not for long. They seemed in no hurry, now the outcome was inevitable. They didn't even bark; they didn't need to. They knew there was an ending.

The stag looked at them, and they looked at the stag. Hunter and hunted faced each other. The deer looked as if he was posing for one of those portraits you've seen reproduced a million times on shitty souvenir plates or watercolours, or stitched onto cushions in twee tea shops: The Stag at Bay. He looked so noble and beautiful, so much more noble and more beautiful than any of us. I could have cried. 'Down,' said Henry, fingers spread, palms facing the ground. 'Everybody down.' And we all got down onto the cold, prickly heather, on our elbows like commandos, hardly breathing.

'Greer,' said Henry, in a low, slow voice like a hypnotist, never taking his eyes off the stag, 'looks like you'll be our dispatcher.'

'Me?' I gasped, incredulous.

He smiled. 'You're at the right place in the line. It's your kill.' Perfect darted forward, bent double, head low, to hand me a weapon, but before he could get to me Henry handed me his own gun. 'Use mine.'

I kind of stopped worrying about the stag at that point, because if *I* was going to be the one to shoot at him, he'd never been safer in his life. But then Henry slid over to me, and said, 'Look, like this.' He practically lay on top of me, on my back, arms around me, showing me how to hold the gun. The wooden stock felt warm from his hands, the metal barrel cold against my cheek. I was warmer than I'd been all afternoon, but still shivering. It was like that moment in *The Color of Money* – when Tom Cruise shows Mary Elizabeth Mastrantonio how to hold a pool cue just so he can put his arms around her. You see it in films a lot – a guy showing a girl how to hold a tennis racket or a sword or something. It can be really creepy if the girl doesn't like the guy, or if he is old or ugly or evil, but if she does and the guy is hot then it can be very romantic. Right then, I was feeling all kinds of things: that it was lovely having Henry's weight on me and his arms around me, that it was horrible that I was holding a gun; that I'd never felt so alive, that I was about to kill something; that I wanted to push him off me and scream, that I wanted him to hold me even closer. It was the most thrilling and romantic and disgusting and sickening moment of my life and I wanted to laugh and vomit all at once. If I was the person I wanted to be, the person I think I am, then I'd have pushed Henry off and chased the stag away. But I just lay there, feeling Henry de Warlencourt's sweet damson-gin breath on me – hearing him saying, *Rest the barrel on that tussock so you've a steady shot . . . lay your cheek on the barrel, bend your elbow a bit, that's right.* He pointed the gun for me, right at the deer's flank; furry warm flesh, full of blood and nerve and sinew and life, but only for a few more seconds. Henry closed his warm hand over my cold one.

Now close one eye, he said.

I could tell myself – I *do* tell myself, that it was really Henry shooting that deer, but I know it was me, my finger was the one below his on the trigger; he was the maestro, but I was the instrument.

In that long, stretched moment before he, I, we pulled the trigger, the story of Aidan's stag popped into my head. I could hear the Abbot reading the lesson in the STAGS chapel that last Mass before we broke up for Justitium. '*The blessed saint, when the hounds were running close, held up his hand to the stag and rendered him invisible. In such wise the hounds did pass him by, and their tooth did not touch him.*'

I'm not religious at all, but at that moment I prayed. I don't know if I was praying to God, or St Aidan, or who, but I prayed. *Make him invisible*, I said inside my head, gazing at the stag with the one eye that was looking down the barrel. *Make him invisible, for Christ's sake. It's the only thing that will save him now.*

But this time my Jedi powers didn't work. Henry's finger squeezed mine on the trigger; hard, hurting. There was an enormous bang in my ear and the gun kicked back into my cheek and shoulder like a blow.

At the last second I closed my eyes, unable to watch.

chapter thirteen

I thought the hunt was over. But it wasn't.

Suddenly deathly tired from exercise and about a million emotions, I sat on the cold shingle and gazed at the dead stag in the shallow water, one side of his body and one of the great antlers clearing the surface of the lake. He'd looked noble in life, but almost mythical now. All you could see was half a silhouette above the silver water, and the other half a perfect reflection again, but this time completing the antlers and the bulk of the body to make some strange alien creature. It was like one of those paintings you do in nursery school – you know, when you paint on one half, then fold the paper over. The lake was all shimmery in the dusk and it looked like that one in *Excalibur*, the one where Arthur gets his sword and then chucks it back at the end. The lake suddenly flashed and blurred as my eyes filled with tears. As I wiped my eyes I thought, *They should leave him there. It's a fitting place for him.*

But no. As I watched, the beat keepers and Perfect waded into the lake to drag the dead stag to the foreshore. They did this by pulling his antlers like bike handlebars. Once the deer was on the shingle Perfect drew his own sword – a hunting knife that flashed in the twilight – and cut the stag's throat. As the stag bled out on the pebbles Perfect shanked him in the belly, and proceeded to cut him open with a sort of sawing action. Then, as if I was watching some sort of horror film, I watched him shove both hands inside the stag and sort of flop the guts out into this plastic-lined hunting bag. The innards looked like blue snakes and seemed to move as they shifted and settled, smoking with the last warmth of life. The pearly steam in the twilight gave the corpse an even more magical appearance, although now the butchered stag looked more Halloween than legendary. I shivered as Henry wandered over with his lieutenant Cookson. 'You cold, Greer?' he asked solicitously. He could hardly give me his jacket as he'd already given it away. Instead he made a considerably less charming offer. 'If the game bag wasn't so heavy I'd ask if you wanted to carry it. The guts stay pretty warm all the way home.'

'It's like a hot handbag,' said Cookson, with his usual gift for saying what Henry had already said but taking it down to the next level.

I recoiled from this gross image, but then, to show that I wasn't entirely ignorant of the traditions of hunting, I said, 'Better leave them to the hounds. I wouldn't want to deprive them of their prize.'

Henry and Cookson wandered back to the kill, and it was then that I noticed something odd. The hounds weren't there. They'd just vanished; there wasn't a single dog to be seen. It was really weird. Perhaps they knew the hunt was over and had just slunk back up the hillside like ghosts, ready to be kennelled for the night. It seemed strange that they hadn't hung around for their reward, but at the same time I was glad I didn't have to watch them feasting on the stag's innards.

But the horror wasn't over. Perfect seemed to be juggling something slimy in his hand, cutting bits off and handing them round. He put a piece in my palm – it was like hot red jelly. 'Thanks, I guess,' I said. 'What is it?' Of course Perfect didn't answer; I never heard him speak to anyone but his master.

'It's the deer's liver,' said Shafeen at my elbow. 'You're supposed to eat it. Everyone in at the kill gets a bit.'

'Raw?' I said. 'Really?'

'They don't call it a blood sport for nothing,' said Shafeen, putting it gingerly in his mouth.

I dropped mine on the shingle in disgust and wiped my hand on a tissue. I know I'd had black pudding for breakfast, but this was a step too far. The Medievals, though, were all munching away happily, like it was Haribos or something.

As the butchery on the shore continued Piers wandered over. 'I say, want one of the hoofs? Traditional to give one to the first-timers, you know?'

I felt sick. 'I'm good,' I said.

'Please yourself,' said Piers, clearly displeased at my disrespect for tradition. 'Dashed odd. What about you, Punjabi? Nice souvenir to have. One for you and one for Carphone, eh?'

'I'm not a first-timer,' said Shafeen coldly. 'Chanel might, but I doubt it.' He looked around. 'Where *is* Chanel?'

Chanel had gone. She'd completely disappeared.

We looked all around the lake, walking round in groups of two or three. I went with Shafeen and we called her name until it echoed off the water and the mountains. We met the others coming back, without any of us having laid eyes on Chanel. While we were doing that, Perfect went up to check the bothy and the cars, but he came back shaking his head.

It was frightening. The terrain had totally changed with the setting of the sun – the lake was a black slick, the night air smelled of butchered beast. Hills were dark hunched shoulders and the trees, lacking their summer leaves, were black antlers against the purple sky. The search was on for real, as soon it would be night.

I expected the Medievals to groan and roll their eyes. I expected Piers to say, 'Dashed girl,' and Cookson to call her a 'bloody nuisance'. I expected the girls, at least, to opt to go home and bathe while the boys and the servants searched the estate. But, perhaps prompted by their new friendship, they were all apparently keen to help look. In fact, the Medievals swung into action like a machine. Hunters for centuries, this was their moment. They armed themselves with field torches and hip flasks and hunting knives. 'Right,' said Henry, 'who saw her last? And where?'

'She went to the loo after lunch,' I said, too concerned to worry if I'd used the correct term for toilet. 'But she was with us when we set off down the valley for the lake.'

'She was definitely with us in the gorge,' stated Shafeen flatly. 'You gave her your jacket.'

'So I did,' said Henry. 'Let's go back up to the gorge then – it's as good a starting place as any.'

So I wasn't the only one to have noticed the jacket thing; neither, it seemed, was Henry the only one who liked Chanel. Shafeen had leaped in to save her from humiliation with his tiger-mother story, and he'd apparently been watching over her today. Certainly on the search he appeared more concerned about her than any of us. While I couldn't help thinking that the Medievals were enjoying this unexpected twilight expedition as an extension of their day, Shafeen seemed properly worried. He was watchful and silent as a stone, listening intently. Watching him in the half-light tracking Chanel, I could almost believe he was a tiger's son. He was stealthy, but he missed nothing. Just as earlier in the day we'd searched the terrain for signs of the stag's 'slot', Shafeen followed Chanel's trail as surely as a big cat. While the Medievals swigged from their hip flasks and chattered, it was Shafeen who found the only clues we had. It was Shafeen who saw, tangled in a gorse bush, a long wiry blonde strand from Chanel's hair extensions. And it was Shafeen who saw, trodden in the mud, Chanel's flat cap of too-natty ginger tartan. He wrung it in his hands like a cloth – he looked ill.

'At least we know she came this way,' I consoled him. 'Pity we don't have the hounds. We could get them to sniff it or something and find her.' My remark was met by a weird silence from all the Medievals, but Shafeen turned to look at me, and even in the twilight I could see this strange expression on his face as if he'd just realised something. He opened his mouth to speak, but just at that moment we heard two dreadful sounds from the black hills.

The baying of hounds.

And a human scream.

With torch beams crossing in crazy patterns, we ran in the direction of the noise. The sound of the barking was eerie as hell, and a memory of seeing an old version of *The Hound of the Baskervilles*, featuring this massive hound with blood-dripping jaws, didn't help me. Worse still was the screaming, a sound I knew to be Chanel. And worse than all that was the moment when the screaming stopped. Like Hannibal Lecter said in *The Silence of the Lambs*, it's when the screaming stops that you have to worry.

In the dark and the confusion, and by some weird trick of the acoustics up in those the hills, it was difficult to know exactly where the sound was coming from. Eventually Shafeen led us to a narrow stony gorge, where limestone crevasses sliced into the hill, kind of like caves that had fallen on their side. They looked exactly like some huge monster had clawed three gashes in the landscape. At the mouth of the biggest one the hounds crowded, frenzied with bloodlust. Shafeen and I rushed forward, with Henry close behind, pushing our way through the dogs. 'Chanel!' we shouted. 'Chanel!' and then fell silent, straining to listen.

And somewhere, below the frantic baying of the hounds, I heard a tiny voice. 'Here!'

Shafeen was ahead of me, cramming his body into the longest crevasse. 'I'm too tall,' he gasped.

'Let me.' I pulled him out of the way and crawled into the tiny space. I couldn't see a thing. 'Torch,' I said, impatiently clicking my fingers outside of the cave. Shafeen put a torch in my hand and I shone it into the crevasse. There, bunched up small, filthy and tear-stained, was Chanel. I nearly cried with relief. I hadn't realised, up until that very moment, that ever since the screaming had stopped I'd thought she might be dead.

I gave her my hand. 'Come on,' I said. 'You're safe now.'

She shook her head over and over again, as if she would shake it off. 'I can't go out there,' she said, more definitely than I'd ever heard her say anything. 'The dogs.'

'Chanel,' I said, 'you're fine. We're all here.'

But she just kept shaking and shaking her head and stayed huddled up in her corner.

I crawled back out to Shafeen and Henry. They were wearing identical expressions of waiting and worry. 'She's fine,' I yelled over the baying. 'But she won't come out while the dogs are here.'

'Can you call them off?' shouted Shafeen to Henry. Somehow, in an emergency, they'd become allies.

'Certainly,' said Henry. 'Leave it to me.' He nodded in my direction. 'Tell her to get ready.'

I ducked my head back into the cave and held out my hand. 'Henry's taking care of the dogs,' I said. 'He says to get ready.' Evidently she trusted Henry more than me, because this time she put her hand in mine. It was icy cold.

I pulled her to the mouth of the crevasse, my body between the dogs and her. The noise was really deafening. I don't mind dogs at all, but even I was freaked by them. There must have been fifty, and they were utterly transformed from the friendly, slobbery, tail-waggy creatures I'd met this morning. Their teeth were pin sharp and white, their tongues red, their jaws foaming like that Hound of the Baskervilles. This, then, was the hounds in the 'riot' mode Shafeen had told me about. And I remembered something else too, from further back, from a Latin lesson at STAGS. The fifty hounds that had devoured poor Actaeon had entered a 'wolf's frenzy'. Well, this was a wolf's frenzy if ever I saw one. Something about Chanel was driving them crazy.

Then I saw Henry walk out of the darkness behind them, holding the game bag on his shoulder. '*Now!*' he shouted, and opened the bag. He tipped the deer's guts out, still steaming as Cookson had promised, and threw them right into the middle of the pack of dogs. In a fervour, they ripped the innards apart, blood flying everywhere. At the same moment I pulled Chanel out of the cave and past them, but great streaks of red splashed onto Henry's jacket, making her shriek with horror. It wasn't exactly *Carrie*, but it wasn't far off. I dragged her as far as I could away down the hillside, but her legs gave out and she collapsed on the grass. Beat, I flopped down next to her. Shafeen ran over at once and fell to his knees. 'Are you OK?' he said.

Chanel was craning round him to make sure the dogs weren't following. But the animals were otherwise engaged. They were now quiet, feeding like a silent wolf pack, calmed by blood.

Still, it was only once the beat keepers had dragged them off a fair distance away that Chanel could bring herself to speak. She nodded shakily, the opposite to the head-shaking in the cave. '*Now* I'm all right.'

Henry came over and knelt too. He and Shafeen looked like rival suitors for the princess's hand, one dark, one fair. And even though the princess was now pretty ragged, her long blonde hair everywhere, her beautiful new clothes ruined, they still had eyes for no one but her. Then Henry did a weird thing. He reached out and I thought he was going to embrace her, but instead he took his jacket back. He pulled it right off her shoulders. 'It's all covered in blood,' he said, by way of explanation. 'I'll get Perfect to bring one of the Land Rovers as close as he can to pick you up. You'll be warm and dry in no time.'

He went to instruct his headkeeper, and the dogs, spotting him at once, swarmed around him devotedly, playful as puppies once again. They stayed at Henry's heels as he gave his orders to Perfect, but as it turned out the headkeeper's transportation was not needed. Shafeen literally took matters into his own hands. 'Come on,' he said to Chanel. 'No point waiting for protocol. You'll freeze.' And in one fluid motion he picked her up and strode up the mountain with her in the direction of the cars, with all the Medievals looking on, open-mouthed. He looked all dark and tall and masterful, and she looked all blonde and pretty and pathetic draped in his arms. It was like that bit in *Sense and Sensibility* when Willoughby carries Marianne out of the rainstorm.

I collapsed onto the cold grass, full length, gazing at the stars. I was absolutely exhausted by the day. A whole morning of walking. The stag at bay. The shooting. And then, before I'd even processed the reality of being a stag murderer, all the drama of the search for Chanel. (By the way, if you're thinking that the killing of the stag was the murder I committed and that he was my only victim, you'd be wrong. I wish.)

I got to my feet eventually, only the fear that I'd be left behind giving me the strength to shift my weary bones. On legs that could barely hold me up, I followed the torches back to the cars. And all that time, after everything that had happened, all that I was thinking (and I realise that for a Buzzfeed feminist this doesn't paint me in a very good light) was that what I would *really* like would be for someone to carry *me* up a mountain like that.

chapter fourteen

It's unbelievable really, the reviving power of a hot bath, a cup of tea and a roaring fire.

In under an hour after we'd got back to the house in our Land Rover convoy, I actually felt human again. And it was just as well, since apparently it was business as usual at Longcross.

Dress laid out. Drinks at seven thirty. Dinner at eight.

I fiddled with the dress on the bed. This one was the dark red of arterial blood. I remembered the stag's blood on the shingle, the warm liver I was supposed to eat. Jeffrey watched me from the wall, and I found myself actually *wishing* for sulky Betty to come. It was hard to be alone in Lowther with Jeffrey, and I felt that night that the stag's head wore a particularly judgemental expression. 'I'm *sorry*,' I said.

And I was. Now I knew Jeffrey wasn't a joke. Now I knew that he hadn't come into this world as a head on a plaque. I knew how he'd died, and that he was once a living, breathing creature. Like the one who had run right past me and stirred the autumn air, and like the one I'd dispatched as he stood at bay in that Camelot lake. I hoped Jeffrey knew I wouldn't have pulled the trigger on my own. But did that make it any better? More than ever I felt the lack of a TV to fill the accusing silence. Instead I dried my hair in front of the fire, watching that instead. It was really quite absorbing. Historical telly.

When Betty came to dress me, my greeting was a bit over the top with relief. Used to how it went by now, I let her help me into my dress. The blood colour suited me, making me feel even more guilty. As she sat me before the mirror to do my hair I said, hesitantly, 'Betty . . . could I have it a bit less, well, ringlety than last night? You know, wavy rather than curly? Please?' I wasn't really sure, as you can probably tell, how to talk to servants, but I needn't have worried; she was very obliging in her sullen way. 'Of course, miss.' And she did a good job. Soft waves this time, with my heavy fringe parted in the middle. The strong colour of the red dress required a bit more make-up than last night's soft rose, so I swept some smoky grey over my eyelids. I was pleased with my appearance, till I thought suddenly of Chanel getting ready, and what the hell *she* must be feeling.

Amazingly, after all the drama, we weren't even very late sitting down to dinner. I saw at once though that the table was only set for eight.

Chanel wasn't there, and there was no place set for her, as if the servants had known.

I sat down at the now familiar array of silver cutlery. Tonight I was seated between Esme (meh) and Cookson (yuck).

'Is Chanel OK?' I asked Esme.

'She's fine,' she said soothingly. 'She was just a bit shaken up, so she had a bath and got into bed. Henry's having dinner sent up to her room.'

I suddenly felt a little pang of envy – I could have handled dinner in bed myself. It suddenly seemed an impossible task to have to endure all those fancy courses while making chat with random Medievals. Shafeen and Henry, my only allies and fellow Chanel-rescuers, were at the other end of the table. Shafeen was talking, guardedly, to Piers, when he wasn't having to endure Charlotte pawing at him from his other side. She had clearly been impressed, too, by his Willoughby-chivalry on the mountain. Henry and Lara were talking with their blond heads together, low-voiced. She seemed pretty salty about something – maybe she hadn't liked Henry giving Chanel his jacket or, even more likely, him practically lying on top of me when we shot the stag. He certainly didn't seem like a one-woman man.

I remembered the feeling of his arms around me, that warm sensation which had died with the stag. And, as if my memory had prompted him, Henry stood up, glass in hand.

'A very special toast,' he said, 'to Greer, a novice hunter who dispatched a stag on her first outing.' He looked at me with his very direct blue eyes and the warm feeling returned. 'Ladies and gentlemen, I give you Greer MacDonald, the dispatcher of the stag.'

I wasn't sure what to do, so I just sat there like a dumbass while they all stood up and raised their glasses. They repeated my name, and my new bizarre title, all staring at me. Then they all drained their glasses and sat down and there was a ripple of applause. It was surreal. I'd never been toasted before, but I kind of wished it wasn't for that. At the time I believed Henry thought he was being gallant, but I'd so much rather he hadn't – I would have preferred it if he'd taken the credit, as with the credit went the guilt.

Then it got worse. Two footman types brought out this big black book between them and opened it in front of Henry at the right page. The volume looked really old, with one of those aged greenish-black leather covers that in books they call 'morocco'. A third footman handed Henry a pen. It wasn't exactly a quill, but it looked like the oldest working pen you could get; one of those wartime fountain pens ministers used for signing peace treaties.

'What's happening?' I asked Esme.

'Henry's writing you down in the game book,' she said.

Jesus. 'Just me?'

'No, silly,' she said. 'The date. Who was there. What we killed, and how many. And your name, as the dispatcher.'

Great, I thought. My murder was *literally* going down in the history books. 'Oh, wonderful,' I said. 'I'm so glad my noble achievement will be recorded for posterity.'

She didn't get the sarcasm. 'I know, it's tremendous, isn't it? You must be very proud.'

The servants were handing round the main course on gold-rimmed plates. 'It's not the stag I killed, is it?' I said, not entirely joking. I wasn't sure that I could bear to eat my victim.

Esme looked at me as if I was mad. 'You can't eat venison straight away,' she said, scandalised. 'It's game. It has to be hung.'

Apparently the deer hadn't suffered enough. '*Hung?*'

'So it starts to rot. It tenderises the meat.'

The conversation was taking a bit of a gross turn so I gave up on Esme and concentrated on my dinner. I was suddenly starving after all the drama. I tucked into whatever was in front of me – some sort of chickeny meat in a wine sauce. It was really nice at first, not as good as Nando's but pretty tasty. Then I bit down on something small and hard.

My mind flashed to all those stories you read online about kids who have found a filling in their KFC. I discreetly spat the thing onto my plate, where it made a sharp metallic *ting* on the china. There lay a little ball, about the size and colour of one of those little silver balls you get on cupcakes at kids' parties. 'What the *hell?*'

Cookson, on my other side, turned to me. 'Whatever's the matter?'

I pointed my knife at the little metal ball. 'I think Henry might be firing his chef tomorrow.'

'It's shot,' he said. 'You're eating pheasant. It's just shot.'

I was getting a bit cheesed. I didn't need an autopsy. 'I don't need to know how it *died*. There's just metal in it.'

He started to laugh, rather unpleasantly. He had one of those silent, shoulder-shaking laughs. 'No, I mean, it's shot. You're *eating shot*. The pellets that killed the pheasant.'

I was shocked. 'Can't they take them out first?'

'Of course they try. But they rarely get all of them. When you're shootin', you use a shotgun. Not like the rifle you used today to bag that stag.' God – did people have to keep reminding me? 'Every gun cartridge has a ton of those little pellets inside. When you discharge the shotgun, the pellets go out in a wide arc.' He described their trajectory with his two hands, parting them in a wide cone. 'Gives you the best chance of baggin' something. Little buggers get everywhere.' He took a drink. 'You'll see tomorrow.'

I didn't know then how true his words were.

After my blooper I kept my head down for a bit and listened to the general conversation. I expected the chat to be all about Chanel and what had happened on the hillside. But here's the weird thing: no one mentioned it at *all*, to the point where I wondered if it was a manners thing. Perhaps it was ill-bred to refer, in front of your host, to the fact that said host's stag hunt had turned into a man hunt. Not wanting to be Savage, I didn't mention the incident either, until Cookson got stuck into the wine and eventually brought it up.

'Pretty rotten luck for your friend,' he said.

'I wouldn't say she was my friend,' I said pleasantly. 'I only met her properly yesterday.'

'Thing about hounds,' Cookson went on as if he hadn't heard me, 'is they follow their nature. They are creatures of instinct.'

Then he leaned in close enough for me to smell his sour wine breath and said one of the most unpleasant things that had ever been whispered in my ear in all my seventeen years.

'Ask your chum if she was on her period,' he said. 'They sniff it out, the old hounds. It's the blood they're after.'

Gross. It had been a Day of Blood: black pudding, deer murder, liver all round, a handbag full of guts, a red dress and now this lovely little factoid. After that choice piece of female biology, from the lips of Cookson of all people, I pretty much lost my appetite, as well as my capacity for making small talk.

I was relieved when the sirens went off to the drawing room and I could excuse myself and go to bed.

I was so tired I could barely climb the Wayne Manor stairs. They seemed, with their thick scarlet carpets and massive oppressive paintings, suddenly higher than the hills we'd been trudging up and down all day. When I finally reached the top, all I had to do was to turn right to Lowther, shed the red dress like a snakeskin and get into my lovely bed.

I hesitated for just a moment, deliberating, swaying with tiredness.

Then the sisterhood won.

Shit, I said under my breath, and turned left towards Chanel's room.

chapter fifteen

Chanel's room had a name too.

It was etched in faded gilt on a wooden panel over her door. It said Cheviot. I know because I read it while I was waiting for her to answer my knock. Turns out I was waiting for a long time; she never did answer, so after a bit I just turned the handle and went in.

Chanel was sitting up in bed, still awake. The dinner tray was next to her on the bedspread. Without being invited, I closed the door and went to sit on the bed. I had to move the tray a bit to sit down, and I could see that it was totally untouched.

The fire was burning merrily, and the room was warm, but Chanel was wearing her thick white towelling robe in bed. Her face above it was the same colour as the towelling. She was ghost pale and wore a haunted look that was vaguely familiar. Suddenly, like a blow to the stomach, it struck me where I'd seen it before. It was on the face of Gemma Delaney, the girl from my old school who'd stopped me outside chapel at STAGS and warned me not, on any account, to go huntin' shootin' fishin'.

Chanel didn't say anything when I sat down. She just shrank back onto her pillows. I wasn't really expecting a warm greeting, or a thank you for hauling her out of that cave, and it was a good job I wasn't. She pursed her lips in a line and said nothing.

'Nice room,' I said, trying to break the ice. And it was – her walls and bedcovers were duck-egg blue and faded gold. I looked instinctively above the fireplace, and noticed an empty space with a brighter patch of wallpaper in the spot where Jeffrey was in my room. I thought she'd been spared the head of a dead animal companion, until I saw, on the floor next to the wastepaper basket, a mangy fox's head with bared teeth lying where Chanel had taken it down.

'Cheviot,' I said, nodding. 'Mine's called Lowther.'

Nothing.

'Who names their rooms, really?' I said. Still Chanel said nothing, so I started riffing nervously. 'I mean, I've heard of people naming their houses – people even do it on our street, and it's just a crappy terrace. They put up these dinky little oval china plaques, with "Dunroamin'" or something painted on there, to try to kid themselves that they aren't living on a street with like five hundred identical houses. But a room in a house with a name? Never. I mean it's like –'

She cut across my monologue. 'They were hunting *me*, Greer.'

'Who were? The hounds?'

'No,' she said, quite clearly. 'The Medievals.'

I sat quietly for a moment, taking this in. I hadn't realised until that moment what a psychological toll the afternoon had obviously taken on Chanel. Frankly, she was talking crazy. I said, gently, 'Thing is, Chanel, there may be a simple explanation for it all. Are you . . . ? Is it . . . ? Is it your time of the month?'

Now, I hate this phrase and always have – I think it's because it's the phrase my dad used when he tried to tell me about periods. In the absence of my mum it all fell to him, and he was so squirmy and uncomfortable, bless him, that although I love him to bits, I came to hate that phrase.

Chanel didn't seem to mind it though. 'Esme said that to me too.'

'And . . . *is* it,' Jeez, I had to say it *again*, 'your time of the month?'

'Yes,' she said.

'Well, there you go then. The hounds were confused, all hyped up by the scent of blood. That's what they're trained for after all,' I finished clumsily.

'*No*,' she said. It was almost a shout. She started to shake her head just as she'd done in the cave. 'No. They were hunting *me*. I was really cold coming down the hill, even though Henry gave me his jacket.' Her voice warmed a little. 'Those new Hunter wellies I'd bought were killing me, stupid things, and I fell behind. I was separated off from the pack, just like the stag was.' She scraped her hand through her hair, trying subconsciously to flip it like the Medieval girls did. It didn't work. 'I lost sight of you all. So I thought I'd just go back to the cars, but I must've got lost. Then they came for me.' She huddled further down into her dressing gown. 'It was horrible, Greer. Like a nightmare. They came streaking out of the dark, twenty, thirty of them, barking crazily. I just ran.' She shivered. 'I keep thinking about Actaeon in Latin yesterday.'

Could it have been only the day before? That last morning of lessons at STAGS seemed years ago.

'Remember? Actaeon saw the goddess Diana naked, and as a punishment fifty hounds tore him to pieces.'

'I remember,' I said softly.

'I thought that was going to happen to *me*, Greer. I kept trying to get away, going places they couldn't go, into woods, across streams, but they kept finding me. If I hadn't found that cave . . .' She stopped and looked down at her hands, and I saw that her beautiful nails, those white crescent moons, were all dirty and chipped. Weirdly it was the sight of the fingernails, more than anything else she'd told me, that made me want to cry. She'd probably ripped them desperately trying to crawl into the cave. But what she was saying *couldn't* be true. Could it?

Chanel was talking again, low-voiced. 'When Dad invented the Saros smartphone we got really rich really quickly. By the time the Saros 7S came along, I was too rich for my old school – my old friends didn't want to know me. They all thought I was stuck up. Dad and Mum thought I'd fit in better at STAGS. Dad said they were our sort of people now. But it didn't turn out that way. No one's talked to me all term.'

Now it was my turn to look down at my hands. If I'd only known that Chanel was feeling just like me, I'd have tried harder to befriend her.

'And then when I got The Invitation to come here, I was so happy. I thought that meant I'd made it, that I'd made the breakthrough. I got all the right clothes, everything. I practised how I would speak, studied manners and etiquette and which fork to use and all that crap. If I don't fit here, and I don't fit there, where do I fit? Did they bring me here as *game*, to hunt? Is that all I am to them, prey?' When she wasn't trying so hard to sound posh, she had a really nice soft Cheshire accent. But what she was saying was insane.

'You're nuts,' I said gently. 'Coconuts. You're letting your imagination run away with you. Listen. If you're honest, you were already frightened of the hounds, weren't you?' I remembered her wary expression in the drive before the hunt, her avoidance of their slapping tails.

'Yes,' she admitted. 'I didn't like them, even this morning.'

'Well then. All that happened is that once the stag was down they got bored, picked up another scent and followed you. Of course it was scary for you, but it's just a game for them.'

'And for the Medievals,' she said bitterly. 'They *planned* it. I *know* they did. The stag hunt was just the warm-up. How did they seem, when they came to look for me?'

Truthfully, only Shafeen had seemed genuinely worried, but after Chanel's speech, and her ridiculous paranoia about being hunted, I didn't want to undermine her further by suggesting that the Medievals were not her true friends. So I told part of the truth. 'They were very keen to find you. They all came along, every one of them. In fact, it was Henry who distracted the dogs.'

'I'm not talking about Henry. Henry's fine.' There it was again – the warmth in her voice. 'It's the others.'

I patted the blue-and-gold bedspread under my hand. 'You just need to sleep.'

She looked at me appealingly with her reddened eyes. 'Will you stay with me? Just till I'm asleep?'

I was deathly tired, but I nodded. 'Of course. Everything'll be fine in the morning. You'll see this afternoon for what it was, a horrible accident.' I took one of her hands, with the raggedy nails. It was clenched into a tense little fist. Smiling, making a joke of it, I prised it open, finger by finger, trying to make her relax so I could hold it properly.

There was something in her clammy palm.

Several somethings.

I unfolded her hand fully and looked. They were long, pale seeds. 'What are those?'

She shrugged her bath-robed shoulders. 'I dunno. They were in the pocket of Henry's jacket. When I was in the cave I was looking in the pockets for something to throw at the hounds, anything foody to distract them. But there was nothing but these seeds.'

I looked at them closely – they were a bit bigger than rice grains, with little ridges running the full length. For all I knew they were the sort of thing countrymen always carried in their pockets; grass seeds or something. 'Well, you don't need them now.'

I picked them off her palm one by one and put them in this tiny little enamelled Chinese-style jar on the bedside table. 'They're quite safe there. Lie back.'

I took one pillow away and helped her snuggle down in the bed. Then I took her hand again as she closed her eyes, only letting go of it when I was sure she was breathing easily and steadily. I suddenly felt a real affection for her – she looked like a little girl. If Cookson called her my friend now, I wouldn't correct him. 'Goodnight, Chanel,' I whispered. I was already at the door when I heard her answer.

'Greer.'

I turned, my hand on the doorknob. Her eyes were still closed, her voice really sleepy.

'It's Nel,' she said. 'I tried to tell everyone all term, but it just didn't stick.'

I smiled. 'Sleep well, Nel,' I said.

chapter sixteen

As I closed the door gently behind me and turned to go back to my room, I nearly jumped out of my skin.

Henry was there in the passageway, right behind me. He was leaning on the oak panelling, feet crossed, hands in pockets, his white bow tie untied and his shirt open at the throat. He looked like a model.

I put my hand on my thumping heart. 'Jeez, you gave me a fright!'

He smiled, and sort of pushed himself off the wall in this graceful way using just his back. 'I'm sorry. Is she all right? I was just going to check on her.'

He was all concern, and I couldn't help feeling a little jealous. Perhaps Nel *was* the reason why Lara was so salty at dinner, and not me at all. 'She's sleeping,' I said. 'Best leave it for tonight.' I promise you I wasn't trying to keep them apart; I genuinely was thinking of Nel, although I know you won't believe me when you hear what happened next.

Henry nodded, looking at me intently all the time. 'Come on,' he said. 'I want to show you something.' He took my hand.

Clearly this was the night that wouldn't die, but suddenly I wasn't at all tired.

He led me up some stairs, and I didn't resist. I let my hand rest in his, feeling, as I often did, that I was in some movie. He in his white tie, me in my evening gown, him leading me through the darkened house, upward, ever upward. *Twilight*, I thought; Edward and Bella. And just like in that movie, it was dangerous, it was all kinds of wrong, but somehow it was right. At the very top of the house there was a long sort of gallery, with a polished floor that would be brilliant for skidding in your socks. All down both sides were Olde Worlde paintings of people who all looked like Henry. They stared down their de Warlencourt noses along the moonlit floorboards, which had a sheen like a tempting skating rink, looking like they certainly wouldn't approve of skidding in socks. But Henry turned to me with a sparkle in his eyes and a wicked smile on his face. He kicked off his shoes. He'd clearly been thinking the same thing. 'Come on,' he said.

We skidded past their disapproving eyes and under their de Warlencourt noses, shrieking like kids. 'I used to do this with my cousins all the time when I was little,' Henry called down the gallery. 'They're twins, a boy and a girl, a bit younger than me. They'd go like lightning down here. It was so funny.' We skidded up and down ten, twenty times until we collapsed under a particularly snooty portrait, breathing hard and giggling.

'Was that what you wanted to show me?' I gasped.

'No,' he said. 'That was just a diversion. Put your shoes on.'

He led me past the curious painted eyes, and then, I'm not kidding, he opened a hidden door in the panelled wall.

Behind it was a winding staircase with a little *Alice in Wonderland* door at the top. Henry opened it, we stepped through and suddenly we were on the roof.

The wind buffeted me, but Henry still had hold of my hand. I breathed in the cold, and let go of him, turning around and around, gazing open-mouthed at the view.

Everything was blue in the moonlight. I could see miles and miles of silvery roofs, turrets and chimney stacks; and beyond that, acres of forests, frothy like sea-foam, and the rising hills in the distance.

'Let's sit over here,' Henry said. 'It's a bit sheltered. Do you mind the cold?'

'I like it,' I said. And I did. I needed to feel something, after the numbing shock of the day, and the cold was like a reviving slap in the face. Still, he took off his tailcoat and put it around my shoulders. It was warm from him, and smelled of the scent he wore. It could easily have been part of the movie I was living, but the gesture actually jolted me out of my stupid fantasy – he'd done the same earlier in the day, for Nel, just before she was hunted like a stag.

We sat down together, with a sheltering stone balustrade at our back, and an uninterrupted view ahead of us of the manicured lawns and gardens at the front of the house.

'Look,' Henry said, and pointed down. A fox was trotting confidently across the silvery lawn, followed by its sharp moonlit shadow. 'It's a vixen,' he said.

As if she could hear Henry's voice she stopped, one paw raised, her tail thrust straight out behind her. Watching and listening for danger.

'She's safe from you then?' I asked drily.

'Yes.' There was a smile in his voice. 'We don't foxhunt at Longcross. We don't keep any foxhounds.'

You do, I thought, thinking of Piers and Cookson. I looked out at the view, all the way to the horizon. 'Is *all* this yours?'

'Well, my father's.'

'Yours one day.'

'Yes.' He said it almost wistfully, as if it was never going to happen.

'How far does your land go?' I asked incredulously. He pointed – a spire in the far distance, milky blue in the moonlight, stuck up like the blade of a sundial. 'That far,' he said. 'That's Longcross church. It dates back to 1188. When Conrad de Warlencourt came back from the Crusades, it was said he brought the True Cross with him, the actual cross on which Jesus was crucified. He set it in the hillside at dawn and the long shadow of a cross fell across the land. Long-cross, you see? Where the shadow fell he made a vow to build a church.' He stretched out his long legs so they actually dangled off the edge of the roof. 'A village grew up around the church, as villages do, and Conrad built a manor house. Subsequent generations added to it, and in the reign of Queen Anne, Edward de Warlencourt built this main bit of the house. It's quite a nice little family project.'

His understatement didn't fool me. I could tell by the warmth in his voice that he was enormously proud of his birthright. I thought of our little home in Arkwright Terrace in Manchester, in a red row of houses that actually did look a lot like *Coronation Street*. I responded with an understatement of my own. 'You're so *lucky*.'

Strangely, he didn't agree at once, as I thought he would. Instead he let a long silence fall. An owl had time to hoot twice before he spoke again. 'This world is disappearing,' he said. It seemed like an odd thing for a seventeen-year-old to say, but he obviously meant it.

'I don't think so,' I said reassuringly. 'Half the people in the cabinet went to a school like ours. People like you run the country.'

'That's all changing,' he said. 'Privilege is becoming a dirty word. Estates like this are being turned into theme parks. Tradition is becoming irrelevant. The whole world is online.' He spoke of the Internet as though it was a foreign land. He picked a clump of moss off the roof and whipped it over the balustrade. You couldn't hear it land. 'It doesn't matter what school you went to any more, just how many followers you have on YouTube.' He said it scornfully, a Savage tone for a Savage word. But there was a waver in his voice and I thought for a moment that he might even cry.

And here's the weird thing. I felt *sorry* for him. In that moment I forgot about Nel and the drama of the day and I sat there on this fricking huge palace of his, in the middle of his acres of land, with those thousands of millions of bricks that he owned cold under my bum, and I felt *sorry* for Henry de Warlencourt. He was right. He was trying to hold back something that couldn't be held back. I might have felt even sorrier for him if I'd known he wouldn't live to inherit Longcross.

'I'm so sorry Chanel got scared,' he said. 'I feel utterly responsible, as she is my guest.' He sounded sincere. 'It could be that . . . I don't know if anyone explained . . . It might be that . . .' Good manners fought with the need to present himself as the host with the most.

I rescued him. 'That it was the wrong time of the month. That's what Cookson said.'

He caught my tone. 'You don't believe it?'

I rested my chin on my knees. 'Do you ever watch movies?' I asked. 'Or does the monastic rule of the Medievals not allow it?'

'Yes, I watch films. Not very often, but sometimes.' He sounded vaguely amused.

'Ever seen a film called *The Shooting Party*?'

'No,' he said politely. 'No, I haven't seen that one.'

'It's set in a big manor house like this one, just before the outbreak of the First World War. The lord of the manor has a shooting party, and his little grandson is staying at the house. Well, the grandson has this pet duck, and they establish this duck really early on, and the kid's relationship with it.' There was a sudden breeze and I pulled Henry's coat closer around my shoulders. 'They keep coming back to this duck, and it does stuff like gatecrashing their tea party in the drawing room – you know, all this cutesy stuff. Well, of course the duck goes missing just before the shoot, and the kid is distraught, and he and his maid go looking for it, and all the time you're thinking, *There's no way that duck is making it to the end of this movie*. It's going to end up as a pile of feathers, and the kid will be devastated, and the score will swell, and everyone will cry, and it will be some big premonition of the carnage of the Great War, blah blah blah.'

'And what happens?'

'Well, the duck survives. But on the last shoot of the weekend, a *person* gets shot. A peasant who happens to be in the wrong place at the wrong time.'

There was a long silence, then Henry spoke. 'I give you my solemn promise,' he said, 'no, my word as a *gentleman*: you are not going to get shot. And nor is Chanel.' He sounded genuine. 'In fact,' he went on, 'here's a notion: tomorrow, for the shoot, would you like to take your time? You don't have to participate at all. You could meet us for lunch after the first drive.'

'Is that how things used to be?' I mocked gently.

'Yes,' he said a little stiffly. 'But I wasn't trying to be sexist. On this occasion I was considering your feelings more than ancient traditions. The guns all have to be up at six. Chanel has had a shock; maybe she'd like to sleep a little later. You could have a leisurely morning, and then join us at the folly for lunch.'

It must have been after midnight, so a lie-in, and, I'd bet, another breakfast on a silver tray, did sound nice.

'OK,' I said.

'That's settled then,' he said, saying in his Medieval way exactly what I'd said in two letters. 'Lara will collect you at noon.'

The third siren. I'd wondered when she'd come into play. I don't know whether it was the champagne or the moonlight, but I felt kind of brave. 'She's very beautiful, Lara,' I said, quite truthfully. Then he turned and took my face in his hands. Somehow, even though I was wearing his jacket, the hands were warm.

'She's not as beautiful as you,' he said.

I defy you to know what to do with your face if someone is holding it and says that to you. I'm not saying I didn't like the compliment; it's just that I'm pretty sure I adopted a dopey expression.

'You're the fairest of them all,' he said.

I felt as if I was melting. The language fitted exactly into the fairy-tale setting. It was pretty romantic, but I had to call him on it. 'Aren't you and Lara . . .' I didn't know how to match his courtly language – 'going out?'

Suddenly his face was very close to mine. 'Not any more,' he said.

And then Henry de Warlencourt kissed me, right on the mouth.

SHOOTIN'

chapter seventeen

As usually happens to me when I mean to sleep in, I woke up really early.

I lay there in the dim light, Jeffrey watching me, thinking about The Kiss, A Happening So Significant It Deserved Capital Letters. I relived The Kiss about a hundred times, and then ran through every second of Henry escorting me, like a perfect gentleman, to the door of this very room, kissing me again on this very threshold, and saying goodnight.

I wondered now if it was a drunken kiss, but he had seemed entirely sober. Maybe then it was a consequence of the day of drama, a releasing of tension. But it didn't feel that way – if it was, why didn't he go and find Lara? *You're the fairest of them all*, he'd said. I hugged the compliment to myself – but then I had another thought. Would Henry want, you know, *more*? We were here for the rest of the weekend. There were no parents, we had our own rooms, and the only adults that were here, the kids told *them* what to do, not the other way round. My stomach felt really icky and I put my hands on the place, which felt sort of fizzy inside, over the soft cotton of my pyjamas. What if there was a time when Henry didn't say goodnight and go, when his feet crossed the threshold of Lowther? What if he *stopped* being a gentleman?

The thought was so terrifying, and so exciting, that I was suddenly wide awake and I had to get up. 'Morning, Jeffrey,' I said to the stag's head and went to open the curtains.

The view looked quite different to how it had yesterday. It was still knock-your-eyes-out beautiful, but the sky was grey and overcast; one of those days where if it wasn't raining yet, it would be soon.

The Cogsworth clock on the mantel said 7 a.m. I groaned. It had been after midnight when I'd left Nel's room, so God knows what time it had been by the time Henry brought me back to Lowther. I must have had zero sleep.

I thought about waking Nel; such a luxury, after weeks of isolation, to have someone to talk to. But it was too early. Let her sleep. Besides, I felt a bit guilty – had she liked Henry too, before I stole him away? She'd seemed weirdly ready to exempt him from her paranoid notions of being hunted.

I got that fizzy feeling in my stomach again at the thought of Henry, and decided I must be hungry. But there was no sign of Betty – she had no doubt been instructed to let me sleep. Emboldened by The Kiss from her master, I looked around the room for something I knew must be there. Behind one of the curtain ties I found it: a marble button in an ornamental gilt surround. I pressed it, and in less than two minutes there was a knock at the door and Betty was in the room. She looked properly pissed off at being summoned by the likes of me, and gave me the evils even worse than usual, her lips pressed into their customary disapproving line. 'Could I have some breakfast, please?' I asked.

'Of course, miss,' she said stiffly. 'I'll bring it right away.'

And she did – the same silver tray, and silver dome, and silver coffee pot. In less time than it seemed humanly possible to make it. As she set it on the bed she said, 'I'll light the fire when you're bathing, miss, so as not to disturb you.'

That was. Betty's deal. Everything she said was perfectly considerate and obliging, but I could tell she absolutely hated me underneath. She did it all with a look, old Betty. And the funny thing was, I was much nicer to her than any of the Medievals were. I never heard any of them saying please or thank you; they just barked orders at the servants. But if anything I overdid it, because she made me nervous.

I overdid it now. 'Thank you *so* much, Betty,' I said, gravely rehearsing, in my head, a *Rebecca*-type fantasy where I was the new bride of the lord of the manor, and Betty was that scary old bat of a maid. Except instead of being the young Mrs de Winter I was the young Lady de Warlencourt.

The idea of being the lady of the house wouldn't leave my head. When I'd got dressed in the shootin' gear that Betty had left out – similar to the huntin' clobber except everything had about fifty pockets – I decided that since I had time to kill (it was a long time before lunch, before I saw Henry), I would explore the house.

As I looked around Longcross, at some point as I moved from one enormous, gilded room to another, I morphed from Joan Fontaine in *Rebecca* to Keira Knightley in *Pride and Prejudice*. I was Elizabeth Bennet, nosing around Pemberley, absolutely gobsmacked at Mr Darcy's riches. I wasn't thinking Henry and I would really get married or anything dumb like that, but I did think, all the way round, what it would be like to be Henry's girlfriend and have access to this place 365 days a year. Long summer holidays, Christmases; wow, Longcross would make a fantastic Christmas house, holly everywhere and a huge tree in the atrium reaching right to the top of the grand stairs. I imagined myself under such a tree, in a Christmas jumper, drinking mulled wine with Henry. Keira and Joan fled as I cast myself in the picture. It suddenly seemed totally possible. When Henry'd said he wasn't with Lara any more, didn't that mean he was with *me*?

From then on I went over the house like I owned the place. Now and then I'd see a servant, a maid, a butler, a secretary or something, but they would just say, 'Good morning, miss,' and respectfully stop what they were doing and sort of stand to attention until I'd left the room. It was as if the servants thought I was too lofty to be allowed to see them doing their menial tasks, and their behaviour just fuelled my fantasy – for that one morning, when there was no one around to challenge me, I was mistress of the place.

I went up to the long gallery at the top of the house, where I'd skated with Henry, but I couldn't find the door in the panelling through which he'd led me to the roof. It was like in *The Lion, the Witch and the Wardrobe*, where one time you can find a door to Narnia in the wardrobe, and then when you look in the same place you can't find it again. For a minute I wondered if I'd imagined the whole thing: that incredible view, Henry giving me his coat, that conversation about *The*

Shooting Party, and of course The Kiss. The thought of him never kissing me again, the door being closed on that too, made me suddenly go cold.

I continued my tour. There were dozens, hundreds, of rooms in the place, many of them bedrooms. Every one of them had a name – Grey, Bamburgh, Levens, Clifford, Fenwick. I didn't know whether they were people or places but they all seemed to come from the world that Henry revered. There were no modern names. No room was called Kanye.

I went back downstairs and wandered around the ground floor. At the end of one flagged passageway I found a room with one wall entirely covered in an enormous, ancient-looking map, a huge walnut desk in front of it that looked like it belonged on a ship, and an antique-looking globe standing on that, as if Henry owned the whole world. I found kitchens, storerooms, laundry rooms, wine cellars, and all the time I didn't see any technology anywhere. This cruise ship, this *nation*, of a house was obviously run without the aid of any state-of-the-art equipment. The kitchens had those old-fashioned Aga ovens. The wine cellars had dusty bottles on racks as you'd expect, but no electronic humidifiers or digital thermometers. And here's another funny thing. I never once saw a phone. Not even a landline. Not even one of those old-fashioned ones with the rotary dial and curly flex, nor those even older ones you see in Ealing comedies, those black upright ones with the funny little trumpet that you unhook and hold to your ear. Maybe all phones were considered Savage, not just mobiles.

After the lower decks I went out of a back door and toured the stables, the kennels and the gun rooms behind the house.

I stroked the velvety noses of the horses when they put their heads over the half-doors to greet me, enjoying their lovely hay-and-horse-poo smell. Their flanks steamed in the cold, but I imagined riding out with Henry through flower meadows on summer days, in jodhpurs and matching white shirts. *Jeez.* My fantasies were as old-fashioned as the world Henry inhabited.

I greeted the tumbling, tail-wagging crowd of black-and-tan hounds in their kennels. 'Hello, Arcas. Hello, Tigris,' I called, assuming the three dogs I'd met with Henry were somewhere in the seething mass. I couldn't remember the other name. The dogs looked happy, harmless and completely different to how they'd looked in their Baskerville-mode, when they'd come baying after Nel. After a bit I turned away, and that's when I saw a figure way across the stable-yard, watching me.

I knew him straight away by his sheer height and bulk. It was Perfect, dressed in his padded waistcoat that looked like a Kevlar vest, all ready for the shoot. I wondered why, if the shoot started as early as Henry said it did, he was back at the house. All his clothes were mud brown or moss green, and in the woods and spinneys I'm sure he'd be well camouflaged, but in the limestone courtyard he stuck out like a sore thumb. He didn't seem to be trying to hide though. You know when you catch someone's eye and they immediately turn away? Well, he didn't do that. He just kept on staring. Perfect alone, of all the servants who had seen me nosing around, didn't greet me or avert his eyes respectfully or stop what he was doing. He'd been staring before I spotted him, and he went on staring afterwards. I couldn't tell whether he didn't like me hanging with the hounds, or just didn't like *me*. Either way it was unnerving. I quickly scuttled out of the stable-yard and out of his eyeline.

By now I was shivering a bit, partly because I'd left my waxed jacket in my room, and partly because of Perfect's creepy gaze. So I ducked inside a place called the Orangery. (Most of the rooms at Longcross, not just the bedrooms, were helpfully named, like a Cluedo set.) The Orangery was blessedly warm, like a greenhouse, and crowded with vines and fruit trees. I counted the bright oranges and bunches of grapes dangling from the branches even this far into autumn. I went into the ice cellars, great subterranean stone rooms, now empty of ice and littered with old sledges and ice skates, but somehow still holding close a winter of their own. It was so cold there that I soon scurried back inside the main house.

There I found, on the ground floor, more drawing rooms with empty fireplaces, and a music room with silver-framed black-and-white photographs on the piano, of blond boys who might be Henry when young, or Henry's father when young, or even Henry's grandfather when young. I saw an armoury bristling with bows and arrows, and, best of all, a massive library, a vast room covered floor to ceiling with books.

I like libraries, with their leathery-papery-dusty smell, and this one was a good one, so I spent quite a bit of time in there. There was a polished wood floor, with small floorboards laid in a sort of herringbone pattern. There was a huge chandelier suspended from a soaring frescoed ceiling. A pair of big glass doors opened out onto the grounds, with an uninterrupted view across the lawn to a huge fountain. There was a little mezzanine deck above the main bit, with loads more books and little wooden ladders to reach them.

I looked at the shelves, and pictured the tiny blond Henry from the silver-framed piano pictures climbing on the ladders to reach the volumes he wanted to read. Sometimes it was hard, particularly when you saw Piers and Cookson at play, to remember how intelligent the Medievals were. But they all knew loads about everything and I thought I now knew why. If they all grew up with a crap-ton of books like this, no wonder they were brainy.

I had a look at some of the spines. Coleridge. De Quincey. Wordsworth. Southey. The poets I recognised from English lessons, the ones who'd been as knocked out by the Lake District as I was and couldn't stop rabbiting on about it. And then I found other poets from further afield: Dante, Baudelaire, and our old friend Ovid. I browsed though some of the books for a while – man, they were old, probably should've been in a museum. But then again, Longcross kind of *was* a museum.

I climbed up to the mezzanine and had a little bit of a mooch around. The leather-paper-dust smell was most intense up there, as if that was where the real treasure lay. I had a browse and saw that, running along the bottom shelf of that whole level, almost hidden in the shadow of the balustrade, there was a whole bunch of books with no names but with dates. Rows upon rows there were, a whole collection of black books with tooled gold numbers on the spine, bound in that morocco leather. I ran my finger along the spines. They each represented a decade, and they spanned centuries, from the Middle Ages to the present day. I wondered if they were photo albums, and then told myself not to be a dummy; photographs weren't invented back then, duh. I was about to pull one out and take a look when the chime of a wall clock brought me to myself. I had got so used to the library-silence that I jumped about a mile in the air, and looked at the clock.

It was twelve noon, and I was supposed to meet Lara in my room.

I slid the book back into place with a satisfying *thunk*, and while I clattered down the spiral staircase the twelve metallic chimes spurred me on like some sort of reverse Cinderella. It had taken just one morning to transform me, not from riches to rags, but from rags to riches. I was utterly sold on Henry's world. What was not to like about a world uncluttered by TV, Google, YouTube, iTunes, the ringing of phones, the beeping of microwaves? Who couldn't live like this, without all the noise and craziness of the modern world? If you needed a little excitement, there was always huntin' shootin' fishin'.

chapter eighteen

On the bottom step of the grand staircase Lara Petrova, the third siren, was lolling like an expensive cat.

She stood up at my approach and blocked my path, almost as if she was guarding the upper reaches of the house. She half closed her ice-blue eyes at me. 'Where have you been?' she demanded.

'Just looking around,' I said.

'What*ever* for?'

I wasn't scared of Lara any more. I had the talisman of Henry's Kiss still printed on my lips, like some invisible superpower from a Marvel movie. So I shrugged insolently before I answered her question. 'Just plain nosey, I guess.'

She looked at me sharply. 'And what did you find?' It was a funny question.

I thought about the Narnia thing, and felt like telling her I'd found another world. Then I thought of all those poets. 'Beauty,' I said.

She looked relieved and you could see she thawed a little. She said, a bit huffily, 'I'd already been to collect you, but you weren't there. I was just on the way to call for Chanel.'

I smiled at her pleasantly. I didn't think she was on the way to anywhere. I think she was waiting for me. I wondered if Henry had already told her about last night.

'I'll go and get her if you like,' I offered. I felt a bit uncomfortable being alone with Lara. Either she already knew Henry had kissed me, and was styling it out, or she didn't know a thing and was ignorant of the fact that she was about to be dumped. Either way I felt, unexpectedly, a little bit sorry for her.

'Let's go together, shall we?' she said breezily, smiling her charming smile at me, in a complete one-eighty from the cold, suspicious attitude she'd greeted me with. I don't know why, but I got the distinct feeling she didn't want to allow Nel and me to be alone together. She took my arm conspiratorially and we climbed the stairs like that, her hanging on as if she was my best mate. Henry evidently hadn't told her a thing.

Nel was sitting on her bed, ready but subdued. Because all her lovely new gear had been wrecked yesterday, she was wearing Longcross clothes, and they washed her out. She looked pale and not quite herself. I could now see that Nel's own style – brand-new, colourful – really suited her. Now that she looked like the Medievals, it seemed as if something had been lost. I grabbed my jacket from my room, and, as it had started drizzling, gave in to wearing a cap today. In a trio, like some bizarre variety act, we all trooped down the staircase and out of the front door.

Then Lara led us into the woods.

The shootin' day was entirely different from the huntin' one. Yesterday it had been crisp and sunny; today it was grey and drizzling. Yesterday we'd been out in the open, high in the hills, with the heather peaks above and the lakes below. Now we were in the deep woods of the estate, under a dripping canopy. But today was just as beautiful in its own way. The autumn colours of the Longcross woods were like fire. A pearly mist lay low in the clearings like smoke. The leaf mould underfoot gave off a rich earthy smell, and it was soft like a thick carpet, muffling our footsteps. In fact, so far, shootin' was weirdly quiet. Nothing could be heard apart from the cocky, confident cawing of rooks overhead and, in the undergrowth, the shy clucking of the hiding birds who were about to meet their maker.

Nothing, that is, apart from Lara's hypnotic drawl. All the way, Lara talked. I didn't get a chance to talk to Nel at all – Lara planted herself in the middle of us, and we never got a chance to say more than a quick 'Hi'.

I knew Lara was from a Russian family, and before she'd deigned to talk to me, I'd always imagined she'd speak like some arch-villain; like Xenia Onatopp in *GoldenEye*. Actually she was posher than all the Medievals, even Henry. She had one of those voices that is so upper class it sounds lazy, almost as if she couldn't be bothered to finish her words. Her drawl fitted with her whole vibe – she had the air of finding everything deathly boring, as if it was all a giant waste of time. She was quite different from the other Medieval girls – she wasn't over-the-top friendly like Esme or an italicising enthusiast like Charlotte. She never made sudden movements, but sort of drooped around the place. The only time I'd heard her sound sharp and alert was when she questioned me about looking around the house. The rest of the time she seemed half asleep, but she wasn't, because now and again she'd say something that reminded you how clever she was. The whole effect was pretty annoying. It was lucky she was so beautiful to look at, or I couldn't see why anyone would want her around. The only similarity between her and the other sirens was the inevitable hair flick; she did it just the same as they did, and every time her hair fell perfectly. Chanel, I noticed, had stopped doing it.

Lara filled the dripping silence by telling us, in her lazy drawl, all about what went down at a pheasant shoot. 'They've got famously good coverts at Longcross,' she said. 'People come from all over to shoot here, including British royalty, foreign royalty . . . you know . . .' She tailed off as if she couldn't be bothered to finish the sentence, then gathered the energy to speak again. 'Basically you have the guns, that's the guests at the party who are going to shoot, and each gun has a loader, that's their kind of helper, who holds the spare guns, makes sure they're loaded, counts the birds they've shot. That can get quite competitive. You're not really supposed to count how many you've bagged, it's not considered good form, but of course people do. Most people don't stand a chance against Hen though.'

At first I didn't know who she meant – I thought a Hen might be a kind of super-wily pheasant. But then it dawned on me she was talking about *Henry*. Hen. I'd never heard anyone call him anything but Henry before; he didn't seem the type to go for the more informal *Harry* or the Shakespearean *Hal*. This wasn't part of Lara's lazy thing, that she literally couldn't be arsed to finish his name; it was more than that. It was her special name for Henry. It was a badge of ownership. For a moment that fizzy feeling returned to my stomach. How would she take it, I wondered, when she found out that *Hen* wasn't hers any more?

'Hen's a brilliant shot,' she said, more forcefully than she'd said anything else. 'There's this legend that he once had seven birds dead in the air at the same time. That was before my time though,' she said, as if this was still her time. Suddenly I couldn't wait to see him. I wanted her to know.

'Each shoot is called a drive,' she continued, 'and the guns place themselves in a long, strung-out line in a clearing. The position of the guns in a drive is called a stand. Then the beaters, who are all from the Longcross village, walk through the woods with long sticks, basically beating the undergrowth and generally making a row until the pheasants fly out over the heads of the guns. Each gun will only shoot in the area of sky over their head – they mustn't poach another gun's bird; that's strictly against shooting etiquette. The loader reloads, so that the gun can bag the maximum number of birds in each drive. Then, as the birds fall, each loader's dog picks up the birds.'

'Dogs?' It was the first word Nel had uttered besides 'Hi'.

'Yes, dogs.' Lara put her hand to her mouth. 'God, I forgot. Not *those* kind of dogs sweetie. Just little gun dogs – spaniels. They pick up the fallen birds and that's it.'

Nel didn't look comforted, but she strode on with us – there was nothing else she could do.

Suddenly there was a tremendous report of gunfire, which ricocheted all around, the sound bouncing off the dense trees. Nel and I jumped about a foot into the air. The 'guns' weren't quite ready for us – they were still shooting, strung out in a long line across the clearing. As we approached, my longing to see Henry turned into something like fear. I spotted him at once – as you always can when you like someone; if you're at a party or something, you can be four rooms away and sense when they've arrived. He was shooting away in total concentration; a flat cap on his blond hair, his waxed-jacketed shoulders hunched under the gun, his cheek along the barrel that was pointed skyward. I'm a peaceful person and not a huge fan of guns, but I had to admit he looked amazing. Skilful and dangerous at the same time.

The gunfire rattled on and on, like fireworks night. The noise was deafening, and I couldn't believe that back in the woods I'd thought that shootin' was peaceful and quiet. I could see Nel give a little jump every time the guns discharged. She really wasn't in a good state. Lara took her arm and sort of pulled her to one side, and I got the distinct feeling, once again, that she had been told not to leave us alone together. But Nel could relax, as that was apparently the last salvo for now. All the guns were handing their weapons to their loaders and leaving their carefully held positions, walking down the hillside towards us.

The lure of her own kind was too much for Lara and she left our side to greet Charlotte and Esme, who were flat-capped and armed just like the boys. It gave Nel and me a brief chance to chat.

'Did you sleep OK?' I asked.

'Terribly.' She turned to me and I could see violet shadows under her eyes. She'd not fully returned to her previous Queen's English; you could now hear the Cheshire in there. I liked her voice a lot better this way.

'Nightmares?' I asked sympathetically, suddenly guilty. My dreams had been filled with Henry on the rooftop and ball gowns and foxes and moonlight.

She hesitated. 'I *guess* they were nightmares. That is –' she pulled at my sleeve and spoke, low-voiced, close to my ear – 'I think there were *dogs* at my door in the night.'

'Dogs? What were they doing?'

'Just sniffing, and sort of *whining*.'

Even under the jacket and the jumper and the shirt, my skin chilled. 'Are you sure?'

'Yes,' she said. 'No. I *could* have been dreaming, I suppose. But I'm almost sure I was awake. I could see the slice of light from the passageway under the door, and their feet sort of interrupting it. They were walking about, trying to get in.'

'But they didn't?'

'No. I wanted to lock the door, but I didn't get out of bed. I couldn't – I was too scared. I just put the quilt over my head and eventually I must have gone back to sleep.'

My heart went out to her – a little girl, hiding under the covers from the monsters in her mind.

'Sounds like a bad dream to me,' I said gently. 'Understandable after what you went through yesterday.'

She gave herself a little shake. 'I guess so.'

As we got closer I could see the shooting party had dogs, and I glanced at Nel. They were quite different to yesterday's dogs; these were pretty cute, spaniel types with curly coats. They took no interest in us as they were busy working, looking around for fallen birds. Nel kept her distance, and looked terrified of the dogs, which was to be expected.

I said, 'Are you sure you're going to be OK? Would you rather go back?'

She shook her head, brave girl. 'No, I'll be all right. It's just that I wish . . .' She stopped.

'You wish what?' I prompted.

'This is going to sound really stupid. But I wish I'd brought the seeds with me.'

'That does sound really stupid,' I agreed, but nicely. 'What seeds?'

'The lucky seeds. The ones I found in the pocket of Henry's jacket. They stopped the hounds from getting me yesterday, and in the night too.'

I rejected the idea of pointing out that it was a narrow cave entrance and a closed door that had kept the dogs away. If the magic seeds were a comfort to her, then fair enough. 'I wonder what they are,' I said, to take her mind off the dogs.

'I thought I might ask Shafeen,' she said. 'I bet he'd know.'

I looked at her sideways, surprised. 'Why Shafeen?'

She looked at the ground.

'Just because he's *Indian*?'

She shrugged, and said defensively, 'OK, *yes*. They cook with a lot of seeds and spices, don't they?' She was getting mad at me, and I was glad. Her spirit was returning. 'I just thought he might know, that's all.'

I shook my head, smiling. 'Nel, Nel, Nel.' For just a second my eyes left Henry and travelled up the line. I fixed my eyes on the tall figure of Shafeen where he stood silhouetted on the horizon, handling his gun competently. 'He's not some throwback maharajah, you know. He probably eats McDonald's when he's not at school just like we do.' I repeated what Shafeen had said to me, that first night after dinner. 'His father runs a bank in Jaipur. You're as bad as they are.'

'*Sorry,*' she said sulkily. And we walked on to catch Lara up. I smiled to myself. I should've felt bad but I didn't; at least Nel wasn't thinking about the dogs any more.

chapter nineteen

At the end of the last drive of the morning, the dead pheasants were laid out neatly on the leaves, poor victims of the morning's carnage.

They were perfectly in line, little dead soldiers still wearing their feathery battledress. Perfect was standing over them, as if he'd done something clever. He saw me, but this time didn't stare me down. Now, in the presence of his master, he was perfectly proper, and just touched his cap to me. Then he went along the ranks, counting (aloud, the moron) and pulling every tenth bird forward a little, interrupting the perfect rank, for easy reckoning. Henry was standing at the end of them all – he hadn't seen me yet; he was totally focused on Perfect, like a general waiting for his sergeant major's report from the battlefield.

'Fifty-two, my lord.'

Henry nodded. 'And Mr Jadeja?'

'Forty-eight.'

Perfect didn't even bother to count the other guns' birds. It was clear that there were only two dogs in the fight that morning.

Shafeen took the news pretty well, shrugging his shoulders

and breaking his gun so both the cartridges jumped out, like little smoke bombs. The smoke had an acrid, not-unpleasant smell. 'Plenty of the day left,' he said, philosophically. Weirdly, Henry took the news that he was Top Gun of the morning less well. Clearly he didn't like having competition at all. Maybe his mythical gun skills were not as unique as he thought. I wondered where Shafeen had learned to shoot, and remembered what he'd said the day before about shooting tigers. *Tigers*, I said to myself. *Don't be an idiot*.

I went over to Henry, unable to wait any longer for him to notice me. The sight of me seemed to improve his temper. 'Greer!' he said, just as he'd done that first night at Longcross when he'd greeted me in the Boot Room. It was a way he had, like I was always a nice surprise, as if I'd just jumped out of a cake. It was the first time our eyes had met since The Kiss, and I could feel my cheeks heating up. I could feel Shafeen's eyes on me too, looking from myself to Henry with an interested look, and that of course made me even redder.

'Walk with me?' said Henry, and even though it sounded like it had a question mark, it was an order, not a request. That was another way Henry had, of saying things with a built-in assumption that people would obey him, centuries of baked-in entitlement. This time, of course, I was only too happy to comply.

We walked through the wood together and out the other side. I couldn't tell you what we talked about – little bits of nothing, because everyone else was walking around us, the Medievals, Shafeen walking by himself like a lone gunman and Lara the jailer, arm in arm with her captive Nel. We couldn't say anything private, we certainly couldn't talk about the night before and our rooftop hook-up, but as we walked through the undergrowth his knuckles grazed mine and it was like electricity jumping through me.

We came out of the trees on a little hill, with a beautiful stone building right on the top. 'The folly,' said Henry, pointing. The folly was octagonal, with pillars and curly stone decorations, and those kind of long windows that were actually doors opening out on to eight different views. I know the word 'folly' makes it sound like some tiny whimsical thing, like a tree house or one of those little temples you find in public parks. Only it wasn't some tiny thing; it was bigger than my whole house in Arkwright Terrace.

Inside, the floor was stone, so no one had to worry about muddy boots, and there was the inevitable fire burning, so it was toasty and warm. No antlers here, but a pair of stuffed pheasants mounted on the mantelpiece over the bright flames. The table was a lovely sight, set, as ever, with a snowy-white tablecloth, and all the crystal and cutlery, but this time the silver salvers were piled high with nothing but oranges, in perfect pyramids. Their colour picked out the trees in the autumnal landscape, a palette of flame. It occurred to me that these were probably the very oranges I'd seen in the Orangery this morning, innocently hanging from their branches, looking pretty, not knowing this was their last morning on earth. Just like the pheasants – the poor dead pheasants. There was a lot of death around today.

Lara was placed opposite Henry, but there were people on either side of them, as if seven people had gatecrashed their romantic dinner. I was actually sitting next to Henry. I'd never sat so close to him before – I'd kind of moved up the table since

Friday night and now at Sunday lunch I was in pole position.

As the soup was served, some kind of nice spicy wintery vegetable broth, Henry turned to me. 'I hear you've been over the house.'

I smiled at him playfully. 'Now, who could have told you that?' I was kidding. There were servants in every fricking *room* of that place. I'd have been more surprised if he *hadn't* heard about my grand tour.

He caught my tone. 'My spies are everywhere,' he said deliciously, blue eyes twinkling.

'I bet they are.'

'I would have liked to show you around myself.'

'You still can,' I said, taking a sip of water. 'I probably saw about a hundredth of it.'

Henry tipped his soup plate, away from him of course. 'What did you think of the hundredth that you saw?'

'I loved it,' I said simply.

'I love it too.' It wasn't just one of those things you say to agree with the person you're talking to. He *really* loved it. You could tell by his voice.

'I know you do,' I whispered. 'You told me on the roof.'

'I meant *everything* I told you on the roof,' he said pointedly and a bit loudly, and I could feel myself going red again. I noticed Shafeen pause in his conversation and shoot him a look. Henry had given us away. But he was oblivious. 'Where did you go? Around Longcross, I mean.'

As the courses went by – lobster vol-au-vents, chicken mayonnaise with boiled potatoes, pear crumble – I told Henry about his house. I told him about the icehouse, the Orangery, the stable block and the kennels. I told him about the room with the map all over one wall, the piano room, the armoury and the wine cellars.

Now and again he'd interrupt me, to tell me the name of something I didn't know ('The room with the map is the estate room') or slip in a little factoid about his ancestry ('That silver chain mail belonged to Conrad de Warlencourt. He was wearing it when he captured the True Cross').

Then I told him about the library and he got a bit weird. He sat up, all alert, just as Lara had been. 'The library?'

'Yes. The library.'

'What did you see?' he asked, sharply.

'Books,' I said, but he didn't laugh.

I attempted to change what I could see was, for some reason, a touchy subject. 'I'll tell you what I *didn't* see,' I said. 'Any tech. Anywhere in the house. Not one computer, not one phone. No TVs. You're really thorough with this Medieval thing, aren't you?'

'Sometimes the old ways are the best.' He took a sip from his glass with a satisfied expression, and I couldn't tell whether he was savouring the wine or his life. 'Ever heard of the Luddites?'

'Luddites?'

'The Luddites were textile workers in the North, not very far from here. When the Industrial Revolution came along they felt challenged by the coming of machines.' Henry spooned his dessert. 'They thought that technology was "a threat to commonality". In other words, they were afraid of it. They thought machines threatened the way they lived their lives. One chap by the name of Ned Ludd decided to do something about it. In 1779 he smashed two stocking frames in the factory where he worked and gave his name to a movement. The movement spread and pretty soon organised groups of workers were smashing machines.'

'*You* don't go around smashing machines,' I said.

'No.' He smiled gently. 'But we can choose not to use them. Look,' he said reasonably, 'we're not cavemen. We have cars, we have electricity. We just choose to reject the aspects of technology that we think have damaged society and the natural order of things. Teenagers can become YouTube billionaires from their bedrooms without ever having had a decent education. A reality-TV star can become president of the United States without any experience of government.'

'So you say no to *some* tech, not all of it.'

'Precisely.'

'Like the Internet.'

'That's one, yes.'

'And smartphones.'

'That's another.'

'And TV.'

'That's a third.'

'But can you *do* that?' I asked. 'These things have been invented; they are with us, like it or not. Can you put the genie back in the bottle?'

'I'd challenge your analogy there,' he said. 'The genie was a force for good, a benevolent spirit offering three wishes to fulfil your heart's desire. I'd use a different analogy. You know the story of Pandora's box?'

I did. 'Pandora was given a box which contained all the evils of the world. She opened it from curiosity, let the evils loose, and was unable to close the box again. But that's what I mean. Once this stuff is out there, it's out there.'

Henry nodded slowly. 'The Luddites found that too. They were fighting a losing battle. The machines rolled over them and crushed them, and within less than a century, technology had taken over the world. But are we any the better for it?'

'Yes,' I said, 'because not all of it is evil. And here's why I like the genie analogy better than Pandora. The wishes can be good or bad; what we wish for is up to us. I think tech is like that. It's not all bad. Some of it is good.'

'What's so good about it? Name me three things?'

I was having fun – this was combative but friendly. He knew much more about this stuff than I'd given him credit for, and it made me realise that Henry wasn't ignorant about modern tech, he'd just chosen to reject it. He was very clever, and I enjoyed debating with him. Maybe this was what it would be like to be Henry's girlfriend. I thought of The Kiss and our hands grazing in the wood. Maybe I already was.

I thought about his question. 'Three good things about tech ... OK: Skype. Skype brings people together. It telescopes the world. You can talk to your old granny in the outback in Australia. A surgeon in London can oversee keyhole surgery in Cowshitville in the middle of nowhere, if there's no one there qualified to do it. And what about all those online campaigns, for democracy in Arab states, rights for women, finding missing people. They can change the world for the better.'

'Skype and online campaigning,' said Henry. 'That's two. What about a third?'

I thought for a moment. 'Funny videos of cats.'

Henry nearly spat out his wine. 'Are you serious?'

'Yes,' I said firmly. 'In a way, all the funny stuff on the Internet, all the amazing tricks, all the memes, all the stupid photos, that's all valid too. If it makes millions of people smile, or de-stress, or relax, isn't that a force for good?'

'All right,' he said, smiling himself. 'You've listed three – arguable – benefits. Your three genie wishes, if you will. Let me match that with the infinite evils of Pandora's box. The Deep Web. The proliferation of paedophilia, hard-core porn, you name it. And then, in the shallow end of the pool, even social media has its evils. Look at trolling. Trolling is the new blood sport.'

He motioned to the world outside, and I followed his gesture to see the stunning view; the flame-coloured trees, the lush green hillside and, far in the distance, the heartbreakingly lovely house nestling in the valley.

'Lots of people wouldn't approve of what we are doing this weekend. But trolling is much more destructive than what we get up to here for a few days a year. The kind of hunting that trolls do is in every home, every day, threatening every young person's mental health. No,' he said, smoothing his napkin, 'I think we're better off without tech. It "threatens commonality", just like the Luddites said.'

I didn't necessarily disagree with him. I'd found that morning – this whole weekend – very seductive. The peace of it, the real-world pursuits. But I didn't think we had the choice. 'You said it though. This stuff is in every home. You're fighting a losing battle with keyboard warriors.'

'Maybe I am,' said Henry with a sad smile. 'But I'll fight it as long as I can.'

'How will you know if you've lost?' I asked, interested.

'If the day comes,' he said, 'I'll know. But until then, I'm happy being a Luddite.' He lifted his glass, and I lifted mine to chink his. I didn't wholly agree with him, or wholly disagree, but the gesture said we'd park the argument amicably for now.

But Shafeen had other ideas. He cut across the friendliness.

'You're not a Luddite,' he said to Henry scornfully. 'It's not the same thing at all.'

Suddenly everyone else was listening. Piers actually put down his glass and Cookson paused with (ironically) a silver spoon in his mouth. Lara rested her chin charmingly on her hand. Nel stopped pushing her pudding around her bowl, and Esme and Charlotte flipped their hair and turned their heads to listen too.

'The Luddites were a working-class movement.' Shafeen addressed the pyramid of oranges in front of him, looking neither right nor left. 'They thought machines would replace them and take their wages. Not threaten some long-dead way of life filled with privilege and luxury and leisure. They wanted to *work*.' He looked straight at Henry. 'Have you ever worked?'

'Have *you*?' asked Henry smoothly.

Shafeen shifted a little. '*I'm* not claiming to be a Luddite. All I'm saying is, *you're* not one either.'

Henry stretched, supremely confident. 'Well, Shafeen, you've known me for . . . how many years?'

'Ten,' said Shafeen shortly.

'You've known me for ten years. You're as well qualified to judge as anyone. What would *you* say I am?'

We were all dead silent, waiting and listening.

Shafeen thought for a moment, studying Henry as if he'd

never seen him before. 'You're King Sisyphus,' he said, 'trying to push a boulder up a hill. Sisyphus was a king from Greek myth who thought he was cleverer than everyone else, even the gods. He spent eternity pushing an immense boulder up a steep hill.' He shook his head. 'Trying to fight technology is like trying to fight gravity. Some day, when you and your kind aren't there to push it, that boulder's going to come rolling back down the hill again.' There was a dangerous silence.

I glanced at Henry nervously, but just as at the end of the tiger-mother story, he started to laugh. And said unexpectedly, 'You're absolutely right.' Then he clapped his hands together. 'Well, if everyone's had their fill, it's time to push a boulder up a hill.' He shoved back his chair and stood up. 'Shafeen and I have a score to settle.' He glanced out of the windows.

The light was fading, and the sky was turning the same orange as the fruits on the table and the trees outside. 'There's time for one more drive before dark,' announced Henry.

I'd almost forgotten the shoot, and the pheasant-slaughtering competition; for a moment it was almost as if the score to be settled was about the Luddites.

Henry raised his hand, and one of the servants sprang forward with one of the ever-present silver trays they seemed always to have to hand at Longcross.

On this tray was a large silver flask, with sort of a tan leather base reaching halfway up it. Around the flask in a neat circle were six little silver cups. Henry poured out some brown liquid into the cups (I never did find out what it was. Brandy? Whisky?) and the servants handed them around, missing out me, Lara and Nel.

'What are we, chopped liver?' I quipped to Lara, on the

other side of the table to me. Again I felt sorry for her – Henry had spent the whole of lunch ignoring her. I didn't really need a drink, but I did need something to say.

'Only the guns get a shooting cup,' she said in her bored, don't-be-stupid voice, and I abruptly stopped feeling sorry for her. 'There's a number on the bottom, which will tell them where they are in this afternoon's stand – their position in the line when they start the next drive.'

'And does it matter?' I asked.

'Not really. It's just a bit of fun,' she said in the least fun-sounding voice ever.

Piers the booze hound was, of course, the first to finish his drink. He did it in the manner of that huge mountain guy from *Raiders of the Lost Ark*, the one who's having a drinking competition with Marion Ravenwood. He drained it, held the little silver cup out in front of him at arm's length and banged it down on the table. I could just about see from my end of the table that there was a little number engraved on the bottom of the cup. 'Three!' he shouted, and everyone cheered.

Cookson wasn't far behind. 'One!' Everyone cheered again. Esme. 'Four!' Cheer.

Charlotte. 'Two!' Cheer.

Then Henry. 'Five!'

'Woohoo!' I said, trying to enter into the spirit.

Shafeen was last – zero suspense of course. Everyone knew he was six, but everyone still cheered politely when he said the number soberly.

I saw Piers and Cookson exchange a look, and felt a sudden little shiver of foreboding.

chapter twenty

Now I thought of *A Knight's Tale* and the lady watching her knight jousting, and beating every other competitor in the lists.

Henry's Crusader blood surfaced again, and I thought it sweet (*sweet!*) that he wanted me to watch him. The only thing was, I was feeling a small, niggling doubt that he could actually *beat* Shafeen. Shafeen had been looking over at us at lunch with a strange set expression, and now he strode to his place in the line with a grim determination. In a western, he'd be twirling his gun right then, not carrying it broken neatly over his arm.

Now we were much closer to the action than we had been before lunch, and the noise was incredible. The guns all wore ear defenders over their flat caps, but we bystanders didn't have any, and I felt as if my ears were bursting. There was that weird smell again, the acrid burning smell of the cartridges, and they popped out of the guns and fell bouncing to the grass. Henry was taking aim and firing in quick succession, and had a pretty good hit rate. But Shafeen was amazing. He was an absolutely crack shot. I would never have thought it of him. He was like Gregory Peck in *To Kill a Mockingbird* – a fine upstanding character, but put a gun in his hand and he was totally accurate and deadly. He tracked the birds with his gun, and shot them cleanly out of the air one after another, swapping his shotgun with his loader like a relay runner without even looking behind him. The pheasants rained down from above, landing on the damp grass with a dull thud. One of them narrowly missed me and lay at my feet like a tribute.

I picked the pheasant up and held it in my hands. It was quite, quite dead but still warm – so weird to think that something could be dead and warm at the same time. The little head lolled over my hand. All I could think about was how beautiful it was – there were about fifty colours in the feathers, from sort of teal green to dark red and loads of different browns in between. As I looked at it, its little golden feet already curling up in death, I felt really sad; like when-you-really-feel-like-you're-going-to-cry sad. I hated both Shafeen and Henry at that moment.

Then a properly strange thing happened – this black spaniel trotted up to me, very politely took the bird from my hands and carried it, careful as a mother, over to Henry's pile of feathered bodies.

Shafeen lowered the barrels of his gun. 'That was *my* bird,' he called furiously.

Henry turned to Perfect, who was, of course, his loader.

'Yours fair and square, m'lord. Right over your head it was.'

'Looks like the score's even, old chap,' said Henry to Shafeen, squinting against the sun.

Shafeen looked from one to the other. 'Oh, well, if you can't win like a gentleman,' he said contemptuously.

I caught a furious look flitting across Henry's face, before he composed his features. There was a horrible moment of tension, broken by the racket of the beaters calling the last drive of the day. Nel, Lara and I retreated back behind the loaders' line for safety, and the sky darkened with birds taking flight. Of course we all looked upwards, our eyes on the birds, to see whether Henry or Shafeen would be victorious, so no one saw exactly what happened next.

I remember a terrific volley of gunshots and watching more poor pheasants cartwheeling out of the sky. Then I remembered a single gunshot, so loud it almost seemed to come from right next to my ear. My hearing dulled instantly, as if the ambient sound had been turned down. My ears were whining with this eerie ringing sound. Muted under the ringing, almost like it was underwater, I heard a cry. It was as if everything was happening in slow motion. I looked down and to my right in the direction of the shout, in time to see Shafeen spinning around with the force of a blow and falling to the grass.

He'd been shot.

The Shooting Party, I thought, and started to run. I was absolutely convinced that, just like the guy who gets in the line of fire in the movie, Shafeen was dead. By the time we girls got there, there was already a small knot of loaders and dogs and Medievals around him. I had to fight my way through wellies and dogs to get close.

He was a horrible colour – his dark skin almost green. He was on his side, clutching his arm and rolling slightly, so at least he was alive. No one else was touching him, so I knelt and prised his hand from his arm and saw an ugly tear in the arm of his jacket. I folded back the material and could see that the tear went through the jumper, through the shirt.

Through the skin.

I nearly puked. A horrid gash was seeping blood.

'Shot grazed him,' observed Piers casually, peering down. 'Dashed good job.'

I looked up at him incredulously. 'A graze is what you get on your knee when you fall over at primary school. This is not *that*.' It was deep, and the blood kept coming.

Piers shifted his feet and said sulkily, 'I just meant there'll be no pellets to dig out. Painful business that.'

Cookson nodded. 'Doctor'll patch him up and he'll be right as rain.'

I flapped my hand impatiently. 'Never mind all the chat,' I said. 'We've got to tie something round his arm.' I'd seen it in movies.

I looked up and no one was moving. The servants all stood well back, as if they didn't feel that it was their place to intrude on the doings of their betters. All the Medievals were in this semicircle, looking down at Shafeen writhing and moaning. At that moment I assumed they simply didn't know what to do. I remembered seeing this film called *The Admirable Crichton*, where this aristocratic family goes on a sea voyage and gets shipwrecked, and then when they're on this desert island it turns out the rich family don't have any survival skills and so they're at the mercy of this really resourceful butler called Crichton, who effectively becomes the boss on the island. Here in the covert it was Nel who woke up from her stupor and was more use than the rest of them put together. She took off her brand-new Hermès belt, dropped to her knees and helped me tie it tightly round Shafeen's upper arm. Esme and Charlotte, who'd been perfectly happy to shoot birds into a million pieces a minute ago, were making a hysterical fuss about blood. The boys just sort of stood about, as if they didn't know how to help – or didn't want to. Shafeen was now shivering, and his eyes were half closed. I took my jacket off and Nel did too, and we draped them over him. That shamed Cookson and Piers into action, and they did the same. Strangely Henry, the king of jacket-lending, kept his on. It was almost as if he was in shock too.

'What the hell happened?' I yelled, hoping to shake him out of his stupor.

He didn't reply or even look at me.

'Dashed difficult to say,' said Piers, filling the silence. 'Someone mis-shot, I think. Punjabi was edging out of his line. Getting a bit competitive with old Henry, don't you know.'

'Impossible to say who,' said Cookson smoothly. 'Just an unfortunate accident.'

Henry said nothing, but looked down at Shafeen with an unreadable expression on his face. Then he knelt and put out a hand. 'Come on, old man. I'll help you up.'

Shafeen's dark eyes focused. 'No,' he said quite clearly. 'Not you.'

Henry recoiled as if he was the one who'd been shot. He stood up and stumbled backwards.

This wasn't the time for their childish feud. 'Someone's got to take you!' I exclaimed, worry making me shout at poor Shafeen. 'What if you collapse?' What I really wanted to do was pick him up and carry him down the mountain myself, as he'd done to Nel. I turned to Henry. 'Can we get a car up here?'

Henry shook his head.

'*I'll* take him.' Piers put his hands under Shafeen's armpits. 'Come on, Punjabi. *Jeldi, jeldi.*'

But Shafeen was tall, and drifting in and out of consciousness. He was a deadweight. Piers and Cookson between them couldn't carry him. 'Perfect,' called Henry calmly, 'have the beaters take the gate off.'

I thought it was some kind of ill-timed joke, but, unbelievably, Perfect and the beaters literally took a gate out of the nearby dry-stone wall, and laid Shafeen on it. Like coffin bearers, we all lifted it between us, and that's how we got Shafeen down the hill.

All the way down I looked at his pinched face growing paler and his tweed sleeve darkening with blood. Nel smiled at him. 'Now I'm carrying *you* down the hill,' she said.

He looked at her, focused and half smiled. Then his head lolled sideways again and his eyes closed.

Back at the house, a swarm of servants flooded out of the grand entrance at our approach, followed by Henry's fat Labradors. The menfolk lifted Shafeen from the gate. By this point he was conscious and could walk with help, and two of the under-butlers took him into the Boot Room. We all followed.

They laid Shafeen down by the fire, in the midst of the detritus of walking sticks and an old wetsuit and the rows of wellingtons. The Labradors sniffed him and Nel, despite the dogs, crouched down next to him like Florence Nightingale.

'Shall I go outside and wait for the ambulance?' I said.

Henry looked strangely blank.

'You've called an *ambulance*, right?'

Henry turned to the mammoth headkeeper. 'Perfect, go to the village for the doctor.'

'For Chrissake!' I shouted. 'Wake up!' I had. It was as if that shot on the hillside had wakened me from a dream, a lovely dream of the past. It had ripped a jagged hole through the fantasy of this morning. I took hold of Henry's arm and dragged him outside. Perfect, the shadow, followed.

In the fresh air I could say what I hadn't wanted Shafeen to hear. 'Your lovely antiquated life is all very well, but this is an actual *emergency*! He's losing blood! What if he dies?'

'He's not going to *die*,' said Henry. 'It's a flesh wound.' But, in concession to me, he said, 'Be as quick as you can, Perfect.' Perfect touched his cap and walked, not very fast, I have to say, in the direction of the stables.

'What, are you going to send him on a *horse*?' I yelled. That's exactly what they did in *The Shooting Party*, but that was set before the First freaking World *War*.

'Of *course* not,' he snapped. 'In the estate car.'

'But Shafeen needs *hospital* treatment.'

'The nearest hospital is an hour and a half away.'

Then I calmed down a bit. If that was true, then I supposed Henry's plan was the quickest way to get Shafeen medical attention.

But I was still breathing hard. Henry laid his hand on mine, but this time I didn't get the electric shock. 'It's better this way,' he said gently. 'Trust me.'

Thing is, I wasn't sure I did any more.

chapter twenty-one

The night Shafeen got shot, I didn't really expect there to be a dinner.

But I should have known better. It would take more than a human shooting to keep the upper classes from their meals.

I sat on my bed in Lowther for a long, long time, cold despite the merry fire, thinking and gazing unseeing at the dying light outside. Jeffrey watched me, saying nothing. That's what I liked about Jeffrey. He knew when to keep quiet and let a person think.

When Betty came with my clothes, I didn't even let her get as far as laying them out on the bed. 'Betty,' I said curtly, 'I'll dress myself tonight. That will be all.' Weirdly, she looked a lot less fierce as she nodded and left. Maybe she preferred a world without pleases and thank-yous, a world where her masters knew their place and she knew hers. Was she more comfortable that way? With commands, rather than requests? Was Henry right about the natural order of things?

Either way, I didn't need her tonight. I knew exactly what I was going to wear and how I was going to have my hair and do my make-up. I shook my mother's dress out of the case – luckily it was the kind of material that fell perfectly, with no creases.

I put it on, and decided there would be no princess ringlets tonight. I warmed up my tongs and ironed my black hair dead straight, fringe to my eyelashes, bob skimming my shoulders. I looked in the mirror with a kind of grim satisfaction. The Dress was perfection – silver grey, strapless, with thousands of tiny jet-black beads swirling and clustering down the front like a murmuration of starlings. My mother might not have been much of a mother, but she sure as hell could make a dress, and I respected her for that. There was a lot of work in it, every bead sewn on by hand. I thought then that she must have loved me a *little*, to make this dress for me.

I rummaged in my make-up bag for my blackest eyeliner and drew two smooth wings over my eyelids, flicked up at the outer edges. I took one last look in the mirror. The princess was gone. I looked like myself again, and, I was pleased to see, a little bit dangerous.

I decided I couldn't face drinks in the drawing room, if they were even happening, so I went straight down to dinner, alone. I wasn't surprised to see at once that Shafeen was missing. I had half expected Nel to stay away too, so that there would be one less at dinner every night, like in that Agatha Christie film *And Then There Were None*. But she was there, or at least half there, a ghost of what she'd been.

Now I was sitting one place away from Henry, with Lara in between us. At lunch I'd been next to him. I expected that I was being punished for shouting at him about the ambulance.

The dinner was very serious to start with, but within the space of a couple of courses, once the wine started to flow, the Medievals were as rowdy as ever, chattering away and shrieking with laughter. It was as if nothing had happened to Shafeen.

I toyed with my food. It was fish soup, which I'm not a fan of at the best of times, but especially when I remembered that this was what they did – we'd had venison the night before we killed the deer, pheasant with lead shot garnish before the shoot, and tomorrow we were to go fishing. I couldn't believe the sports would continue after what had happened, but apparently, from what I was hearing around the table, such incidents were not uncommon. I must have heard the words 'these things happen' about a hundred times.

These things happen. These things happen. Everyone had a story about an uncle, cousin, guest, who had been shot during a drive. I was not convinced.

The only direct reference to Shafeen came when Henry stood up, tapped his silver knife on his glass till everyone fell quiet and said, 'I will not, of course, be giving the shootin' toast tonight, out of respect for Shafeen, who sustained a *slight* injury.'

I thought of the blood seeping through Shafeen's jacket and had to bite my tongue. 'Instead I give you Shafeen, and our best wishes for his speedy recovery.'

'*Shafeen*,' they all said, seriously and respectfully. Then Piers added, glass high in the air, 'The Punjabi Playboy!' And they all fell about laughing. I put down my glass. I felt the wine would choke me.

Then two servants approached Henry. One placed the morocco-bound black book in front of Henry, open at the right page, and the other one handed him a fountain pen. *Oh*, I thought, *he's still going to write in the game book though.*

From where I was sitting I couldn't see exactly what he was writing, but I knew he'd be recording the number of pheasants massacred that day. Then he wrote one last entry, and he turned the book to face Lara. Their eyes met and they both smirked. That was his mistake, because when he showed the book to her, he also showed it to me.

I'll never forget what I read there. I can still, to this day, see the scrawl of ink, drying on the paper in the candlelight.

1 x Shafeen Jadeja

That was when I knew.

All the terrible thoughts I'd tried to keep at bay upstairs, sitting on the bed while night fell outside, crowded in on me, gathering like the darkness had outside my window. Henry de Warlencourt had listed Shafeen in the book as *prey*. He was of no more value than those pheasants. Henry had not just written his name down, but had entered him as a *quantity*. '1 x Shafeen Jadeja', as though there were thousands of him in the world. Pheasants and peasants, both expendable and worthless.

I thought I was going to be sick.

Fortunately, as soon as the game book was closed, the table all rose as we ladies retired into the drawing room for coffee, giving me an escape. Nel, the three sirens and I settled into various chairs and sofas, the Medieval girls absorbed in the ritual of handing round and lighting cigarettes. I wondered how the hell I'd be able to make conversation now I knew what I knew. I made sure I sat next to Nel. I had to speak to her, had to apologise for not believing her. I was a very new friend to her, but I had already been a totally rubbish one. And I had been an even worse feminist, dismissing her as a hysterical, crazy psycho.

I looked for a distraction, and when the maid came in with the silver coffee tray, and there was all the milk-and-sugar kerfuffle, I seized my chance.

I grabbed Nel's arm, hard enough to hurt. I had to wake her from her zombified state – had to let her know that I was serious. 'I'm *so sorry* I didn't believe you. You were right all along,' I muttered in a low voice.

'Wha—'

I cut across her. 'No time. Don't ask any questions. Tell them you're going to bed. Meet me in Shafeen's room in ten minutes. Bring the seeds.'

'The *seeds?*'

'Yes. The seeds.'

chapter twenty-two

Shafeen's room was on a different floor to mine and Nel's – probably some weird morality thing, even though Longcross was turning out to be the least moral place I'd ever been.

His room had a name too – it was Raby. When I knocked on the door and went in, Nel was already there. We both sat on Shafeen's bed, in a weird mirroring of last night when I'd sat on Nel's.

Except he wasn't in a dressing gown. He was sitting up, the bed sheets to his waist, smooth brown chest and broad shoulders rising above. His dark hair was all bed-head messy and falling all round his face. I thought, completely irrelevantly, how handsome he was. *Some feminist, Greer.* A white bandage was wrapped around the top of his arm, and a bottle of painkillers sat on the bedside table.

He smiled tightly when I entered, and said, 'What's going on?'

Now we were here, I wasn't sure what to say. Now Nel and I were *both* going to sound like a couple of hysterical fantasists. But one shared look across Shafeen's legs was enough to tell me we were on the same page. I didn't really know how to start, but I knew someone had to.

'Look, Shafeen, I've . . . We've got something to tell you.'

His face became set and stern – he suddenly reminded me of a hawk; a hunter, not prey.

Nel took over. 'Thing is,' she said, 'we think the Medievals *meant* to shoot you.'

'*God*, yes,' he said. 'Of course they abso*lute*ly meant to shoot me.'

Nel and I glanced at each other in a mixture of shock and relief. 'You think so too?'

'Oh yes. They gave me the number-six shooting cup at lunch so I'd be at the end of the line, where they could turn their guns on me without hitting each other. I was aiming at a pheasant over my head and it jinked in the air at the last minute, and I swung round to try to hit it. And if I hadn't, I'd be dead now.'

My mouth gaped open. 'But they'd be *murderers*.'

'No,' he said, 'it would have been a "terrible accident". An inexperienced Indian boy, didn't know what he was doing, got himself in the line of fire. Henry and Piers and Cookson and the rest have been shooting since they were knee high.' He gestured, and winced. 'They are all good shots. The verdict would be accidental death and everyone would move on with their lives.'

I was shocked at the harsh words.

'Two things went wrong for them. One: I've been shooting since I was knee high too. Game hunting is a big thing in Rajasthan. Two: they missed.'

'But they must *know* you would talk,' said Nel.

He shook his head. 'They rely on people being frightened of them, of their money, of their status. I'm not frightened. But even if I talked, what then? It's my word against all of theirs. You two were to be scared into silence, and who else was there on the shoot? A bunch of Medievals, a few village fellows on the Longcross payroll and Frankenstein's monster, aka Perfect, who has been the de Warlencourts' creature for generations.'

'So who did shoot you?' I asked, with a sick feeling of dread sitting in my stomach.

'I didn't see,' he admitted. 'I was looking up the whole time. But I'm pretty sure it was Henry.'

Somehow I'd known he was going to say that. But I still found myself wanting it not to be true. 'Why him?'

'One, the trajectory of the shot. He was number five, he had a clear aim at close range. Two, when I was hit, the force spun me round before I fell. His gun had just discharged. I saw him break it and the cartridges jump out. He was literally holding a smoking gun.' He shifted his weight a little and took a drink of water. 'How did you two figure it out?'

'Nel knew yesterday,' I admitted.

'When the hounds came for me,' she said, 'I knew they were hunting me. But I thought it was just the other Medievals. I didn't think it was Henry.' She was echoing my own thoughts. 'I thought Henry was the good guy,' she said sadly. 'He gave me his jacket.'

'Then took it back again,' said Shafeen drily.

'Actually –' Nel and I exchanged a nod – 'we have something to show you.' Nel snapped open the cerise clutch bag she was holding and counted her magic seeds into the palm of Shafeen's good hand. 'These were in the pockets of Henry's jacket.'

'We thought you might know what they are,' I said.

He peered at his palm. 'I do,' he said grimly. 'They're called aniseeds.'

The name made a connection in my mind. 'Aniseeds? You mean, like liquorice?'

'Yes. Dogs can't resist it. In some parts of the country they drag a bag of aniseed over the hillside for the hounds to follow. It's called a drag hunt. Dogs go mental for aniseed. It makes them crazy.'

'I *thought* there were dogs sniffing at the door last night,' said Nel triumphantly.

'There would have been. The stag hounds and the shooting dogs are kennelled, of course, but even Henry's fat old Labradors would make it up the stairs for a sniff of aniseed. And if you don't get rid of those, they'll be round again tonight.'

It was still hard to believe. 'They seemed so *nice* as well, those dogs. When they weren't in their "wolf's frenzy", I mean. Arcas and Tigris even came to greet me this morning when I . . .' I stopped.

'When you what?'

'The names,' I said. 'The names of the hounds.' I turned to Shafeen. 'That last day at STAGS, Friar Mowbray told us in Latin about Actaeon being ripped apart by fifty hounds. She started to tell us the names. They were called Arcas, Ladon and Tigris.' I looked to Nel. 'Henry's hounds have those three names. He called them by them yesterday. And I bet the others are all named after the other forty-seven.'

'I bet they are.' Shafeen shifted, wincing slightly with pain as he did so. 'So are you convinced now, Greer?'

I nodded. 'Yes. I wasn't convinced last night,' I admitted. 'That is, I knew Nel'd had a fright, but I couldn't quite believe she was being hunted. I met Henry outside Nel's room – he was coming to check on her. He . . . convinced me of his concern.'

I couldn't quite look at Nel for the next bit. For all I knew, she'd liked Henry too, and had been as horribly disillusioned on the huntin' day as I'd been on the shootin' one. 'He took me on the roof, and we had this really good chat. He reassured me we were quite safe. He said – and this I remember – he said, "I give you my word as a gentleman that you are not going to get shot. And neither is Chanel."'

'Well, he wasn't lying; you have to give him that,' said Shafeen. 'I was the target of the day.' He narrowed his dark eyes at me. 'Did he tell you that you're beautiful?'

'Yes,' I said in a small voice. I guess Henry *was* lying about *that*.

'Did he kiss you?'

Man, he was clever. 'Yes.'

'So what changed your mind about him?' he asked, much more gently. 'When did the scales fall from your eyes?'

'At dinner tonight,' I said. 'You know that big black book they wrote in after the stag hunt?'

'The game book? Yes. They write up their kill for the day.'

'Well, you're in it. They wrote your name down too, under all the pheasants.'

Even the sardonic Shafeen looked shocked. 'You're *sure*?'

I nodded. 'I saw it, in black and white.'

'That probably means they wrote *me* in it yesterday,' said Nel. She looked like she was tearing up, as if she couldn't quite believe such cruelty existed.

I put my hand over hers. 'Yes. And I saw something else too. The way that Henry showed Lara. They were smirking. They thought it was funny.'

In that look, my whole world had changed. You see, all that time I'd been trying to convince myself, like Nel had, that the cruelty had come from all the *other* Medievals. Not him, never him. But in the end I had to wake up. It had been Henry's jacket, Henry's house, Henry's weekend. Henry's doctor. No hospitals. I looked at the neat white bandage at the top of Shafeen's arm, contrasting with his brown skin, and the bottle of painkillers on the bedside table.

'Looks like the doctor patched you up pretty good.'

'Oh yes. He looked after me *very* well, for a guy who was clearly the wrong side of eighty,' he said with a tinge of irony.

I looked at the tightly wrapped dressing.

Nel said, 'You mean, he *didn't* look after you?'

'Oh no, he made *sure* I was comfortable. He looked after me all right, like he's been looking after the family for fifty years. Had to make sure there was nothing to tell, and no need for a hospital, just like he does every time.'

There it was again. '*Every time?*'

'Yes. You haven't quite caught on yet, have you?' He looked at Nel. 'Either of you. It's bigger than just this weekend. They've been doing this for *years*.'

Nel and I were silent for a minute, taking this in. 'Shafeen,'

I said gently, 'if what you're saying is true, we have to go to the police.'

'No,' he said, more decidedly than he'd said anything.

'But –' began Nel.

He cut across her. 'We don't have enough on them yet. I'm not leaving till we've got proof. What do you think I'm doing here?'

I opened my eyes wide at him. 'You mean, you *knew*?'

'I've had my suspicions for years. Kids go off for the weekend at Justitium and they come back like ghosts. Shattered creatures who move around the school like zombies, not daring to say anything to the Medievals. They just keep their heads down and graduate.'

'Gemma Delaney!' I said suddenly.

He nodded. 'She's one of them.'

Nel said, 'Who's Gemma Delaney?'

'This girl from my old school. She told me not to come to Longcross. She must have been here last year.'

'She was,' said Shafeen. 'And she's not the only one. Some of them come back injured, some of them just thoroughly scared. All of them are put back into their place; the carefully marked-out place the Medievals have decided for them. Sometimes,' he said, 'they don't come back at all.'

'*What?*' Nel and I chorused.

'There's this legend going around the school. Some kid in the nineties – went to Longcross and never came back. They chose him well: boy from a Third World country, here on a scholarship. Brown skin, funny name –' he pointed to himself; 'at STAGS on a scholarship –' he pointed at me; 'not the right type –' he pointed to Nel. 'Sound familiar? The story goes he was killed in a hunting accident at Longcross.'

'But that *can't* have been Henry,' I protested, still not quite able to stop defending him, to let my fantasy go. 'He wasn't born even.'

'You don't get it, do you? This has been going on for *years*. Christ, my *father* even came here.'

Then I remembered – there was some longstanding beef between Henry's dad and Shafeen's.

'What happened?'

Shafeen shrugged his bare shoulders. 'He never told me. It was like he was ashamed. But now I'm sure it had something to do with this.'

'Why would he send you to STAGS, if something so terrible had happened to him there?'

'Nothing happened to him there. It happened at Longcross – nothing to do with the school. He got a great education. He went on to Oxford, then Sandhurst, then took up his governorship in Rajasthan. I guess he wasn't to know that the son of his nemesis, Rollo de Warlencourt, would be at STAGS at the exact same time as me. They didn't exactly keep in touch. My dad thought STAGS was a great school, full of the right people. He was half right.'

'Which half?'

'STAGS is a great school. That is, the education is great, and the friars are good teachers, but the kids are all in on it.'

'On what?' said Nel.

'On the huntin' shootin' fishin' thing.'

'Who is?' I said.

'All of them. Your roommate for example. What's her name?'

I nearly said Jesus. 'Becca.'

'She's in on it. And yours, Nel.'

'What are you talking about?' I said slowly.

'Was your roommate there when you got The Invitation?'

I thought back. 'Yes.'

'Did she encourage you to go?'

'Yes.'

'Did she say you might become a Medieval?'

'Yes,' I said, shamefaced.

Shafeen struck the snowy sheets with his good hand. '*That's* the carrot. They have their elite little group which rules the school, and everyone is so desperate to join them they're easy to fool. Even me,' he admitted. 'The truth is, Becca will probably become a Medieval now, for helping them trap you. Was it the first conversation she'd had with you all term?'

I nodded.

'Same for you, Nel?'

'Yes.'

'You see?' Shafeen sat up straighter, all animated. 'This is what they do. They make you feel unwelcome; starve you of friends, of smiles, of conversation. Then, when they finally talk to you, it's like the sun has come out. Believe me, I understand. They've invited me a few times over the years. Apparently they couldn't even wait for the sixth form for me. They *hate* me.'

'Why?' I asked, interested.

He shrugged, and grimaced, and I could see for the first time that it hurt him. Not his arm, although I'm sure that killed him too – but the fact that the Medievals didn't like him. I saw then the years of bullying and exclusion he must have endured at STAGS. 'I don't know why,' he said, in this sort of small voice, suddenly sounding like a little boy. 'Maybe it's because I don't fit their idea of a misfit, if that makes any sense. They don't quite know what to do with me.' He glanced at me quickly. 'I wasn't fair to you, Greer, that first night at dinner. My father *does* run a bank in Jaipur, but he's its president. And we *are* from Indian royalty, and we *do* have a palace in the hills. We have the right money; the Jadejas are as old as the de Warlencourts, and probably as wealthy. We have the right background – my father went to STAGS, then Oxford, then Sandhurst. I live like them, I speak like them, I hunt and shoot and fish like them. I guess it's just the brown skin and the funny name that aren't quite right. I'm still a Savage, in the truest sense, from the days of the Raj and the Empire. No; even further back. You heard them in history, Greer. Henry will always be one of the Crusaders, and I'll always be an Infidel.'

I thought about this for a minute, then picked up on something he'd said. 'You said they've invited you before?'

'Oh, yes. Lots of times.'

'But you didn't come till now?'

'No.'

'Why *this* year?'

He looked at me pointedly, like someone does when they're trying to shut you up. 'I had my reasons.' I got the message, and backed off. Besides, I thought I knew the truth. He was here because Nel had been invited. He was here to protect her.

That night of the tiger-mother story, he'd said what he said to shield Nel. He'd been the one to notice when she'd gone missing at the stag hunt. He'd carried her up the hill. I think he liked her. I looked at Nel now, sitting next to Shafeen in her cerise gown, all pretty and pink and white, her streaked blonde hair tumbling all over her shoulders. They would make a gorgeous couple, him all dark, her all light. I swallowed what felt like a stone in my throat. This morning I'd thought I had a boyfriend. By nightfall I'd discovered the same prospective boyfriend was a homicidal maniac. Suddenly I needed to go, to get as far away as I could from Longcross.

'We need to get the hell out of here,' I said. 'We can pack now and just leave, before any of them are up.'

'Go where?' asked Nel. 'Remember this evening when you were trying to get Shafeen an ambulance?'

I glanced at Shafeen. I wasn't sure he knew this bit.

'Henry said the hospital was an hour and a half away,' Nel went on. 'That might be the nearest town too, and the nearest police station.'

'And even if we did get to a village,' said Shafeen, 'it would probably be stuffed with Henry's backwoods tenants.'

They were right. Ever seen *The Wicker Man*? The last thing we needed would be for some hillbilly Lake District community to start doing weird witchcraft and setting fire to us in some straw effigy of Conrad de Warlencourt.

'So now what?' I asked.

'We need evidence,' said Shafeen grimly, 'and I'm not leaving till I get it. This has to end *now*.'

'What kind of evidence?'

'The kind that's written down in black and white.'

White paper, and black ink shining in firelight. Letters that spelled out Shafeen's name. 'The game book!' I said.

'Yes.'

Another image came into my mind; that morning in the library, up in the mezzanine. The rows and rows of black books bound in morocco leather, the books which had dates but no titles.

'I'm fairly sure I know where to find your evidence,' I said. But we couldn't go down there and start snooping around with all the lights on, alerting Longcross's fifty million servants to our search. *My spies are everywhere*, Henry'd said. And he'd meant it. 'Thing is, we'd need a torch.'

'How about a Saros 7S?'

Nel opened her clutch bag again and slid out a slim, beautiful tablet of smooth glass and metal, rounded at the corners and glowing like treasure. She touched the screen and it sprang into life, showing a gorgeous picture of Nel cuddling a cute fluffy cat (might've known she'd be a cat person) and the date and time. 'You brought your phone with you?'

Nel nodded, a light of mischief in her eye that I was really happy to see. They hadn't beaten her after all. She'd disobeyed the Medieval girls too. I'd brought my mother's dress to Longcross and I was wearing it now. Nel too had broken the rules, but for something a bit more useful, her own brand of rebellion.

Tech.

'You little *beauty*,' Shafeen said admiringly, and I knew he meant Nel, not the phone. For a moment we all stared at the

Saros 7S as if it was the Holy Grail in *Indiana Jones and the Last Crusade*. It seemed almost miraculous, this little piece of technology no bigger than a handspan. We'd all been starved of it for so long.

'Does it have a torch on it?'

Expertly, Nel touched the screen a couple of times and the camera's eye emitted a piercingly bright beam.

Shafeen's eyes lit up almost as brightly. He threw back the covers and shrugged on a white towelling robe over his pyjama bottoms. His huntin' look was back. 'Let's go,' he said.

chapter twenty-three

I'm not going to lie.

Creeping down to the library at Longcross in the pitch dark was the scariest thing I'd ever had to do. (At that point in my life, I mean. Of course much scarier things happened to me the next day.)

We'd decided to go separately, so that if any of the Stepford Servants saw us we could make some excuse about going for a drink of water or something. I remembered the way from my snooping session that morning, and briefed the other two in Shafeen's doorway. The passageway was mercifully empty, because by the time we'd finished all our chat it must have been the small hours of the morning. 'You go down the grand staircase,' I whispered, 'and turn right. It's through a set of huge double doors on your left. Oh God . . .'

'What?' whispered Shafeen and Nel as one.

'What if it's locked? It's got properly valuable books in there. I don't mean just first editions; I mean actual *manuscripts*.'

Shafeen considered. 'I don't think it will be,' he said. 'Rich people trust each other. It's a club. They'd never dream that someone they've invited for a weekend would try to rip them off.'

'We're here though, aren't we?' put in Nel. 'We're not part of the club. They've made that very clear. They *might* lock the doors against lowlifes like us.'

Shafeen frowned. 'True. OK, I'll go first. If it's open, I'll go in and close the door behind me. If I'm not back in five minutes, follow me, one at a time. If it's locked, I'll come back and we'll just have to try in the morning. Of course that will be much trickier.'

I privately thought searching in the morning would be pretty impossible. One: the place was crawling with servants. Two: weren't we supposed to be going fishing? But we had no option, so we had to try Shafeen's plan.

'OK,' I said. 'If you're not back, Nel will come down.'

'Wait, why me?' said Nel.

'You've already been badly spooked once,' I said. 'This way you're always with someone, except for on the stairs. Shafeen's in the library, I'm here. It's the fox, the chicken and the corn.'

'I guess I'm the chicken,' said Nel ruefully.

'You're the bravest girl I know,' I said truthfully. 'Go on, Shafeen.'

I don't think we breathed while we waited that five minutes to see if Shafeen would come back. I counted in my head, and when I got to three hundred seconds I gave Nel a little nod. She nodded back, and set off down the great staircase on silent feet. She'd taken off her posh shoes to go barefoot and when my turn came I did the same. Luckily the carpet on the grand stairs was thick, and I moved soundlessly. It was pretty creepy though, I can tell you – hardly any light at all, just the knowledge that those enormous landscape paintings loomed above my head, with the cows and the shepherdesses staring down at me, and, above that, the huge great hulking chandelier ready to drop on my head out of the dark like something from *The Phantom of the Opera*.

We all met up just inside the grand double doors in a white pathway of moonlight streaming in through the glass doors to the garden. Anyone entering would see us at once, especially Shafeen, who looked like a white ghost in his towelling dressing gown.

'This way,' I said, and I led them both up the little spiral staircase to the mezzanine, my bare feet hurting a bit on the cold wrought iron. I went straight to the long low shelf I'd seen that morning, the shelf full of books which were all leather-bound, and all had dates instead of titles. They went in decades, tens and hundreds of them. I knew what they were now. They were game books from all the weekends, all the years and all the centuries that the de Warlencourts had been killing for fun. We walked right to the far end, and found the most recent book, with the current decade tooled in gold on the spine. I pulled it out, remembering that I'd done the same this morning. If I'd managed to look at it then, and I hadn't been interrupted by the Cinderella chimes of the clock, would I have seen Nel's name written there? Would I have seen the truth then, and run up the hill to warn Shafeen? I turned the pages, riffling the heavy-grade, top-quality paper, the other two hanging over my shoulders, until I found today's entry. Nel shone the torch in close. There were the damning words in Henry's neat calligraphy:

Sunday 30th October
122 x Pheasants
1 x Shafeen Jadeja

'Jeeeesus,' breathed Shafeen. 'I mean, I believed you, but . . . wow.' He shook his head.

Nel tapped the screen of the Saros and it flashed a couple of times. 'Photos,' she said. 'They upload to the Orbit, which is the Saros's satellite storage. We have evidence now, even if they take the phone off me.'

Then she put out her broken-nailed finger and turned the page back one. There she was too.

Saturday 29th October
1 x Warrantable Stag
1 x Chanel Ashton

I saw her face in the white light of the phone. I feared she was going to be sick.

But instead she took a deep breath and tapped the screen again, taking another photo. 'Gotcha,' she said.

I had a sudden thought. I turned back the pages to last year's Michaelmas Justitium. 'Look!' I exclaimed.

They both looked.

Saturday 31st October
1 x Warrantable Stag
1 x Gemma Delaney

Wordlessly, Nel took another photo, and I had to lean on the balustrade. I couldn't breathe. I remembered Gemma, that shining girl from Bewley Park Comp, all glossy hair and confidence. She'd been reduced to a shadow of her former self, a broken girl, but still with the kindness and the courage to come to me after chapel at STAGS, because I was another Bewley Park old girl, and beg me not to go to Longcross. And now the Medievals had tried to break Nel and Shafeen.

'Well,' I said to Shafeen softly, so angry I could hardly speak, 'you wanted proof. You got proof. We've got the photos. Let's go.'

'Wait,' he said. He prised the Saros 7S from Nel's hand and started to walk back down the line of books. He was running his fingers down the spines and counting softly. We followed him and the wavering light, and stopped where he stopped. He shone the Saros at the spine of the book and the gold-tooled lettering shone out from the matte black leather.

1960–1969

Then I knew.

Shafeen was looking for his father.

He prised out the book and riffled through the pages, going back and forth as though desperate to find something, but dreading it too. At last he stopped and Nel and I crowded in. Shafeen crumpled cross-legged on the floor of the mezzanine, and we had to kneel to read over his shoulder.

I started to say, 'Shafeen –'

'He never told me,' he interrupted in a small, broken voice. 'He never said.'

I put my hand on his towelling-clad shoulder. I knew why he hadn't. What man wants to admit such a thing to the son he loves? That he'd come to England in the 1960s, to a prestigious school, and was included and accepted as an Indian boy so far as to be invited to a country-house weekend. He must have been so excited. It made me want to cry. I wanted to stand right there and weep for young Aadhish Jadeja, an Indian princeling but still, always and forever, an outsider.

Shafeen slammed the book shut so hard that both we girls jumped. 'They have to be stopped,' he said, in quite a different voice.

Nel put a hand on his other shoulder. 'We will stop them. We have the photos now.'

'It's not enough,' Shafeen said. 'They could say these entries are a joke. Or they could say it's like an accident book, you know, like the one we have in woodwork at STAGS if you cut your finger and you have to write it down.'

'But it's all *here*,' protested Nel loudly. 'They're hunting *kids*! Shooting *kids*!'

'Shhh.' I calmed her down. 'You don't want the minions to hear us.' But just as I said this, the room darkened as a huge silhouette blocked the moonlight from the garden doors.

A silhouette with heavy boots and a flat cap.

Perfect.

The headkeeper stood there for a long moment, still as one of the statues outside, just watching. His long, grim shadow stretched out across the polished floor, giving him giant proportions. Then he reached out and turned the handle of the doors.

I signalled wildly for Nel to kill the torch and for both of them to get down. I flattened myself on my front on the narrow balcony. The little beads of my mum's dress dug into my stomach, but I could see perfectly between the banisters of the balustrade and just prayed that, as Perfect was far below us, the angle of the mezzanine would hide us from sight. I was most worried about Shafeen. Not only was he taller and broader than Nel and me, but in the white towelling robe he stuck out like a polar bear in a coal mine. If Perfect looked up, he would see us at once.

From my viewpoint I saw the headkeeper step quietly into the room, his hobnailed boots barely sounding on the polished floorboards. An icy autumn draught entered with him, and I gave an involuntary shiver. The dangling crystals of the huge chandelier tinkled a little in the night breeze and, as if summoned by the sound, Perfect walked into the middle of the room and stood right under it. (He moved surprisingly quietly for such a big lunk. Probably he'd had years of practice stalking innocent creatures through the undergrowth.) Then he slowly turned around under the chandelier, scanning through three hundred and sixty degrees. It was like that bit in *Beauty and the Beast* when the Beast dances with Belle.

Except there was no Belle.

And no music.

And no candlelight.

Just a beast.

In the moonlight I could see that Perfect was holding something in one arm, a something that he was resting casually on his shoulder. As he turned, I could see the dull metallic gleam of two long barrels. A shotgun.

Perfect raised his chin. I swear he was sniffing the air, like a hound. Then he looked in our direction, and it felt like he looked right at me. It was as if he'd spent so long staring at me throughout the weekend that he could now sense where I was. It was all I could do not to cry out.

Then Perfect did something that made my heart nearly leap out of my frock. He took the gun from his shoulder, held it in both hands and cocked the hammer. Then he walked slowly and silently towards the spiral staircase.

I didn't breathe.

Perfect laid a hand on the iron stair rail, and put his foot on the first step. Just then an owl hooted loudly outside, and he turned, quick as a cat, both barrels pointing out the door. Then he moved quickly and quietly back across the room and went out into the grounds, closing the doors carefully behind him.

chapter twenty-four

We all waited a good five minutes before we dared speak.

I rolled onto my back and breathed out a soft *whooooo* of relief. Shafeen raised himself up on his elbow, hair flopping in his eyes. Nel sat up and tapped the Saros to make the torch come back on. 'Sheesh!' she said shakily. 'D'you think he saw us?'

Privately I was almost sure he had; how could he *not* have done when he'd looked right at me? But if he *had* seen us, why would he just leave us and go? Not wanting to spook Nel, I said, 'Apparently not.'

'What do you think he was doing? Was he looking for us?'

It certainly felt that way, but, again, I didn't want to freak her out. 'For all we know, it's what he does every night. Patrols the place, making sure everything's as it should be. Maybe that's his headkeeper thing.'

'Well, he's gone for now,' said Shafeen, raking his hair back from his face. 'So what do we do about *this*?' He was still clutching the game book from the 1960s. 'It's a good start, but we need more.'

I hauled myself to a sitting position. 'He's right, you know,' I said to Nel. 'It's what they call "circumstantial evidence". Watch any courtroom movie. We need more. We have to catch them at it.'

Shafeen carefully rested his chin on the closed book. 'The thing is, there's only one more opportunity to do that. And that's when we go fishin'. So, Greer, it's down to you. Tomorrow, if we stay, it's your turn. You do know that, don't you?'

'What do you mean?'

'Come on,' he said. 'Huntin' shootin' fishin'. Nel got hunted. I got shot. Tomorrow, it's you. So you have to decide what you want to do.' He got to his feet. 'They invited us because we are misfits. We are upstarts, all at a school where we don't belong. We are to be kept down, to be frightened so much that we won't get ideas above our station in future. We might even be culled, to restore the natural order. Look at all these books.' He waved his arm back along the shelves, embracing centuries of books in the gesture. 'Nel and I were lucky. How many haven't been? How many kids over the centuries, before forensics, and DNA, and all that CSI stuff, have been killed? Even in this century, how many accidents have been covered up, because the de Warlencourts still live this feudal life where they own every tenant on their land and every servant in their house? The little lordlings want their fun, and no one's powerful enough to stop them. Until now.' He turned to Nel. 'You and I have been prey already. It's too late for *us* to trap Henry. It's up to Greer now.' He turned to me. 'If you're willing, it's you who will have to catch him in the act.'

I thought of Gemma Delaney, of Nel, and of Shafeen. But most of all, weirdly, I thought of poor Aadhish Jadeja. 'I'll do it,' I said.

'You're *sure*?'

'I'm sure,' I said.

Shafeen breathed out. 'Then we need a plan.'

'It would help if we knew *where* we were going fishing,' said Nel.

'Well, that's easy,' said Shafeen. 'It must be the lake where we were the other day.'

'The lake where the stag stood at bay?' I asked.

'That's the one. It's on Longcross land so it belongs to Henry. Even the Medievals wouldn't dare to try anything on a public lake. I think it's north-west of here, but I'm not really sure.'

'There's a room with this huge map all over one wall. Just down the passageway.'

'That'll be the estate room. Come on. It would be good to know the lay of the land.' Shafeen still had the game book from the 1960s in his hands.

'Aren't you going to put that back?' Nel asked.

'No way,' he said. 'This one's coming with me.' I couldn't tell if he wanted to have, finally, a long chat about things with his dad, or if he thought the book was somehow shameful, and didn't want the evidence of his dad's defeat to remain at Longcross.

'Won't they notice?' I asked. There was a gap in the long shelf of books like a missing tooth, so Shafeen went along the shelf moving all the books a tiny bit until the gap was closed.

'There,' he said. 'Good as new. They won't notice unless

they're really looking. Come on. And let's be really quiet. That mastodon might still be hanging around.'

Nel tapped off the torch, and we crept down the passageway as I counted the doors – I was pretty sure the map room, as I thought of it, had been at the end of the same passageway the library was on. But things look pretty different when you're swanning down a passageway channelling Elizabeth Bennet, feeling pretty sure that you are the lord of the manor's girlfriend, to when you're stumbling along in the dark, plotting to bring the same lord of the manor down, while his tame heavy is prowling around with a gun. I took a guess and pulled the other two into a doorway.

Nel tapped on the torch again, and I breathed a sigh of relief. It was the room I remembered, with the walnut desk and the antique globe and one wall covered with an old-looking but detailed Ordnance Survey map of every inch of the Longcross estate. I went right up to it, looking at the incredible detail in the powerful white circle of light thrown by the Saros's torch. I traced the house with my finger – the house I'd looked over, and loved, only this morning. Then I let my finger travel to where we'd been huntin' and where we'd been shootin'. And then, in the next valley, I let my finger rest over a long, irregular oval.

The lake.

There were letters written across it, spaced out because the lake was so big. 'L-O-N-G-M-E-R-E,' I spelled out. 'Longmere.' The lake was enclosed at one end, and at the other flowed into a little stream with jagged lines drawn above it. Nel moved the phone closer. 'Conrad's Force,' she read.

Shafeen said, 'It's pronounced "foss". It'll be a waterfall.'

'No doubt named after the famous Conrad de Warlencourt, top knight, thief of the True Cross and all-round scumbag.' My tone was flippant but I don't think anyone was fooled; my voice sounded pretty shaky. My eyes travelled back to the lake as if pulled there, and we all stood in silence looking at the long, dark smudge.

I knew what Shafeen was thinking. Then he said it out loud. 'Can you swim, Greer?'

'Yes,' I said. 'I used to swim for my school. My old school, obviously. Not STAGS.'

I was a good swimmer; actually I'd been one of the best at Bewley, but I'd never tried out for any teams at STAGS, sure there must be lots of baby Olympians who'd been paddling up and down their own vast swimming pools since they were in swim nappies, so I'd never bothered. But, in an environment with no phones and no friends, I had spent quite a few lonely hours thrashing up and down the state-of-the-art pool at school, and now I was glad I had.

'Good,' said Shafeen. 'Because the chances are that before tomorrow is over you'll be making a close acquaintance with that lake.'

'Unless they just shoot me,' I said, thinking of Perfect and the gun.

'No,' said Shafeen. 'It's fishin', remember? Their own rules are the only ones they follow. And they won't just drown you either. It's the chase they crave.'

'But we can't just let Greer be bait.' Nel turned to me. 'I don't want you to go through what I went through,' she said. 'We need a plan.'

So, by the light of the Saros 7S – which, thanks to Nel's dad, had been designed with a battery lasting seven days – we made one.

It must have been 2 a.m. when we left the estate room, ready, we hoped, for the next day.

We dropped Nel back at Cheviot and Shafeen walked me to my room. It was risky but Shafeen, as I was discovering, was the only real gentleman of the party.

At the door he turned to go, hesitated and turned back. 'You asked me why I came to Longcross,' he said. 'I came to protect someone. But it's not Nel. I came because I wasn't going to let them get *you*. And I won't.'

I swallowed. Did he like me in *that* way, in the way I'd thought Henry liked me? What he said gave me a warm feeling but I couldn't process it just now. I was too afraid of tomorrow and what it might bring. I just hoped he was as good as his word. I opened the door to Lowther, but just before I went inside his voice stopped me.

'And in case you're wondering,' he said awkwardly, 'you *are* beautiful. That's the one truth Henry told.'

FISHIN'

chapter twenty-five

I was swimming in Longmere lake, desperately trying to get away from something.

I looked back and saw the Medievals in boats with torches – the girls' blonde hair draping down into the water, as if they were the ladies of the lake. The dark weeds below the surface were pulling at me, choking me, dragging me under. The water closed over my head and I was drowning. Shafeen's head appeared above me. 'We have to get her out,' he said. 'She's beautiful.' Then his dark head changed into Henry's blond one, and Henry reached down to rescue me. But instead of hauling me up, he put out his index finger and pushed it into my mouth, curving it round into my cheek. Then the finger turned into a metal hook that pierced my flesh. Henry pulled and I jerked out of the weeds and rushed up and up, until I broke the surface of the water and my dream.

I didn't wake up hyperventilating and sweating, nor did I sit bolt upright like they do in movies. Just for a moment the dream and last night became confused. For a moment, lying there in my warm bed, I thought that it had *all* been a dream. The conversation on Shafeen's bed, the discovery in the library, the plotting and planning in the estate room till the small hours. But then I saw Jeffrey's head looming out of the half-dark. Today his eyes seemed to be asking me something. Pleading. It was time for the huntin' to stop.

'Don't worry, Jeffrey,' I said. 'I'm on it.' And I threw back the covers and sat up.

The Cogsworth clock on the mantelpiece said ten to six, but I didn't groan; I was relieved. There was something I had to do before the house was awake.

I swung my legs out of bed and scrabbled under the bed for my rucksack. It was one of those outdoorsy ones made of thin tough camouflage material. My dad needed it on a shoot once and gave it to me. It wasn't too bulky so I wrapped it round my waist. Then I grabbed the big white dressing gown from the hook on the back of my door and put it on over the rucksack. It reminded me of Shafeen. He'd been wearing one just like it last night. He was wearing it when he told me he had come to Longcross to save me. He was wearing it when he told me I was beautiful. I shook my head a little. I couldn't think about that now.

I padded downstairs to the Boot Room, the room where I'd first met Henry on Day One, the evening we'd broken up for Justitium. I remembered it well, all the fishing crap and the wellies and the yellowing sporting prints. Fortunately there was no one in there and I found what I was looking for almost at once. It had caught my eye that first day and again yesterday; it was one of the random things propped against the walls of the Boot Room like a discarded piece of junk. I grabbed it, folded it small and put it in my rucksack. Today that discarded piece of junk could save my life.

I put the rucksack back under my dressing gown. The robe was a generous size but I still looked pregnant. I ran back up the stairs two at a time. Two maids were walking down as I went up, but they did no more than murmur, 'Morning, miss,' as I galloped past. They were too well trained to comment, and, as I knew from last night, there were stranger things to ignore at Longcross than a suddenly fat girl running up some stairs.

I slipped into Lowther, ripped off the dressing gown, shoved the rucksack under the bed and dived under the covers. I'd just settled down to fake sleep when Betty knocked and entered. She walked straight to the windows and dragged back the curtains with a particularly vicious scrape, the cow. Light flooded in and I made a show of blinking, as if I hadn't just minutes ago been running all over the house.

'Morning, Betty!' I said breezily.

She shot me one of her evil looks. 'Morning, miss. Shall I bring your tea up?'

'Yes, please, Betty.' I'd decided to revert to my previous manner with her. I didn't want to bark orders like a Medieval. If all went well today, their reign would soon be over. Even a miserable hag like Betty deserved good manners. Everybody does.

Betty brought my breakfast, and today there were bright orange kippers under the silver dome. 'Seems in poor taste on a fishin' day, Jeffrey,' I said, trying to keep things light. My heart was hammering and my appetite levels were at zero, but I forced myself to eat as much as I could stomach of the bread and pastries. I needed to carb-load if things were going to go down as we expected today. No kippers though. I didn't like the way they looked. Or smelled.

Once I was dressed there was a knock on my door and I opened it to ... Esme, Charlotte *and* Lara. 'Well,' I said, being Charlotte for a moment, '*what* an honour.' They bundled in, sat on my bed while I got ready and were all incredibly chatty and friendly. Esme was surprisingly informative about fish: 'We'll be catching brown trout today,' she said. 'Longmere's lousy with it. Good old *salmo trutta*.' (Such a Medieval thing to do, to give the Latin name.) Lara was complimentary about my hair: 'Gorgeous bob today, darling,' she said in her bored voice. 'So 1920s. The original Bright Young Thing.' And Charlotte even said (if you'll believe this), 'Oh my *God*, you look so *nice* in your *fishing* clothes!' A sentence I'm pretty sure had never been uttered before, ever, in the History of the World. The fishing gear wasn't exactly sexy – it consisted of a flannel shirt, thick Aran sweater and waterproof wader trousers.

I was pretty surprised that Lara, in particular, was being so nice, but then I remembered that there was no reason why she shouldn't be. I was absolutely no threat to her and never had been. Henry had been toying with me, flattering me, keeping me on Team Medieval, keeping my Savage suspicions at bay. In all probability Henry and Lara would marry, live at Longcross and raise evil little blond rug rats together.

Even if I hadn't read the game books I like to think that the girls' manner alone would have told me that something was going on. It was, well, *fishy* (sorry). Charlotte, in particular, had barely spoken to me since she'd come to do my Zoella makeover on the first night, and now here she was, acting like my best friend. Then, with a chill, I remembered the huntin' day. They'd all done exactly the same to Nel. This was clearly their brief – to make the poor dumb victim feel secure on the day they were to become prey. I suddenly wondered how nice the boys had been to Shafeen on the shootin' day.

I grabbed my waterproof coat – and the all-important rucksack – and we all clattered down the grand stairs and out into the driveway. As we walked to the estate cars I looked back to the blank windows of the house. I suddenly remembered leaving STAGS for Justitium, and looking back and seeing faces at every window of the school. There were no faces today – and that had been agreed. We couldn't let the Medievals know we were working together. But I knew my new friends were watching me, and knew exactly where I was at every single minute. Although I was going into the lions' den alone, for the first time since the start of Michaelmas term I was *not* alone.

I'm not saying that, as the Land Rovers set off for the lake, I wasn't afraid. But I did take comfort in the fact that we Savages had three things the Medievals didn't know we had.

We had the Saros 7S.

We had the contents of my rucksack.

And we had each other.

chapter twenty-six

I've always thought that the expression 'my heart missed a beat' is utter horseshit.

But once we'd all been decanted from the Land Rovers and taken the long walk down the hillside to Longmere lake, and I saw Henry coming towards me, I swear my heart stopped for a moment. I felt terror, excitement, regret; a whole mess of crap was swimming round in my head. The problem was that no one up there in my brain had bothered to tell my heart that I wasn't supposed to like him any more.

'Greer!' he said in his usual surprised-to-see-me way. 'I missed you after dinner last night. Where did you go?'

'Bed,' I said. 'I was beat after all the drama, you know, what with Shafeen's accident and all.' *Call it an accident. Act like Henry's innocent. Put the plan into motion.*

I looked out at the long, long silver lake where a stag had once died. The purple hills loomed around us, and the orange trees frilled the water. I could see a long wooden jetty reaching out into the lake, with three neat little boats tied up beside it, and waxed-jacketed servants in waders loading up the boats with rods and plastic containers full of God-knows-what. Piers, Cookson and the three sirens were sorting themselves out into groups to head out in the boats. I just hoped to God I'd be with Henry. I began to walk towards the boats to force Henry to fall into step with me. I spoke low in his ear.

'Listen. I wanted to say, well, that I was really emotional yesterday. It was a bit of a shock – I've never seen anyone get shot before. Even though I live in Manchester,' I joked. 'You've got to remember, I didn't grow up with all this.' I waved my arm, taking in the lake, the mountains and the trees of flame – but the gesture meant more than that. It meant privilege. It meant huntin' shootin' fishin'. 'I think it's probably different for you guys. I mean, like Cookson said, these kinds of accidents happen all the time. Inevitable, I suppose, with shotguns spraying those tiny little pellets everywhere, that someone's going to get winged now and again. So I overreacted. I shouldn't have yelled at you about the hospital. Your house, your rules, right?'

His expression softened. 'Thank you,' he said with this little courtly bow. 'I accept your apology, and I appreciate it very much. And I must stress that Dr Morand is an excellent doctor and very well used to dealing with any little incidents that might happen at shooting parties. He's been treating the family since my father was a little boy.'

Gasp. I really wasn't surprised by that, considering how old Shafeen had said the doctor was. But I just nodded. 'How is Shafeen?' This too was part of the plan; I had to hide the fact that I'd even seen Shafeen since dinner, let alone spent half the night with him.

'He's fine.' Henry raised a Roger-Moore-as-James-Bond eyebrow at me and smiled. 'In fact, when I called on him after breakfast he seemed *better* than fine. He had a very pretty nurse already there. Chanel was attending him.'

We'd planned this too: that Nel would go and have breakfast in Shafeen's room, so that the servants or any Medieval who dropped by faking concern would see them, and the idea would be seeded that they were now together. Before last night I'd have said that there wouldn't be much acting required. But underneath all the anxiety of what was to happen today, I held inside of me the warmth of Shafeen's compliment from last night, the fact that he'd called me beautiful. I didn't even know what to do with that, but I sure as hell couldn't think about it now.

'Yes, they looked very cosy together,' Henry went on. 'And as Shafeen can't fish, obviously, with one arm –'

'No epic contest today then,' I said.

'No,' he said, just a tiny bit smugly. He'd eliminated the competition all right. 'So Chanel's stayed to look after him. I think they're joining us for lunch at the boathouse.'

I certainly hoped so, for this too had been agreed last night. Then I launched into the speech we'd planned. 'I don't think Chanel's got the heart for any more blood sports, to be honest with you,' I said conversationally. 'She's pretty shell-shocked after what happened the other day. With the hounds, I mean. She's changed.'

'How has she changed?' Henry seemed genuinely interested.

'She's a bit . . . *deflated* somehow,' I said. 'I don't think she'll be flashing her cash quite as much.' I glanced at Henry sideways. 'Maybe their accidents kind of brought Shafeen and Nel together. Could be a good thing.'

'How so?'

'Well,' I pretended to think. 'Maybe Shafeen won't be pulling that Indian-prince act any more. Maybe he won't be answering you back now. Maybe they've *both* been, sort of, *put in their place*.'

I saw an unmistakable look of satisfaction flit across his face. *Good*, I thought. It'd worked. We wanted Shafeen and Nel to have a good reason not to be with the fishing party, but at the same time allow Henry to think that his plan to suppress the plebs was working. We wanted him to think he'd broken them. But if he thought that, he was wrong.

As we got closer to the jetty I could see that one of the waxed-jacket squad was Perfect. He came to meet us on the shingle beach and touched his cap to his master. I was well wrapped up, but just the sight of him made me go cold. I remembered him in the library last night, turning around with the shotgun on his shoulder, sniffing us out. I steeled myself to meet his eye, but nothing in his expression told me he'd seen us hiding. His pale eyes passed over me without interest.

'Ah, Perfect,' said Henry, 'everything set?' He turned to me. 'Perfect's going to be our gillie today.' I had no idea what that was, but I guessed it meant that the headkeeper was coming with us, and so it seemed. 'He'll pilot the boat and help out just while you get the hang of the fishin'.'

My heart sank like a stone. Perfect was much less frightening by day, but it was possible that his presence in the boat was going to ruin the plan we'd cooked up the night before.

I drew Henry to one side. 'I was kind of hoping that you and I would have some *alone* time?'

He smiled and sort of rubbed his hand up and down the top of my arm. I hate to admit that I kind of liked it. I guess you just can't switch off feelings, even if the boy you thought you liked is a homicidal maniac. 'I was hoping that too,' he said. 'But he'll be with us for the morning. This afternoon we'll find a lonely stretch of water where we can be alone. Sound good?'

'Wonderful,' I said. 'Just what I'd hoped.'

As we walked along the shingle I had a heart-stopping moment when Henry took my bag from me. I hadn't bargained on his chivalry. I clutched at it jealously for a moment but had to let it go – to make a big thing of it would've seemed really suss to him. 'What's in the bag?' he said. 'A life jacket?'

He was almost right. 'No,' I over-laughed. 'Just some spare jumpers. I got pretty chilly yesterday. And the day before, come to that.'

We walked along the jetty to the first of the waiting boats. It was a little glossy wooden vessel with an outboard motor, one of those nice-looking ones you see in seaside postcards. I knew it was time to put another part of the plan into action. Henry got into the boat first, his weight making it rock precariously. He held out one of his hands, and Perfect, on the jetty, held my other hand. As they helped me into the boat I deliberately stumbled and slipped, clutching at Henry as I lurched. He steadied me and I sat down heavily in the bow, making sure, as I did so, that I was reunited with my rucksack. Perfect got in last and the boat pitched with his bulk. I made a show of clutching the sides of the boat nervously.

'Actually, it's a good job Perfect's here,' I said. 'An extra pair of hands to haul me out.'

'Oh?' said Henry.

'Yes. I can't swim. Pathetic, isn't it?'

I was taking a bit of a risk here; I was relying on the fact that none of the Medievals had ever seen me in the pool at STAGS. But I didn't think they had. I tend to get up pretty early to swim, because, having swum competitively, I hated having to stop for people pootling around and splashing each other. I'd certainly never seen any of them in the pool, so I didn't think they could have seen me. Henry didn't call me on it anyway – he just said that most Medieval of words: '*Gosh*.'

'Yes,' I said ruefully. 'Not much chance to learn in Manchester.'

Actually there were tons of public pools in Manchester, for the 'little people' to learn to swim in, but I was banking on Henry's innate snobbery, and him assuming that peasants didn't swim. And it worked.

'I suppose not,' he said. 'Well, it would be my pleasure to teach you that too.'

I laughed a silly little laugh, a bit like Esme's. 'Not today, I hope!'

'God, no,' he said, laughing too. 'Bit chilly, eh?'

It sounds weird to say it, but I actually enjoyed the fishin'. I was pretty sure – all three of us plotters were sure – that nothing was going to happen to me that morning. (Even so, Shafeen and Nel were watching me closely, don't you worry about that.) We thought we had the Medievals' method bossed by now. Jolly morning of blood sports. Everyone very friendly to the prey, everything very relaxed. *Look how nice we are. Look how beautiful the scenery is.* Then a lovely lunch, tons of courses, tons of servants. Tons to drink. Then, in the afternoon, when the night was falling, the dark stuff happened. That was when I'd have to be alert.

And I would be. But for now I had to just act as if nothing was different, as if I was having the time of my life, and as if I was in love with Henry de Warlencourt. I decided that the only way I could get through that morning without descending into the palm-sweating, stomach-churning panic that I was only just managing to keep at bay was to pretend I didn't know what I knew. And it worked.

The thing is, it worked a little *too* well.

Henry spent the morning showing me how to fish. He really couldn't have been nicer, or more normal. He was ever so patient with me; he took his time, and made sure I had fun. I watched as Perfect prepped the rods for us.

'We're after brown trout today,' said Henry, 'so we use a light spinning rod –' he showed me the spooling wheel-thing on the rod's handle – 'which is best for browns. They've got really good eyesight so we use the finest line we can – this is monofilament.' He showed me the line in his fingertips and you could hardly see it – it looked like a piece of glass thread.

'Is this the part where we put worms on hooks?' I asked, suddenly remembering my dream.

'Actually, no. Browns don't really go for bait. That is, they do, but they have pretty sharp teeth, so they can often bite through the line. It's better to use lures, like this one.' He reached into one of the plastic containers and brought out, not a maggot as I'd expected, but something rather beautiful. It was a shiny, tiny fish made of foil and plastic, with coppery, shimmery scales of golds and gilts and bronzes and a little triple hook instead of a tail. It was kind of jointed, so when Henry wiggled it, it looked as if it was swimming. 'Authentic fish-like action,' he said.

I'd happily have worn it as a necklace. 'It's cute,' I said.

'That's a lure. It's called a Rapala. Irresistible to brown trout.'

'So they eat other *fish*?' I wasn't sure about the cannibal angle.

'Worse than that. This lure is supposed to replicate the markings of their own young. Brown trout eat their babies.'

I looked at the poor little shining thing. 'Jesus.'

'Yes,' he said, 'nature can be cruel. Man isn't the only predator.' He stood up in the boat. 'Let's try our luck, Perfect. Greer, sit tight for this one and we'll try you next.'

I won't lie. There was a fair bit of chugging around in the boat, and stopping, and waiting, and *let's try over here*. But the sun was out and I could watch the amazing lake-and-mountain scenery and it was all really nice. Most of the time, if I'm honest, I watched Henry confidently casting the line into the water, looking like he was born to fish, which I guess he was. I remembered seeing Brad Pitt in *A River Runs Through It*. Ever seen that movie? Brad was pretty fine in it, but he had nothing on Henry. I did think about Shafeen and Nel, and hoped they weren't worrying about me. I wished there was a way to tell them that I was fine. That I was finer than fine.

I was really relaxed when suddenly it got all exciting, and the lure bobbed under the water and Henry grabbed the rod and started to pull madly. It looked as if the fish might get the better of him, when he jerked the rod back with a practised little flick and this huge bronze fish flipped out of the water and into the bottom of the boat. I snatched my wellies back out of his way and watched Henry free the lure from the trout's mouth, then bash its head in against the side of the boat. All at once, everything was calm again and the fish was still, lying shining in Henry's hands, scales shimmering in the sun, eyes open and beady, but dead.

'Peace out, brown trout,' I said, a little sadly.

Henry laughed. 'We don't have to feel *too* sorry for him. They're not very nice fish.'

I remembered the kill-your-babies speech. 'OK, but just because you don't like something is not a reason to kill it.' Suddenly I remembered the game books, and the human names, but it all seemed like a far-off nightmare.

'Then how about this for a reason,' said Henry, as Perfect placed the fish in a plastic container and snapped closed the lid. 'They are food, and jolly tasty food at that. You'll find out at lunch. Nothing like eating fresh trout that was swimming around half an hour ago.' He picked up another rod and tested it in his hand. 'You'll notice from our menu this weekend that we eat everything we kill.'

I narrowed my eyes against the sun.

'So you wouldn't just hunt for fun?'

'Of *course* not,' he said. 'Fun is the by-product. You have to hunt for a *reason*.'

He was so believable.

'Come on,' he said. 'Your turn.'

He stood me up in the boat, holding my hands all the time. Then he did that Tom Cruise in *The Color of Money* thing again, getting behind me and putting his arms around me, only this time instead of a pool cue (or a gun) it was the fishing rod. He showed me how to spread my feet for balance and cast the line with a flick of the wrist; how to dangle the lure so it didn't catch under the slipstream of the boat. There was lots of waiting, but to wait in that setting, with Henry's strong arms around me and his warm body at my back, was something I was happy to do for as long as it took.

But then my rod jerked down, bending like an archer's bow.

'Go on, pull,' cried Henry, suddenly animated, yanking at my arms. The fish was incredibly strong, and I didn't know if I could hold on to him, even with Henry's help. Heart beating, I pulled back with all my strength. 'Now reel!' shouted Henry in my ear.

Fumbling, panicking, I reeled the spool and Henry pulled; he reeled and I pulled. We both reeled, we both pulled. I don't know which one of us landed the trout, but at last the silvery fish cleared the water, flicking its tail madly, crystal drops showering from it, glittering like chandelier brilliants in the low autumn sun.

'He's a beauty,' crowed Henry. 'Don't let him go whatever you do.'

I turned so the fish dangled over the boat, and Perfect took him down, dumping him in the bottom of the boat, where he wriggled like a mad thing. He was so strong he actually made a knocking sound on the wood. 'Got 'im.'

'You did it!' said Henry. We clung together, gasping and laughing, both soaked with lake water. The words *He's a beauty – don't let him go whatever you do* were echoing in my head. I was ecstatic. The previous night, and all thoughts of a dark conspiracy, were totally forgotten in that sick moment of triumph. I was one of them. I was a Medieval at that moment and it felt *great*. I loved fishin'. I loved Henry. I even loved grumpy old Perfect, who became almost chatty at the sight of my first catch, as if I'd joined some sort of club or something. He forgot himself so far as to actually speak to me. 'Tek 'old of 'im, miss. Don't let 'im muck yer abart. He's a reet wick one, that un.'

I bent to try to get hold of my prey.

'Watch out, Greer,' warned Henry. 'Brown trout have really sharp teeth. Be careful when you're handling him.'

I managed to pick up the fish. He was surprisingly heavy, and his scales felt very slippery. I held him behind his head, my fingers clear of the gaping jaws, but I didn't know what to do next.

'Shall I?' asked Henry, looking at me very directly with his blue eyes.

'No,' I said, suddenly sure. 'I'll do it.' The fish was wriggling madly, but I bashed his head sharply against the wood of the boat, and, to my great surprise, he fell still, as if he'd been switched off. I held on to him, in a sort of trance, and was still hanging on to him about a minute later. Perfect had to prise him from my hands and place him with the other fishy corpse in the plastic coffin.

I sat back down beside Henry, suddenly in something like shock, and he threw an arm around me. 'You did well there, Greer. Unlike deer or pheasant, trout are the kind of prey that can bite back. They can really do you some damage.'

I thought about that as Perfect turned the boat around to chug back to shore. I'd thought I was going to be the fish today. The prey with the power to bite back. Now I knew it was all stupid. Our plan, cooked up in the estate room in the small hours, was ridiculous. *This* was the way to live. I wasn't afraid, or sorry, I was totally pumped. I'd cried for the stag, I'd mourned the poor feathery pheasants, but the fish I'd killed with my own hands and I'd loved it. I remembered at school, back in Lightfoot with Esme, when I'd thought I wouldn't mind the death of a fish. What I hadn't known then was that I would absolutely revel in it.

Henry, looking at me beadily, saw it straight away. 'Feels good, doesn't it?'

I nodded, speechless for a moment.

'There's a light in your eye,' he said. 'A predator's look. You're beginning to understand.'

'Understand what?'

'Huntin' shootin' fishin', of course,' he said. 'Why we do it.'

'I'm not sure about the other two,' I admitted, 'but I don't really care about fish.'

'Fish can be amazing too,' he said. 'Think about the eels that swim for thousands of miles every year to spawn in the Sargasso Sea. And the salmon, so determined to breed that they will leap up the steepest of waterfalls.'

'I suppose they have a reason,' I said, suddenly aware of his arm still around me. 'They are fulfilling their biological mission. They want to . . . reproduce.'

There was a charged silence. 'Yes,' he said heavily. 'Nature will go to any lengths to replicate itself, to ensure that its kind survives.'

By the time the boat returned to the jetty for lunch, I was almost convinced that Shafeen and Nel and I had made the whole huntin' shootin' fishin' thing up. I'd worked so hard on pretending to have a good time and like Henry that I'd actually had a good time, and I actually liked Henry. All that creeping around at midnight seemed like some stupid gothic fantasy.

At least Shafeen and Nel would be at lunch. I needed to talk to them. Now I had a different plan to the one we'd spent the night crafting. I wanted to *talk* to Henry. Maybe the entries in the game book were some kind of sick joke. Maybe it was some bizarre tradition, or an accident book just like Shafeen had said. Maybe the aniseeds in the jacket were a coincidence. Maybe Henry'd put them there to keep his hounds to heel – it was his jacket, after all – and forgotten all about them when he'd given the jacket to Nel. Perhaps the names of the hounds were just a classical joke; it was just the kind of intellectual gag the Medievals would enjoy. I was reaching, I know, but I just couldn't go through with what we'd planned. I couldn't believe that this shining golden boy, this charming young man who'd taken pains to give me a really nice morning, could be a monster. Maybe, I thought as I walked hand in hand with Henry to the boathouse, *we'd* invented the monster, in the darkness of the midnight library.

chapter twenty-seven

Of the three cool places I'd had lunch on the Longcross estate, the boathouse was the coolest.

It was a long wooden building on the lakeshore, with a kind of planked balcony on stilts that came right out over to the water. Inside there was no fire this time (obvs – not with all that wood about), but there was a bunch of little closed braziers all around the table, which made the place beautifully warm. The coolest thing about it – and this is where the boathouse smacked down the bothy from the huntin' day and the folly from the shootin' day – was that there were actual boats inside with us, rocking in the greenish water, reflecting in the candlelight.

Yes, I said candlelight. Because apart from the fact that there were – well – boats dining with us, everything else was just as if we were in some smart dining room. As ever there was the snowy white tablecloth, the crystal glasses, the rows of silver cutlery and the pyramids of fruit; green apples today, just the colour of the boathouse water. It was a magical setting.

I was so intrigued by the boathouse, and, if I'm honest, so hooked on fishing (sorry), that I almost forgot that I was about to meet Shafeen and Nel again, and that we had a plan to put into action. By now I was well and truly back in the de Warlencourt corner. I know this makes me look really bad, particularly when you hear about what came next, but really, you had to be in Henry's company to understand the sheer charm of the guy.

I was sitting between Henry and Cookson – a Henry sandwich – and nowhere near Shafeen and Nel. They were way down the other end of the table, seated together. They both looked immaculate, but they both also looked tired. Nel was back in her own stuff, all slightly too bright and too tight. I was glad to see it. She suited the hell out of it. She was obviously wearing her 'screw you' to the Medievals clothes, just as I'd done last night when I'd worn my mum's dress. Shafeen had on a cream shirt with a discreet green check and a moss-green waistcoat. His arm was now in a professional-looking sling – I guessed the ancient doctor had called again this morning. He was struggling, wrong-handed, with his soup. His longish layered hair was kind of a bit messy today – I guess grooming was difficult one-handed. But he looked handsome, and noble, what I called his Prince Caspian look, and I suddenly thought, irrelevantly, *You're beautiful too*.

I was torn between happiness to see my new friends – for that was what I considered them now – and a desperate need to tell them to abort our plan. You see, I'd figured that if we went ahead we'd be alienated from this world forever, maybe even expelled from STAGS. It was like the secret door to the Longcross roof that I couldn't find again without Henry, the way to Narnia, which, once closed, could never be opened again. If we turned back from the road we'd taken *now*, we could stay in Narnia forever. We could all go back to STAGS, and have a happy sixth-form experience in the comfort of our new friendship. I knew it would be hard to persuade them to give it up; Nel had been badly scared by the hounds. Shafeen, I guessed, was motivated less by the fact that he'd been shot than that his father had been humiliated in the same way. He was Prince Caspian for real, sworn to vanquish his father's enemies. He had a whole family history to avenge.

The soup had been cleared away and the servants brought out the fish course. Staring up at me from the plate, with one dull eye, was a brown trout, his side slashed three times and neatly fitted with three slices of lemon. I looked at the fish, and the fish looked at me. 'Is this . . . ?'

'Yes,' said Henry. 'It's the one you caught.'

Now this was a novel experience for me. Because of the whole game-hanging, rotting-flesh thing of which Esme had so scornfully informed me, this was the only time we'd eaten what we'd actually killed. Now, I'm not a big fish eater; if I ever have it, it is in the form of the good old Captain Birdseye's Fish Fingers or Filet-o-Fish from the golden arches. I certainly wasn't in the habit of eating the full-on scales-and-tail type. I didn't really know how to cut it up, but, by watching Henry, I sliced through the crispy skin and flaked off some of the pinkish flesh onto my fork. It was super-delicious, but I couldn't really relax and savour my fishy victim. For one thing, I had no appetite, as I was so apprehensive about the afternoon and what would happen at the going down of the sun. For another, I couldn't just sit back and let everyone else carry the conversation. If I was going to send a message to Shafeen and Nel, for once I had to shout the Medievals down and take the lead myself. I didn't know how I was going to find the courage to begin, and then Henry did something which convinced me that I must.

Shafeen had been struggling with the fish in front of him, and Nel clearly had as little idea about how to tackle it as I had, so Henry got up from the table, walked round and crouched down beside Shafeen. As if he was some TV chef he deftly sliced the fish along the backbone, and flaked off the flesh from the two sides, leaving these neat little fillets on the plate, which Shafeen could fork up one-handed.

It was so beautifully done, so kindly and without fuss, that I was convinced, yet again, that Henry was one of the good guys. (I know, I *know*.) Surely he wouldn't bother with the chivalry if he'd wanted us all dead? Surely the hangman doesn't give the condemned man a leg up to the gibbet?

I had to let the others know we were in abort mode. 'It's a beautiful lake, Longmere,' I said to Cookson, but loud enough for the whole table. 'It reminds me of Loch Ness. I went there once with my dad.'

Dad and I had never been near Loch Ness – that is to say, Dad probably had, because he's filmed pretty much everywhere, but I'd never even been to Scotland. Everything I know about Loch Ness came from watching *The Private Life of Sherlock Holmes*, a film not known for its gritty realism.

Cookson swallowed his mouthful. 'Really?' he said in that way the upper classes use when they think you're talking shit but are too polite to say so. 'You think Longmere is like Loch Ness?'

'Well, I mean in the way the mountains surround the water,' I improvised desperately.

Cookson's manners took a dive. 'Like ninety-nine per cent of the lakes in the British Isles, you mean?'

'No, I see what Greer means,' said Henry, coming to my rescue as he walked back around the table. 'Something about the surrounding mountains. Long Fell looks a little bit like Meall Fuar-mhonaidh in the right light.'

I had no idea what Henry'd said – he might as well have been talking Martian – but he was unwittingly helping me to get my point across. I just needed one of the Medievals to mention the most famous thing about Loch Ness. They were certainly smart enough to have heard of *that*.

'I don't know a thing about Loch Ness,' said Esme. Then she shivered deliciously. 'Except for the monster.'

There it was. I thanked the Medieval gods silently.

'Oh, *I* do,' enthused Charlotte. 'Granny's *estate* is near there. And I can *tell* you, all that *monster* stuff is *nonsense*.'

'It's belief either way,' said Henry.

'What do you *mean*?' asked Charlotte.

'Well,' he said, forking up his own fish, 'you either *believe* it exists, or you *believe* it doesn't. There's no proof either way.' He turned to me, looking at me very directly in that way he had. 'What do *you* believe, Greer?'

Just then I had the uncanny feeling that he knew exactly what we were really talking about. Did I believe he was a criminal, potentially a killer? Or not?

He watched me, and Shafeen and Nel watched me. The whole table watched me. 'I believe,' I said slowly, 'that there is no monster.'

I looked straight at Shafeen and Nel. I felt bad for them, as if I was letting them down. But I couldn't go ahead with what we'd planned. These were serious accusations. They would mean police, social services, the ruin of young lives.

I'm not sure if Nel got what I was trying to say. But Shafeen knew all right. 'But there *is* proof,' he almost shouted. Now everyone looked at him. 'Proof of the monster, I mean. There have been sightings. Many, many sightings over decades. People have seen the *evidence with their own eyes*.'

'Drunks.' This, ironically was Piers. 'Scotland's full of 'em.' His voice was thick with the wine.

'Naff *off*, Piers,' said Charlotte fondly, an insult I've genuinely never heard before.

Shafeen took no notice of this sideshow. He wasn't done. 'People have taken photographs. What about the famous Surgeon's Photograph from the 1930s? The one that looks like a brontosaurus swimming – a big body and a little head on a long neck. That's a photograph, Greer. Proof set down in *black and white*.'

Black and white. The same words as he used to me last night, about the game book. *Proof set down in black and white*.

'In *The Private Life of Sherlock Holmes*,' I said, 'the monster turned out to be a submarine.'

'That's fiction though,' insisted Shafeen. 'The guy who took the Surgeon's Photograph was a gynaecologist. Scientists aren't usually given to flights of fancy.'

'It was a fake too though, wasn't it?' put in Lara in her bored voice. 'I thought they proved it was doctored.' I don't think she noticed her pun. 'The "monster" didn't appear on the negative. Scientists may not be given to flights of fancy, it's true, but they *have* been known to falsify data.'

You could always rely on the Medievals for a good conversation. Once again I'd been guilty of forgetting how clever they were. I suppose in a way they'd been well trained – their minds had been nurtured and tutored at great expense; they didn't spend hours staring at screens and they'd been holding their own at table ever since they'd been allowed to stay up to dinner.

'That's true,' said Cookson, taking up the thread. 'You can make circumstantial evidence prove anything.' Once again I got the feeling that the Medievals knew exactly what we Savages were talking about. It was as if Cookson was deliberately casting doubt on what we had found in the game books.

Now, at this point I should explain, as I wished I could've explained to Shafeen and Nel, that it wasn't that I had lost my nerve. I still accepted that something was going on, and I was genuinely ready to tackle Henry about it. But I didn't believe, in the light of day, that the Medievals were killers. Yes, they might be playing jokes, even playing dangerous games. There might even be initiation ceremonies, like you hear about at Ivy League schools in America, testing what lengths STAGS kids would go to for the opportunity to become a Medieval. But committing – or attempting – *murder*? I just couldn't believe it.

Shafeen looked straight at me, his dark eyes pleading. 'Just because no one's seen the monster in action, doesn't mean it doesn't exist.'

'You're right,' I said, trying to reassure him with my own eyes that I wasn't about to drop the whole thing; I just wanted to go about it a different way. That's a lot to say with your eyes, and I was sure he wasn't getting it. But whatever Shafeen felt, I'd made up my mind I was going to take a bit of a left turn. When Henry and I were alone, I'd confront him with what the three of us knew and give him the chance, at least, to explain himself. I said to Shafeen, pointedly, 'I just think the whole thing needs further investigation.'

'That's all very well,' he said, 'but the investigators should still take precautions. A dark lake, a monster. Poke around in those fathomless depths, they don't know what they might find. They really don't know what they're dealing with.'

It was unmistakably a warning. And under the table I could feel, nudging against my foot, the rucksack that I'd packed so carefully and guarded so jealously.

I was pretty sure I wouldn't need what was inside it. It seemed like an awful lot of trouble to use it, when I was now convinced I'd be in no danger from Henry that afternoon. We'd fish some more, we'd have dinner, and by tomorrow afternoon we'd all be back at STAGS. But in the end, more to stop Shafeen glaring at me than anything else, I excused myself to go to the toilet just as we'd planned. I went into the cubicle with a full rucksack, and came out with an empty one.

chapter twenty-eight

The late-afternoon light on the lake was beautiful.

Henry took my hand as we walked along the shingle to the jetty. I wasn't cold at all, too many layers for that, and even my somewhat restricted movement couldn't ruin the stroll. The only thing ruining this idyllic movie I seemed to be living in – *The Notebook* maybe? Or *The Lake House*? – was Perfect striding ahead of us. I'd been promised we'd be free of his shadow this afternoon. I said to Henry, 'Is *he* coming with us?'

'No,' Henry reassured me. 'He's just stocking the boat. I don't think we need him any more. You're quite the expert now. Besides, I think we need some alone time, don't you?'

'Yes,' I said. But not for the reason he thought. We had a lot to talk about.

Henry jumped lightly into the boat and Perfect handed me in after him. We sat side by side, in the stern, Henry taking the tiller. Perfect cast off the rope and Henry started the engine. We idled out into the centre of the lake. The sun was sinking and the sky was turning a sort of rose gold. I thought of my dad – he would have loved this. Magic hour, they called it on his shoots. That precious hour at the end of the day when you had, for a brief time, the most beautiful light, the light the camera loves. I'd seen Dad's work so many times – deer at bay like the one I'd murdered, murmurations of starlings like the jet beads on my mum's dress. I realised, for the first time, that magic hour is so beautiful *because* it's the last hour of the day. It's precious because the day is dying.

Far behind us I could see the other Medievals piling into the other boats, but we had quite the head start. Essentially Henry and I were alone in the middle of the darkening lake. The sun was setting for real and the lake was turning this amazing crimson colour.

Blood, I thought suddenly.

The temperature was dropping and the hills that surrounded us were bruising to black. The rods and the lures were neatly lined up in the bow of the boat, but neither one of us made a move to touch them. It should have been romantic, but there was a weird edgy vibe. Less Helen and Leonard in *Howard's End*, and more Fredo and Neri in *The Godfather II*.

The silence was freaking me out. 'So,' I said, wondering how to begin, 'here we are then. Just the two of us.'

He turned to me and took my hand, like he was going to propose or something. His thumb caressed my fingers, my knuckles, my wrist.

And met, looped over my thumb, the tight cuff of a wetsuit.

I looked at Henry, and he looked at me.

And then I knew.

It was just like that bit in *Primal Fear* when Ed Norton flips from angelic altar boy to homicidal maniac with just one look. He doesn't say anything; it's just the expression in his eyes that changes. Watch it and you'll see. That look won Ed Norton an Oscar nomination and it's chilling enough on screen. I watched Henry de Warlencourt do it for real, and I knew from that look that he was going to kill me. I absolutely knew, without him saying anything, that it was all true. All of it: the huntin', the shootin' and the fishin'.

And now I was truly afraid.

What if Shafeen had understood my message at lunch and abandoned the plan? I'd warned him off, and he'd been disappointed in me. What if he had thought that I wasn't worth saving? What if he and Nel had just gone back to Longcross to pack and had ditched me?

I looked into Henry's ice-blue eyes and faced the fact that I was utterly alone.

I braced myself for what I knew was coming.

The moment stretched out for ages. Then Henry moved towards me and put out his arm. I thought for a moment he was going to change his mind and put it around me. But instead he threw it across me and flipped me backwards, knocking me out of the boat.

The water was colder than anything I have ever known. I'm convinced that the shock would have killed me, if it wasn't for the ace Henry had discovered up my sleeve; literally up my sleeve. The wetsuit saved me.

The wetsuit that I'd seen on that first evening in the Boot Room, lying among the fishing rods like a discarded skin.

The wetsuit my subconscious had clocked again yesterday when we laid Shafeen by the fire, and had stolen at first light this morning.

The wetsuit I'd pulled on in the toilets after lunch, praying that Henry wouldn't notice the bulkiness under my clothes.

Don't get me wrong – it was still *freaking* cold even with the wetsuit, so cold it was hard to catch my breath. I trod water for a minute, gasping with the shock, telling myself not to panic. Then my legs and arms remembered, as muscle memory kicked in, what they were supposed to do, but I had another problem to face. While the waxed jacket was actually quite buoyant, and had trapped some air in it during my fall from the boat, the heavy Aran sweater was becoming waterlogged and in another moment it would drag me down. I kicked off my boots and stripped off the jacket (easy) and the wide wader trousers (harder). Then I tried to push the sodden woollen jumper over my head, which was almost impossible. I had to use my arms, which meant I couldn't use them for swimming, and immediately sank. I had to keep resurfacing and trying again. And here's the weird thing. All the time Henry was sitting in the boat, a dark shape hunched against the sunset, watching me struggle, almost as if he was holding back until I was ready for the chase to start. I think that's when I realised he was crazy: he was still being chivalrous, waiting until I was quite ready for him to kill me. It was like someone holding an elevator door open for you to fall down an empty lift shaft. At last I got free of the jumper and started to swim, and that's when Henry fired up the engine and came after me.

In the dark I worried that the bulky shapes of my clothes in the water would make it hard for Henry to see me. It was important that he followed me. But it was all right – he had a torch. No doubt the efficient Perfect had left it in the stern for him. I saw the broad white beam sweep the water, and I decided to help him a little. 'Help!' I spluttered, waving, not drowning. The torch beam found me, lighting my way. Gasping, but calm, I turned and struck out for the shore. I knew I had to go east, away from the boathouse, to the other side of the lake, as the three of us Savages had arranged.

I hoped to God the plan would work. When we'd been plotting in the estate room our first idea had been that I would take the Saros 7S onto the boat with me and film whatever Henry did. But we had to abandon that idea when Nel had said that although the Saros had been designed to be water resistant – it would survive being dropped accidentally in the bath or the toilet – it couldn't survive a prolonged immersion. So we'd made a Plan B: I was to lure Henry to a pre-arranged place where Shafeen and Nel would be waiting to witness my trial. And – hopefully – intervene before it was too late.

We were confident that Henry would chase me. We had no doubt that he would do anything to defend his lifestyle. And we were right. He chugged after me, the boat idling quite slowly, not attempting to run me down. But he was relentless – he kept on coming.

And the others came too. 'She's in!' I heard him call out to the Medievals, his voice carrying across the water. I saw other torches go on, and multiple beams of light sweep the water, illuminating the blonde hair of the Medieval girls hanging over the side of the boats and almost sweeping the water's surface as they looked for me. They were sirens for real today, evil nymphs who brought watery death. Well, I wasn't going to let them claim me. Not today.

I swam just fast enough to keep me ahead of the boats. I was making good headway to the shore when I heard a whistle and plop to my right. Surely they weren't shooting at me? But no – the Medievals obeyed their own rules. Henry was casting a hook for me. He was still fishin'.

I swam a little faster, but the next moment a wicked hook snagged the wetsuit at my left shoulder. I struck out strongly, diving under the surface for a moment, to pull the hook loose. I was free, for now, but as I glanced around I could see a jagged a little tear in my wetsuit, and feel a sting in my shoulder as if I'd been cut. I knew that if they all tried to catch me with their fishing hooks they could make a real mess of me.

I swam faster.

The three boats nosed towards me, and two of them pulled ahead of me, Piers and Cookson on one side, the girls on the other. I realised with a rush of panic that there was worse to fear than the fishing hooks. If they decided to surround me they could just wait till I drowned, wetsuit or no wetsuit.

I was too tired to try to escape them.

They had me trapped. I trod water in the middle of the enclosed triangle of boats, spinning this way and that in a panic, looking at each of their ghoulish, torchlit faces in turn. They didn't say anything. They didn't even look at me in an evil way. They were just watching me, with mildly curious, dispassionate expressions as if I was wildlife, a rare fish they'd been lucky to catch. I don't know why I did this, but I held out a dripping hand so they could haul me up, hoping for a shred of humanity in any one of them. But no one took it.

I realised then that our plan was lunacy, and I was finished. My limbs were frozen and tired, and I had no more strength left.

And then, in that moment of despair, I saw a light far away on the shore. The light was piercingly bright. My panicked mind thought of the Bethlehem star, magically appearing in the Christmas night. Then I knew the truth.

It was the white-hot torch of the Saros 7S.

And, like the Bethlehem star, it was there to show the way. Like the Bethlehem star, it had risen in the east, where I was supposed to go. All I had to do was follow it.

Suddenly energised, I jinked and dived under Henry's boat, striking out desperately in the murky freezing depths. I surfaced again with nothing but clear water between me and the star. I swam for the shore until my muscles ached and my lungs burned. I could hear the boat engines behind me. I didn't dare to turn, sure they would catch me up and run me down. I determinedly looked forward. *If I can just reach the shore . . . If I can just reach the shore . . .* Then at last I felt the scrape of shingle under my knees. I hauled myself out of the water, the wetsuit dragging me down, the water streaming from my body. I was standing in a little freezing brook, my feet blocks of ice. I stumbled upstream, wherever it took me, frantic to get away from the torch beams and the boats and the voices. I stumbled on for I don't know how long, the Saros star always up and ahead of me, leading the way, until I came out into a wide pool. Beyond the pool I heard a rushing and a roaring and made my way towards the sound. Then I heard splashing footsteps behind me, and Henry burst out of the darkness, his torch swinging wildly. I turned and ran, and his broad torch beam illuminated a white wall of spray ahead of me.

It was a waterfall.

chapter twenty-nine

This, I knew, was Conrad's Force, and the light of the Saros was at the top of it.

I knew now that Shafeen and Nel hadn't abandoned me. They were waiting, like the faithful friends they were, at the meeting place we'd arranged last night: the packhorse bridge at the top of Conrad's Force, which was the closest place to the lake that you could drive a vehicle. Shafeen and Nel were going to borrow a Land Rover to bring them to lunch and leave it there as my getaway car. Nel, who was full of surprises, already had her licence. (She'd passed her test on her seventeenth birthday and her dad had given her a brand-new Mini tied up with a big red bow.) On the map in the estate room the bridge had looked so close to the lakeshore. But what we hadn't appreciated was the sheer *height* that those little jagged lines on the map had represented. I had expected some little ornamental fall like you see in public parks. This was the real deal, as high as a building, and as fierce as a flood. The bridge *was* close to the lake as the crow flies. But I wasn't a crow. I was going to have to climb.

I got myself as close to the falling water as possible, right at the edge of the spray. It was impossible to stand in the full force of the falls without the water beating me back down, so I sought out rocks and footholds up one side. I knew that Henry had to follow me – he couldn't let me go now, knowing what I knew. But it was a relief to me that, because he was climbing too, at least he couldn't catch me with his vicious fishing hook. He'd have to abandon the rod and use both hands.

That climb was probably the hardest thing I've ever done. My hands and feet were like ice. I cut them often on the rocks and tough gorse of the falls and didn't even notice – my flesh was so cold it neither bled nor hurt. The wetsuit restricted my movement but it protected me too – not just from the water but from the sharp rocks. Henry was slower than me; I was smaller and lighter and I was no longer wearing my fishing gear. His sodden clothes must have been dragging him down, his heavy boots slipping on the rocks in a way that my bare feet did not. In some ways I had the advantage and it was a good job – if Henry got a hold of me before I reached the others, I'd be finished.

Fear spurred me on, but I had to force myself to climb carefully. If I went too fast, and slipped and fell, I would end up in Henry's clutches. And then, as I climbed higher still, I realised that I had bigger problems than just Henry: the falls were so high that, if I tumbled now, I would die anyway; no one could survive such a fall. A phrase stuck in my head – the STAGS school motto, of all things: *Festina Lente*. Make Haste Slowly. I forced myself to find good footholds on the rocks and careful handholds gouged in the freezing mud, not easy with the icy water beating in my face. As I climbed ever upward I thought of the salmon Henry had told me about, relentlessly hurling themselves up the steepest of waterfalls, struggling upstream to reach their breeding grounds and keep their species going. The fish would do anything to survive.

And so would I.

At last I was at the top of the falls and I saw the packhorse bridge, only seen before as a tiny black arc on a map in the estate room, the size of a sliver of fingernail, but now a massive stone rainbow spanning the river in the moonlight. The bridge was the endpoint – the source of that bright star-of-Bethlehem light. As soon as I'd reached the top of the falls, just as we'd planned, the light from the Saros clicked off, and there was just the moonlight.

Henry scrambled up behind me and I turned to face him. *The stag at bay*, I thought, seeing him standing knee deep in the swirling water. Henry's torch was long gone and it took my eyes a minute to adjust. He was soaked and breathing hard, his trademark hair silver-pale in the moonlight, his eyes mercury-bright. I wanted to lead him away from the noise of the fall, but he stood on its very lip. We'd have to shout at each other to be heard, but that could work out well for the plan.

He spoke first. 'I would have spared you, Greer,' he called. 'You were going to be the only one we left alone. I even talked to the others about it. I thought you understood. I thought you loved Longcross.'

'I did,' I said. I had to keep him talking. 'I do.'

'Then Perfect saw you in the library last night, with the game books –'

'So he *did* see us,' I exclaimed, before I could stop myself.

'Of course,' said Henry. 'He's a gamekeeper. Tracking animals is his job.'

I didn't rise to the insult, and he went on. 'I knew you'd gone over to their side, the side of those who don't belong, who think they can be like us but never will be. The side of the Savages.' He shrugged. 'No matter. The game books will be gone by tomorrow. We'll just have to keep them somewhere else. Can't leave evidence lying around now, can we?'

'Why didn't Perfect just use the gun on us then?' I asked. 'He could have taken out all three of us, problem solved.' I knew the answer, but I wanted Henry to say it.

'Oh, Greer, you still don't understand, do you? Even you, my clever little scholarship girl. It has to look like an accident, don't you see? How do you think we've managed to get away with it for so long? Because they always look like accidents. Even the deaths.'

I was already shivering and didn't think I could get any colder, but it turned out I could. His words gave me an extra chill. 'So there *have* been deaths then?'

'Of course there have been deaths.' He sounded surprised I would even ask. 'Quite a few over the years. Terrible "accidents", all of them. All from families who wouldn't be able to stand up to us. The son of some tin-pot African royal family. They wouldn't dare to go up against the British establishment. We had a scholarship girl once before too; she was one of the deaths. Her family was too poor to pay for an enquiry. Dr Morand fills in the death certificates, and my father squares things with the police commissioner and the coroner. They all come for the shooting, you know.'

'Of course they do,' I said bitterly.

'It was easier in the old days. My father, my grandfather, his grandfather.'

I swallowed. All those blond boys in the silver frames on the piano. All of them grew up to be murderers. 'Just how long *has* this been going on?'

'Conrad de Warlencourt started it. When he came back from the Crusades. I guess he just missed killing the savages. So he found more savages to kill on his own doorstep. And then he found like-minded people to carry on the tradition. Tradition's *so* important, isn't it, Greer? You need continuity, and order. I think Conrad would like it that you will meet your end here, at Conrad's Force. His own waterfall.'

My body started to shudder uncontrollably. 'So I am to die now?'

'Oh yes, I think so,' he answered, just as if I'd asked him whether he thought it would rain later. 'I was even considering sparing you – this morning when I saw you kill that fish. I thought you could be a Medieval after all. But then I saw the wetsuit, and I knew you'd prepared yourself against me. Under the clothes you were a Savage all along, through and through.'

'Are you going to make my death look like an accident too?' I said, teeth chattering with cold and fear.

'Naturally. It's harder now, of course. In the feudal days no one would even challenge us. Much harder now. More agencies asking more questions. DNA, post mortems – all that technology you people love so much. But we're still able to convince the police. A gentleman's word still counts for something at Longcross. A terrible fall, and a drowning. Case closed.'

He took a step towards me, away from the lip of the waterfall.

What a Sherlock Holmesian time we'd had of it, my fear-crazed mind thought. *The Hound of the Baskervilles*. The Loch Ness film. Then this ending, a tussle between two mortal enemies on a waterfall.

'Have you seen *Sherlock Holmes: A Game of Shadows*?' I asked, playing for time.

'What do you think?' he said, his predator's eyes on me.

'It's not a great film,' I said. 'And it's not super-faithful to the books. But there's one bit that is. Sherlock and Moriarty are in Switzerland, and Robert Downey Jr – he's Sherlock Holmes (bear with me, I was doubtful too – but he's actually good) – he lures Moriarty to the head of the Reichenbach Falls. Well, they have this tussle and they both go over the edge together.' I was babbling, and backing away, and Henry was creeping towards me like that game you play in primary school, when you try to move without anyone seeing you. 'And Watson, who is played by Jude Law (again, you wouldn't pick him for it, but he's really OK too) goes back to London all sad, and they actually have Sherlock's funeral, and then Watson is writing up Sherlock's last adventure, and he types "THE END". And then the doorbell goes and it's the postman, so Watson leaves the room, and when he comes back, it turns out that someone has typed a question mark so that it says "THE END?" And Watson smiles. Because that one little bit of punctuation, that question mark, tells him that although the bad guy is dead, the good guy survived. And you, Henry, are the bad guy.'

Henry just shook his head and kept on coming. 'You've just demonstrated the problem with living your life through screens,' he called over the sound of the rushing water. 'Children nowadays spend *four hours a night* online. They live in headphones, cut off from the world. No one can eat a meal without taking a picture of it. No one can enjoy a concert without filming it or meet a so-called celebrity without taking a selfie. You don't even have to retain your own memories any more; Facebook does it for you. Everything has to be recorded; people experience life through a screen the size of a playing card, instead of *living* it. And for what? Not everything is a movie, Greer.'

'Not everything,' I agreed. 'But *this* is.'

In a much louder shout, directed to the packhorse bridge where I could see the Saros 7S's little red recording light, I yelled, 'Did you get all that?'

'Oh yes,' shouted Nel from up on the bridge. 'We got it.'

Shafeen and Nel stood up and leaned over the parapet. Nel had the Saros in her hand and turned the torch beam full on Henry. The water swirling around our ankles turned to white milk.

She tapped the phone and held it high. It began to speak, in Henry's voice. '*Of course there have been deaths. Quite a few over the years. Terrible "accidents", all of them. All from families who wouldn't be able to stand up to us.*'

Henry held his hand high, just as I'd done when I'd reached my hand out of the lake. But he wasn't asking for help. He was commanding. 'Give me that thing,' he said, low and deadly, like a furious teacher confiscating something from an errant child. The force of his personality was such that I almost expected Nel to drop the gadget into his hand.

But she just shook her head. 'Wouldn't do any good,' she said. 'You could take this phone from me, but the video's already been uploaded to the Saros Orbit. It's a satellite storage system, totally secure.'

'Isn't technology wonderful, when you find the right application for it?' called Shafeen.

Henry should have been beaten. He should have been deflated. He should have broken down, and sobbed, and begged us not to go public. But he did none of these things. He drew himself up, more powerful than ever, his eyes shining with this freaky, almost religious light. 'You can't win,' he said. 'You can't upset the order.'

'Oh yeah?' said Nel. That girl was a badass. 'One touch of this screen and this video will be uploaded to YouTube, Facebook, Snapchat, Twitter and Instagram. By morning your confession will have gone viral. You'll be an Internet sensation. It's over, Henry. Your world is over. We're in my world now.'

Henry backed away towards the lip of the falls, as if seeking to put some distance between himself and these terrible new words. But he was still defiant. 'The order will go on, even without me,' he cried.

Shafeen called back, grim, mocking. 'There's a new order now,' he said.

I think I'll remember the next few seconds for as long as I live. People say the end of a life slows down, as if it's playing in slo-mo, and I'm here to tell you that's perfectly true. I turned my head to Shafeen when he shouted from the bridge, and that took my eye off Henry long enough for him to back right up to the edge of the falls. Then, and only then, did I process what Henry had said.

Even without me.

I knew what he was going to do.

I spun around, my wet hair stinging my face like a whip, and half waded, half stumbled to him as fast as I could, the water impeding my progress like quicksand, my own voice, loud in my head, screaming 'NO!'

I'll swear on my life, forever afterwards, that my fingertips caught at Henry's, linked, slipped and lost him. I saw him for a second, an hour, a lifetime, suspended in space: immensely strong, immensely powerful. For one split second our eyes met and locked, his gaze undefeated. Then, his arms flung out like a cross, he tipped back over the lip of the falls.

Suddenly I was back in Paulinus quad, dropping a coin down the medieval well. The coin was falling down and down into the darkness, and I was waiting for it to hit the surface of the water. Henry and the coin falling together. At Conrad's Force, too, time stretched out to infinity, and the roar of the waterfall was so loud that we couldn't even hear when Henry hit the rocks below.

chapter thirty

To be honest, I don't remember much about what happened after that.

Nel told me that I collapsed in the water and Shafeen had to wade in and fish me out, only just catching me before I slipped over the lip of the falls myself. He'd picked me up and carried me to the Land Rover, which was parked on the packhorse bridge. I have a vague memory of being in his arms, but it was far from romantic. I was numb with cold and shock and actually thought I could still die.

Apparently it was Nel who drove the Land Rover back to Longcross in the dark. I don't remember that either. Nor do I remember Shafeen and Nel dressing me in enough of their clothes to conceal the wetsuit and carrying me shivering into the house, or the servants swarming around me and fetching me a dressing gown and blankets and wrapping me up in front of the roaring Great Hall fire, or the same ancient family doctor coming to check me over.

I *do* remember, though, the Medievals trooping back in, *much* later, and the unmistakable flare of surprise in their eyes when they saw me alive. I remember the smooth lies they told, one for each of them:

'*Oh* my *God*, we've been so *worried* about you . . .'

'Don't you remember falling in? We were all trying to fish you out . . .'

'Then you just slipped under Henry's boat and disappeared . . .'

'We thought you'd drowned . . .'

'We've been out looking for you ever since . . .'

I could quite believe they'd been looking for me, but not to save me, that was for sure.

Then, a little later, I remember Cookson being the first person to say, *Where's Henry?* And Shafeen looking at me and very slightly shaking his head.

And a couple of them going back out to find him, and Lara coming back and saying, *Hen's not home yet.*

Then Perfect going out to look for him.

Then the police.

Then the hours in front of the Great Hall fire, hours of sipping hot drinks in a white towelling bathrobe, hours of answering questions with lies, and hours of waiting for the results of a torch-lit police search with growing dread for the news we knew would come, before I was finally able to escape and go up to bed.

When I crept into Lowther I didn't switch on the lights. The police cars still crowding in the drive outside illuminated the room every other second with their eerie blue lights. I sat on the bed, exhausted, and Jeffrey looked down at me, his blue-lit expression oddly sympathetic. His eyes seemed softer, his nose rounder, his antlers less pointed. He looked downcast, defeated. 'Yes, you understand,' I said to him, wearily. 'Aidan's stag escaped because he was invisible, but you never quite got the trick of it, did you? And neither did I. All term I kept my head down, never tried to stand out. But I wasn't quite invisible enough. I thought I was just being myself. But being myself was to be *different*, and that was enough to put me in Henry's sights. Better to turn yourself into a mini-Medieval, be exactly like them or be separated from the herd and hunted down.' But Nel had tried that approach and it didn't work; she hadn't quite got it right. And Shafeen was always different, by being another race; he might as well have been another species.

Suddenly I couldn't be in there, just me and Jeffrey. I needed them now: my friends, my new friends. I left Lowther and padded along the passageway to Raby, Shafeen's room. I knocked softly and opened the door. Nel was already there, sitting on the window seat with Shafeen. She'd obviously felt the same way. We didn't say anything. There was nothing to say. Nothing to do but watch and wait. I joined them and we all looked down.

They brought Henry's body back at midnight. I saw the stretcher being transferred from the back of the shooting brake to the waiting ambulance. But you could see that it was too late for any medical attention. In films, you see, if someone's still alive, whatever state they're in, they leave the face uncovered – obvs – so the person can breathe. Henry's body was covered from head to foot. We all watched as the stretcher slid into the ambulance. The doors were slammed, someone signed a form on a clipboard, and the ambulance drove away. We watched it till it was out of sight. A young man was dead, and however evil he undoubtedly was, and however much his death might have prevented countless injuries and even other deaths, he was still someone's son.

I was the first to speak. 'We are murderers,' I said.

'No,' said Shafeen gently, but firmly. 'It was a suicide.'

'We should have gone back for him,' I said. 'We should have gone to find him. What if he was still alive? What if we could have saved him?' The fact that I'd been barely conscious after his fall didn't blunt my guilt.

Nel said, 'How? We couldn't have got back down the falls. You know. It was hard enough for you climbing up. And no one could have survived that fall, from that height.'

I knew that to be true – I'd known when I was climbing that, if I'd fallen, I would have been finished.

'Plus,' said Shafeen, 'we had to get you back. If I hadn't fished you out, you'd have gone over the falls too. And if we hadn't got you back to Longcross, you'd have died of hypothermia.' He must have heard how it sounded. 'I'm not calling myself a hero. I'm just stating a fact.'

'And,' said Nel, 'Henry *wanted* to go. He jumped.'

'Yes, but we *made* him do it,' I persisted. 'We put the noose around his neck. We threatened him with worldwide humiliation at the hands of the very technology he despised. Social media, the police, the press. He couldn't handle that.' I turned to Nel. 'You aren't *really* going to upload his confession, are you?'

'Not now,' said Nel. And I knew what she meant. *Not now he's dead.*

Shafeen closed the heavy curtains against the blue lights and we all collapsed onto his bed in our pyjamas. There was nothing weird – it was like we were all five years old. Nel got out the Saros 7S and we all looked at it where it sat on her palm. In its silver heart lived the technology that had saved me. It had been an integral part of our plan. That miraculous, powerful, friendly little device had turned a 2D Ordnance Survey map on the estate room wall into a 3D digital image of Longmere and its surrounding terrain. It had taken a unique thermal image map of my body and tracked my position every minute of the day when I'd been fishing with Henry, so I was never alone, and Shafeen and Nel knew where I was at all times. It had night-sight capability so Nel was able to film Henry and me at the head of the waterfall even without the light of the torch. It had talked to its mother satellite, uploading to the Saros Orbit every shred of evidence we needed against Henry de Warlencourt, from the photos of the game books to the video of his confession. And now I just felt like I wanted to switch off; and it could help me do that too. I knew exactly what we all needed.

We all crowded round the phone and watched YouTube into the early hours until we fell asleep right there in Shafeen's room. We watched all the crap on the Internet, from piano-playing cats, to skater fails to bottle flips. We watched 'try not to laugh' challenges, mannequin challenges and 24-hour challenges. We watched Vines of people dabbing and animals sneezing, and tons of memes. The brash music and stupid electronic sounds bounced off the damask wallpaper, the garish lights and colours reflected off the heavy silk curtains of the bed that Elizabeth I had slept in. Strange though it might seem, since we were filling his ancient medieval house with Savage rubbish, it was our elegy for Henry.

We let the world in.

In the morning, before we went back to our own rooms, we had a decision to make.

'What do we do?' I didn't need to explain. I meant, *Do we show the video to the police?*

'We keep quiet,' said Shafeen. 'The huntin' shootin' fishin' is over – it can't continue without Henry at Longcross. No point heaping disgrace on the family just to make ourselves feel better. His dad's obviously a shit, but his mum might be OK. She's lost her son – we should let her have her dignity. Let's keep quiet about the footage, unless someone tries to connect us with his death. At the moment, they don't even know that we were with him when he died. If they work that out, then we've got the evidence to show that he took his own life.'

But they never did work it out. The policeman who spoke to me, an inspector with an accent almost as posh as Henry's – treated me very gently, almost as if he was sorry to have to interview me at all. I said I'd fallen over the side of Henry's boat and swum to the shore, and I hadn't seen Henry after that.

'I suppose he went to look for me, and it was dark, and . . .'

Suddenly, totally without warning, I started to cry. I didn't even have to fake it. I suppose after the shock it was just hitting me what had happened.

The inspector cleared his throat in the way that posh people communicate they are uncomfortable. He patted my hand awkwardly. 'You mustn't feel responsible,' he said in his bluff, stiff-upper-lip way.

But I did.

I *was* responsible.

At the end of just a morning of questioning, we were allowed to return to school. The remaining Medievals waited for Lord and Lady de Warlencourt, who were driving up from London, while a police officer drove Shafeen, Nel and me back in a squad car. I was just glad it wasn't Perfect. If he knew what we'd done to his beloved master, he'd have driven us off the road.

For the second time I endured the journey between STAGS and Longcross in silence, but this time I was glad of it.

S.T.A.G.S.

(II)

chapter thirty-one

The police concluded that Henry de Warlencourt, son of Rollo de Warlencourt, 17th Earl of Longcross, had fallen over Conrad's Force and drowned following a night-fishing trip.

No one told us officially, but we read it in the press; now that we'd started to use the Saros 7S we couldn't quite put it back in Pandora's Box, even at school. Maybe Henry had had a point.

So, in our first lunchtime back at STAGS, in an empty practice room in Bede, we read the accounts online on all the major newspapers' websites. They'd got hold of a gorgeous picture of Henry, looking all Gatsby in white tie and tails, and gone to town with it. Even the school didn't escape scrutiny – paps hung around the iron gates training their long lenses at the school; we started seeing headlines like: 'Posh STAGS Mourns Model Pupil . . . Tragic Lordling's 50K-a-year School.' A Facebook page went up, started by someone who didn't even know Henry, just because of his beauty. His looks, his privileged life and the manner in which he died sparked something in the public imagination. Crazy girls from Poland threatened to jump off waterfalls, Oxbridge students had Henry de Warlencourt parties, which were black-tie dinners next to lakes, topped off by a spot of night fishing. Sixth-formers trespassed on the Longcross estate, desperate to take selfies at Conrad's Force. One girl from Portland, Oregon, posted a video of her clutching Henry's photo and crying for the entire four minutes and twenty-three seconds it took for R.E.M. to sing 'Nightswimming'. We all watched it on the Saros in Nel's room, open-mouthed. 'Tragic,' I said. 'Think how mortified Henry would be.'

'He's an Internet sensation,' said Nel, 'without us having to lift a finger.'

'He was King Sisyphus after all,' said Shafeen. 'But he just couldn't get that boulder to the top of the hill. And it rolled down and crushed him in the end.' I knew what he meant. Henry was trying to hold back a world that couldn't be stopped.

But Henry wasn't the only one who wanted to hold back the tide. The Abbot – who was really sweet about the whole thing – wrote to our parents about Henry's death. Didn't phone. Didn't email. He *wrote* a letter home for each of us. Dad was still in South America so I knew the letter would sit in the empty hallway of our little house in Arkwright Terrace until Christmas. I was glad. I wasn't sure how I'd even begin to explain to my father what had happened. I always told him the truth – that was the deal we had – but I didn't think I could tell this particular story. It would have to be the first secret I would keep from him. The other thing was that if Dad knew what had actually happened – the whole huntin' shootin' fishin' deal – he'd be on the first plane home, and I wasn't about to lose him his job. For different reasons, Shafeen and Nel didn't tell their parents the gory deets either. Shafeen, I thought, was trying to spare his father from reliving what he'd gone through all those years ago. Chanel's motives were more complicated. I think she wanted to stay at the school, and knew that if she told her parents she'd be taken away – she'd be snatched from this privileged world, and feel that she'd somehow failed. For that matter, I'm sure all of our parents would have taken us away if they'd known the full story, and none of us wanted that. We'd only just found each other. For our own different reasons, we each kept quiet, and the secret bound the three of us together.

As it turned out, the snail-mail delay worked out well for all of us. The time when we'd needed our folks had come and gone – I could really have done with one of my dad's legendary hugs on the night Henry died. And by the time the other two had communications from their parents, they were over the shock and wanted nothing more than to stay at school with their fellow conspirators. We would all be seeing our parents over the long Christmas break in less than six weeks anyway, when my dad would be back from Chile, Nel would be going to Cheshire and Shafeen to Rajasthan. Till then the three of us needed each other. No one else would understand every single emotion we were going through; how it felt to be murderers, yet not murderers, to be innocent and yet guilty, sorry Henry was dead but glad he was gone.

The school did, however, seem to think that we should all have access to counselling – it was probably the most progressive thing they'd ever done. They engaged this shrink for us. She was the only adult presence at the school – besides the Abbot – who didn't have to be called Friar. She was called Mrs Waller, but insisted we call her Sheila. This was a bit modern even for me. 'Sheila' was a well-intentioned hippy who had messy curly hair and wore lots of scarves and beads. We met in a small office I'd never seen before, which had nothing in it but two chairs and a low table with a box of tissues sitting pointedly on it. I almost felt she would be disappointed if I didn't cry. 'Sheila' was always prodding me – 'How do you *feel?*' But I didn't even know that myself. I could hardly tell her that I'd liked Henry, then I didn't like him, but I sort of still did, and then I'd murdered him. I couldn't tell her that Henry had kissed me and told me I was beautiful but I now thought he'd been lying, and then Shafeen had told me I was beautiful and I thought he was telling the truth. I couldn't share that Shafeen had told me he'd come huntin' shootin' fishin' in order to protect me, having avoided going for years. I couldn't confide that Shafeen hadn't said a word about my beauty since, or the reason that he'd come to Longcross, because we, ya know, had just *murdered* someone between us and had more important things to talk about – like if we were actually going to go to prison. Nor could I say that a tiny part of me still wanted to go up to him and say, *Hey, you know how we killed someone by making him jump off a waterfall? Well, can we just put that to one side for a second while I ask you exactly what you meant when you told me, the night before we committed the most heinous crime in the book, that I was beautiful, and that you came to Longcross to protect me?* I began to dread the therapy sessions, and kind, well-meaning 'Sheila'. I had to tell lie upon lie, and tied myself in knots trying to remember which fibs I'd told, to the point where the sessions were actually more stressful than therapeutic. Shafeen and Nel felt the same. None of us needed Sheila. We only needed each other.

The Abbot seemed to agree with this sentiment. He had us three murderers and the five remaining (weirdly calm) Medievals into his panelled study for sherry – the upper-class equivalent of a nice cup of tea – and preached benevolently at us.

'I've been teaching for a long time,' he said, hitching his gown onto his shoulders and looking over his half-glasses in a fond-uncle kind of way, 'and I have found the best thing for young people in situations like this is normalcy, continuity and a restoration of order.' I exchanged a look with Shafeen and Nel. How many situations like this had he had to face during his time at STAGS? How would he feel – this sweet old Santa Claus of a man – if we told him that every terrible 'accident' he'd had to deal with in his thirty years was probably connected to huntin' shootin' fishin'? Henry's victims. His predecessors' victims. And now Henry. 'We could send you all home on an exeat until after Christmas, but in consultation with the police and Mrs Waller' (Sheila), 'I have concluded that it would not benefit you to be isolated from your contemporaries.'

I certainly wasn't isolated from my contemporaries. Not any more. We three murderers were always together now, bound in guilt. We spent every waking moment in our little group, talking in a little huddle. I tried to concentrate on my schoolwork, but it was pretty difficult. I sometimes wondered, during the rest of that Michaelmas term, if they could take scholarships *away*, as my work was so poor. I think, looking back, that they must've given me a break because of the whole Henry thing, otherwise I would have been on the first train home. My essays made zero sense, and my rubbish efforts were made worse by the fact that I was sort of being *haunted*. You know that movie *The Sixth Sense*, where that goofy little kid sees dead people? Well, that kid was me. I kept thinking I saw glimpses of Henry. Henry playing on the green grass of Bede's Piece in the middle of a rugby scrum, Henry's blond head in chapel, or the tail of Henry's Tudor coat just disappearing around a corner. I'd wondered if he'd attend his own funeral, like Tom Sawyer.

We weren't invited to Henry's funeral. For one thing, we were not considered to be close friends – none of his family had met us, and for all they knew we'd just been one-off weekend guests. I was glad. I don't think I could have stood it. A funeral is no place for the deceased's murderers. It was, we knew, to be held at Longcross, at the church I'd seen from Henry's roof, with all the county families in attendance. The Abbot went, as did the remaining Medievals. We saw them drive away from school that Friday morning in a cortege of long black sedan cars. All that day I imagined what it was like at the funeral; I pictured it like a scene from *The Godfather*. People wailing, and wearing black lace, and throwing handfuls of dirt and roses onto the coffin. A man who looked just like Henry, in profile, looking at his son's coffin, his face a map of pain. A well-dressed lady sat beside him, too well bred to shed a tear. Rollo de Warlencourt and his wife. I never did get to meet Henry's parents.

But the ghost of Henry wouldn't leave me alone. Most of all I became obsessed with that film that I'd told him about in our very last conversation at the top of Conrad's Force, just before he fell. I now wished, since it was going to become our last conversation, and thus assume this enormous significance, that we'd talked about some really worthy movie like *Citizen Kane*. But I suppose last conversations are never like that; you never know when you're going to check out, so people probably quite often drop dead after talking about the shopping list or the laundry. But that last exchange about, of all things, that dumb Sherlock Holmes movie kept coming back to me. I kept thinking about the part where Sherlock tumbles off the Reichenbach Falls but isn't actually dead, and he comes back and hides in Watson's room, and then when Watson finishes Holmes's last adventure and types THE END, Holmes comes out when Watson is answering the door and types a question mark after the word END. When I'd handwrite my essays (no tech, remember) and leave them on my desk in Lightfoot, I kept expecting to come back and find a little question mark written at the bottom in Henry's scrawling handwriting. After all, we hadn't actually seen his body. Just a sealed-up bag. Maybe he wasn't dead. Sometimes, on the rare occasions when I was alone in the room, when Jesus was out playing real tennis or something, I'd go to the windows and quickly whip back the floor-length curtains, to see if Henry was hiding there. Honestly, I was becoming a real fruit loop. I tell you, I almost went back to 'Sheila' to get my head read.

chapter thirty-two

I expected that once we were all back at STAGS after that fateful weekend at Longcross, the Medievals would never speak to us again. I was wrong.

I wouldn't say they treated us nicely, but they certainly never bullied any of us again. It was like there was a strange force field around the three of us. They were almost afraid. They knew I had been pushed out of the boat, and that I had seen them all refuse to help me, but they could not, I suppose, know what had happened between the three of us and Henry. All they knew was that I'd turned up alive, and Henry had turned up dead. I wondered if they were worried about how much I knew; they didn't know how much, if anything, Henry had told me before he pushed me into Longmere, but if they'd ever seen any movies at all they should know how supervillains always feel they're kind of freed up by the fact that their victim is about to die, so it doesn't matter how much they tell them. Like the Six-fingered Man in *The Princess Bride* who describes the pain machine to Westley before he turns it on. For all the Medievals knew, Henry could've done something similar. I could literally know where all the bodies were buried. So they were all carefully civil. The girls were guardedly friendly to Nel and me, and the boys civil to Shafeen. All talk of the Punjabi Playboy and Carphone Chanel was dropped. And life at the school went on as normal.

Actually it was a little bit *too* normal.

In short, although there was an outpouring of grief from strangers online, no one at STAGS seemed to be mourning Henry quite as much as they should. Even Lara didn't seem to be as devastated as she surely should have been. She'd lost her 'Hen', the guy she presumably liked, even loved, along with what she probably loved more: the Longcross package – all those lands and that lovely house and all that cash.

I assumed she must be keeping it all bottled up inside. 'Poor Lara,' I said to Shafeen and Nel on Bede's Piece one day, watching her – quite cheerfully, it has to be said – playing lacrosse.

Nel turned to me in surprise. 'You don't feel sorry for her, do you?'

'No,' I said, 'not for her.'

'For Him then?'

She meant Henry. We always meant Henry when we said Him or He with that extra emphasis that meant the word had a capital letter. Henry, that devil, was now referred to as if he was God.

'You don't feel sorry for him, do you?' Nel prodded again.

I thought about this. I kind of felt sorry that the nice Henry, the one who had kissed me on the rooftop and taught me to fish, didn't have a chance at life. But I wasn't sorry for the bad Henry, the real Henry. So I shook my head. 'No. You?'

'No. I'm glad he's gone. Now other kids are safe. I feel sorrier for that African kid, and that scholarship girl. They were murdered. Not by him, I know. But I still kind of wish he'd been brought to justice.'

'Maybe better not,' said Shafeen. 'If they started poking around into Henry, they might start poking around into *us*. Maybe we're lucky the police were as inefficient as they seemed to be.'

Shafeen was voicing a feeling that had been nagging at me. 'You think so too?'

'What do I think?' he asked.

'Well, do you think it was all a bit, well, *straightforward*? They interviewed all of us, but don't you think they let us get away a bit easy?'

'How do you mean?' asked Nel.

'Well, I've watched a lot of films. A *lot*. And whenever there's an unexplained death, the authorities go into tons of detail – police, coroners, crown prosecutors, you name it. They definitely should have shaken *me* down a little bit more – I mean, I was the last one to see him alive. They should have asked loads more questions. Why was I wearing a wetsuit? Why didn't Henry and I catch any fish before I "accidentally" fell in Longmere? Why was he at the top of the waterfall when we were fishing down on the lake? The police should be interested, the Medievals should be interested, the de Warlencourt family *certainly* should be interested.'

'What are you saying?'

'That there's some sort of cover-up. Obviously the Medievals don't want it to come out about the huntin' shootin' fishin', but it seems like no one else does either. What did Henry call it? "The British establishment"?' I watched Lara score a goal and do a little celebration with Esme and Charlotte, their blonde ponytails flying as they hugged and jumped about. It seemed, well, *wrong*. 'I mean, I'm really *glad* no one probed, as it lets us off the hook –' too late I noticed the fishing pun – 'but it just seems *odd*.'

The lacrosse match was over, and we started to stroll towards school, our black Tudor coats flapping and wrapping round our legs. Shafeen said grimly, 'Well, don't relax just yet. I suppose the next thing will be the inquest. We'll just have to hope that nothing nasty turns up at that.'

I'd forgotten about the inquest. Of course – I should've known from the movies. They always have a court session to discover what happened in a suspicious death. I clutched at my stomach. More waiting, and wondering. I wondered how much more I could take.

Shafeen, Nel and I weren't allowed to go to the inquest, since we were under eighteen. All the Medievals who were in Six Two and *were* eighteen got to go. We watched them leave the school with the Abbot in the school minibus. It looked weird – like they were going on a really dark school trip.

They didn't come back for hours, and the three of us did our best to pretend it was just a normal school day. But just after lunch the minibus came back up the drive and we stopped pretending that we could talk about anything else. 'I'm going to ask,' I said decidedly. 'Come with me?'

Shafeen and Nel shared a look. 'Sure.'

We knew where to find the Medievals. They'd be hanging out, as they always did, at the well in Paulinus quad; and there they were, gathered like crows in the winter sunshine.

For a moment as we approached I could have sworn that Henry was standing there, in the middle of his little cohort. My heart started to thud; the phantom who had been haunting me would show himself at last. But as we got nearer I could see there were only five heads, and the blond one at the centre was actually Cookson. He was leaning on the well just as Henry used to do, in the accepted position of the leader of the Medievals. He even looked like Henry. His hair looked blonder (had he done something to it?) and he was slimmer (had he been working out?). His hair was cut to look like Henry's and he even wore chessboard-check stockings under his black Tudor gown, just as Henry used to do.

'I'll go,' I said, and Nel and Shafeen fell back at the edge of the quad. I felt, as I'd felt ever since we came back from Longcross, that I had a certain power, a cloak of invulnerability like something out of *Clash of the Titans*. I had something on them – that they hadn't helped me out of the lake – and they were wary of me, especially as they didn't know how much more I knew. But as I walked across the grass towards them, feeling their watchful eyes on me, I was as nervous as I'd been on my first day at STAGS. They looked, as a group, as they always had: comfortable, entitled and forbidding. I had to separate one from the pack; and if you want an answer, as my dad always says, go to the top. 'Cookson,' I called, pleasantly enough, 'can I have a word?'

He sort of pushed himself off the well, hands still in his pockets, and I was struck by a memory of Henry at Longcross, pushing himself off the panelled wall in exactly that manner. It was uncanny. Cookson strolled easily to meet me, in the middle of the grass, as if we two were about to fight a duel, with our seconds standing a little way behind.

He stopped, facing me in his duelling stance. I suddenly felt the old hostility return and that my cloak of invulnerability had been stripped away. What had gone down at the inquest? Had we been dropped in it?

'Hi, Cookson,' I said, not really sure how to start.

'It's Henry actually.'

I was a bit taken aback. I'd almost forgotten his first name was Henry. All that time we'd known him as Cookson because there could only ever be one Henry. And now, here was another one, this BTEC version. 'Henry,' I began. It sounded weird. 'I . . . *We* were just wondering what happened at the inquest.'

He stared me down with eyes that looked bluer than usual, eyes that were suddenly like the old Henry's. For a moment I thought he'd refuse to answer. Then he said, grudgingly, 'The coroner ruled it was death by misadventure.'

I needed to be quite sure. 'What's misadventure?'

'An accident due to a dangerous risk taken voluntarily,' he stated in a superior voice. 'The coroner decided that Henry had climbed Conrad's Force voluntarily, so the fact that he fell off it was his own fault. Misadventure.'

Misadventure. It was a good way to describe the whole weekend at Longcross. An adventure gone wrong. 'Did he say anything else?'

'What else could he possibly say? It was a terrible accident,' he said pointedly. 'And that's all.'

So that was it. I stood very still while I processed the information, the sharp breeze stirring our Tudor coats, the rooks cawing in the trees. It took me a minute to realise what it meant.

The matter was closed and we were off the hook.

The thing is, so were they.

I felt massive relief coupled with a keen disappointment. It's not like I had wanted some earth-shattering revelation about the huntin' shootin' fishin' to come out at the inquest, but at the same time I felt weirdly let down. It felt like nothing had changed.

Just then the bell rang from the chapel spire for afternoon lessons. Lara called to Cookson, like the siren I'd always thought her, in an alluring, tempting voice. 'Hen,' she said, 'come *on*. We'll be late for Greek.' I went cold. *Hen* had been her nickname for Henry. As his girlfriend, she had been given the unique privilege of shortening his name. Now she'd passed on the nickname, along with her affection, to this second Henry, who turned and sauntered to join her, supremely confident in his gait. He leaned down – he even seemed to have gotten taller – to kiss her on the mouth. Then, hand in hand, they walked to the Honorius building, leaving me open-mouthed in the middle of the quad. Shafeen and Nel came to meet me, and we all stared after them.

Shafeen gave a long, low whistle. 'The King is Dead,' he said with something like awe. 'Long Live the King.'

Nel sighed. 'Is this another one of those King Sisyphus conversations?'

'No,' he said. 'Yes. *Sort* of. "The King is Dead, Long Live the King" was the traditional proclamation in medieval England when the king died. It meant the people were never without a king. It made everyone feel secure, and there was no opening for a pretender to seize the throne. It represented tradition, continuity, all the things that the Medievals are so fond of.'

'What are you getting at?' said Nel.

'Don't you see what's happened? They've gone seamlessly from one Henry to another. Even the queen, in this case Lara, has hooked up with the new king. It's like *Hamlet*.'

He was right. I hadn't seen the play, but in the Kenneth Branagh version when his dad RIPs, his mum (Julie Christie) starts spooning his uncle Claudius (Derek Jacobi) before you can say, 'To be or not to be.' I nodded. 'And just like that,' I said, 'order is restored.'

At that moment a shaft of weak winter sunlight penetrated the quad, and it was as if the same light, at last, illuminated my stupid brain. '*Order*,' I said. 'That's it.' I grabbed both my friends by their black sleeves.

'Where are we going?' asked Shafeen.

'Nel's room. *Now*.'

chapter thirty-three

Fortunately Nel's roommate wasn't in her room.

We bundled in and I locked the door behind us. I even drew the curtains. Then I sat the other two down on Nel's bed.

'What's the matter?' asked Nel, at exactly the same time Shafeen said, 'Look, what *is* all this?'

'Nel,' I said, breathing heavily, 'where's your phone?'

Nel unlocked a drawer and got out the Saros 7S. With one touch it sprang into life with its friendly but futuristic chime.

'Play me the video,' I said urgently. 'Play me Henry's confession. I just want to check something.'

I hadn't seen it before, and it was a tough watch. Like watching a tragic movie for the second time around, when you know the ending. Like when I saw *The Fault in Our Stars* for the second time, and I couldn't quite believe they were going to let that kid Gus die of cancer, even though I'd seen it before and I knew they did. I watched now, somehow hoping I'd misremembered it all.

I watched myself, soaking and shivering, knee deep in rushing water, talking to Henry at the top of Conrad's Force. I could hear my own voice, raised above the sound of the water, shouting, '*Did you get all that?*' I watched Henry's face, shot from above, as he turned at the sound of Nel's voice, super-loud, right next to the phone, saying, '*Oh yes. We got it.*' I watched his expression change as the Saros 7S's powerful torch was turned on him, the water below him turned to milk and he realised he was being filmed. As he looked directly into the lens I flinched a little. He seemed to be looking right at me, and I was suddenly sure he could see me even now. I shifted uncomfortably on the bed, and watched him extend his dripping hand up to the camera.

'*Give me that thing,*' he said, low and deadly.

Then Nel's voice, louder and bolshie, saying, '*Wouldn't do any good. You could take this phone from me, but the video's already been uploaded to the Saros Orbit. It's a satellite storage system, totally secure.*'

Shafeen joined in: '*Isn't technology wonderful, when you find the right application for it?*'

Then came the moment I'd remembered, the creepy moment when Henry drew himself up, more powerful than ever, his eyes shining with that freaky, almost religious light. '*You can't win,*' he said. '*You can't upset the order.*'

'There!' I said. 'Wind it back.'

Nel scrubbed back along the timeline with her manicured index finger. Henry did a little backwards dance in the water, and then spoke again. '*You can't win,*' he said. '*You can't upset the order.*'

This time Nel let the slider run on past her own barnstorming speech about the powers of social media. Henry's voice said, '*The order will go on, even without me.*'

Then Shafeen's voice. *'There's a new order now.'* Nel stopped the playback, and she and Shafeen looked at me.

'So?' said Shafeen. 'We knew Henry was obsessed with order. Don't you remember the shooting lunch, when he said the lower orders of nature should be culled? *We* were the lower orders of nature, and when we got the better of him, he couldn't take it. He was so obsessed with the concept of natural order that it controlled his life.'

I shook my head. 'Listen again.' This time I took the Saros out of Nel's hand and scrolled it back myself. *'The order will go on,'* Henry said, *'even without me.'* I looked from one to the other. 'Now do you hear? He said, *"The* order." Not order. The Order.'

'I don't get it,' admitted Nel.

But Shafeen turned to me, wide-eyed. 'A *religious* order. It's a freaking *cult*.'

'The order of the *what* though?' asked Nel.

'What's this all about?' I said. 'St Aidan's stag. A school *called* STAGS. Antlers everywhere.' I raised both hands to my head, fingers spread, thumbs to my temples. 'The Order of the Stag.'

'And every one of them is a part of it,' said Shafeen. 'All the Medievals.'

'Not just the Medievals,' said Nel slowly. 'The Friars too.'

'The *Friars*?' I said.

'Yes,' she said. 'I may not be as clever as you two –' she waved away our polite protests – 'but I do know about fashion, and I notice accessories. That ring that Henry wore – the gold signet ring with the antlers? The Friars all wear them, the men *and* the women.'

Then it was Shafeen's turn. 'Come with me,' he said in his commanding voice. He was in full-on Prince Caspian mode and we got up at once and followed him.

We left Lightfoot and the sun was setting as we walked through the chapel cloister, across Paulinus quad – now empty of Medievals – and over Bede's Piece in the direction of Honorius. The whole of STAGS, shadowy and looming, surrounded us in a dark embrace. The lighted windows watched us like eyes. We slipped into Honorius and up the stairs to Shafeen's room. The boys didn't have to share, as there were four boys' houses to the girls' one, so there was no roommate to worry about. Through the heavy oak door there was just an empty room, a room I'd never seen before. It was really nice, all oak panelling and emerald-green curtains, which Shafeen drew.

He unlocked a drawer in the desk and pulled out something heavy and black, and we all sat on the bed together. It was a repeat of how we'd just sat in Nel's room – although now instead of huddling around a phone, we were huddled over a book.

It was a big book, bound in morocco leather, with no title but just a date.

It was the Longcross game book from the 1960s.

'You brought it with you?' I exclaimed.

'I said I would.' He clicked on the bedside lamp and for a moment we all looked at the book in his hands, bathed in a circle of golden light, like it was some sort of holy text.

1960–1969

A decade of huntin' shootin' fishin'. A decade when the rest of the world was changing. Swinging London and the Beatles and England winning the World Cup and Vidal Sassoon haircuts and the moon landings. And all the while, at Longcross, things were fossilised, as they had been for centuries, and dead creatures were written down in ink on paper in books. Shafeen ran his long fingers over the spine almost tenderly, his fingertips caressing the gold-stamped date, as if he was stalling, afraid of what he might find. Then he got all businesslike. 'Now,' he said, 'let's see just how far back this goes.'

He opened the book on his lap and we all crowded around it.

He turned the yellowing paper and our eyes scanned the pages and pages of handwritten inky scrawl. I gave a long, low whistle. There were hundreds of entries. Each one represented a bird, a fish or a deer who had died on that day. It was literally a book of the dead. And, in among them, were names; names of people, of kids who had been tricked and tracked as we had been. And at the top of each page, at the very head of the hierarchy, more names – the hunters who had chased them; broken, injured or even killed them.

Shafeen turned the pages forward until he came to the year he was looking for. '1969,' he said under his breath. 'Michaelmas Justitium.'

He ran his finger down the page, and I could see, over his shoulder, the entry we'd seen that night in the library, when Perfect had almost caught us. The name of an Indian boy whose long-ago fate, even more than Nel's or Shafeen's, had made me risk my life to catch Henry.

'Aadhish Jadeja,' I said, pointing. 'There.'

Shafeen shook his head slightly, not looking up. 'I'm not looking for Dad,' he said. His finger travelled up the page, to the very top. '*Jesus*,' he breathed.

I read over his shoulder. '*Proceedings of the Order of the Stag, Longcross Hall, Michaelmas Justitium 1969.*'

'So it's true,' Nel said.

'Not *that*,' said Shafeen impatiently. 'The *names*.' I followed his finger and read the names of the hunters, of those in attendance on that fateful weekend in 1969.

'The Grand Master, Rollo de Warlencourt.' Henry's dad. No surprise there. But then I read on. 'Charles Skelton, Miranda Petrie, Serena Styles, Francesca Mowbray.

The Friars. *All* Friars.

Friar Skelton, the ancient-history master who'd taught us about the battle of Hattin and was so picky about punctuation that we called him the Punctuation Police. Friar Mowbray, the classics mistress, who'd taught us about Actaeon being torn to pieces by fifty hounds. Friar Styles, who taught modern history (which at STAGS included everything after the Dark Ages) and had told us about Gian Maria Visconti hunting men instead of beasts.

And at the head of them all, Rollo de Warlencourt, the Grand Master.

'Five of them,' I said. 'All the same age, all ex-pupils. They are all in on it. They've all been huntin' shootin' fishin' themselves. They were Medievals when they were at school here, and they all went on to become Friars when they grew up, all except Henry's dad. And the whole cycle keeps on going, the Order sustains itself, and Henry's good old days continue.'

Shafeen looked at me. 'How far did the game books go back, can you remember?'

I considered. 'Middle Ages, easy.'

'Christ,' he said. 'It started when the Medievals were *actually* medieval.'

He was still looking through the book. 'Look.' He turned to random pages. '*Proceedings of the Order of the Stag, Michaelmas Justitium, 1962, Baddesley Manor. Hilary Justitium, 1967, Polesden Cross. Trinity Justitium, 1965, Derbyshire House.*' He looked up. 'It goes much wider than Longcross.'

'It had to, didn't it?' I said. 'There wouldn't always have been a de Warlencourt in the upper school for a thousand years. There must have been gaps. Other leaders of the Medievals, other stately homes hosting the blood sports.'

'But all connected by one thing,' said Shafeen.

'STAGS,' Nel finished.

'The cult is running the school,' I said, 'and the school is running the cult.'

'And now,' Shafeen said, 'there's a new leader: Cookson. Henry said it himself – the Order will go on, even without him.'

'No, it won't.' I stood up. 'Shafeen, bring the game book. Nel, bring the phone.'

'Where are we going?'

I was already at the door. 'It's time to tell the Abbot.' Then I froze with my fingers on the handle. 'No, wait, what if he's in on it too?'

'He's not in the book,' said Shafeen.

'No signet ring either,' said Nel.

'OK,' I said. 'Come on.'

chapter thirty-four

The Abbot watched Henry's confession from beginning to end without saying a word.

As he watched the screen he covered his mouth with his left hand, his expression a mask of shock. Nel had been right. There was no signet ring on his left hand, just a plain gold wedding band. Now I thought about it, I was a bit surprised to see it. I had never met a Mrs Abbot. Maybe she was dead. After all, the Abbot was pretty old. He looked even older by the time he'd finished watching the clip.

When the video was over, there was a long silence, in which we could just hear the muffled tick of the pendulum clock on the mantelpiece.

The three of us were sitting in big leather chairs across the mahogany desk from him. He was in his gown and we were all in our Tudor coats. There was oak panelling on the walls, rows of books on shelves, framed certificates behind his head. We looked like a page in the STAGS prospectus. It should have been the most civilised interview in the world. But what the Abbot had seen couldn't have been more Savage.

He didn't say anything for quite a bit. Then he took off his half-glasses and rubbed the bridge of his nose. He looked very weird, as people do when they always wear glasses and then you see them without them. He looked devastated.

'Poor Henry,' he said sadly. 'He was quite deranged at the end. Forgive me; I did not know it was a suicide.'

He put his glasses back on, blinked owlishly, and eyeballed us.

'And is it true? This dreadful . . . pastime? It seems . . . incredible.'

'Oh, it's true,' I said. 'We lived it, on Justitium weekend, at Longcross Hall.'

'I was hunted,' said Nel.

'I was shot,' continued Shafeen.

'And I was fished in Longmere lake,' I finished.

The Abbot clasped his hands before him, his fingers lacing together. 'Why don't you tell me what happened?'

So we told him the whole story; Nel first, then Shafeen took over, and then me. It took so long that it grew dark outside. The Abbot wrote as we talked, on the block of thick cream paper that sat on his desk.

'And this order that Henry speaks of at the end here –' he indicated the phone with his fountain pen – 'to what does he refer?'

There were no flies on the Abbot. He knew at once that Henry was talking about some sort of sect; he didn't blunder about like we had. I realised then what a clever bloke he was – he wasn't headmaster of such a prestigious school for nothing.

'He was referring to the Order of the Stag, a centuries-old death cult involving the hunting of schoolchildren,' I said. 'It started when the Crusaders, including Conrad de Warlencourt, sent their sons to be educated by Friars after the Crusades. Henry said it himself – Conrad had fought the infidel and was looking for new savages to fight. It's been going on since then,'

'And,' said Shafeen, 'in the sixties, my father went to Longcross too. He was Aadhish Jadeja, the only brown kid in the school. He was invited for Michaelmas Justitium in 1969, for a spot of huntin' shootin' fishin'. And he was shot. Frightened and broken.' Shafeen's voice wobbled and for a moment I thought he was going to cry.

The Abbot turned his kindly eyes on Shafeen. 'And your father told you all this?'

'No,' said Shafeen, almost sadly. 'My father didn't say a *word* all these years. Some misplaced sense of honour – the kid who won't snitch even if it means waterboarding. *He* didn't tell me anything. But *this* did.'

Shafeen placed the black game book on the table. Then, almost as if he couldn't bear to touch it, he turned the volume around with one finger until the gold-tooled date faced the Abbot. He flipped the book open at the right page – 1969.

The Abbot read the page and went totally white. He sat back in his chair and let out a deep sigh.

It was as if the phone, with all its new technology, hadn't quite convinced him, but the game book defeated him because it was from his own world. Books were his kryptonite. Now he got the full extent of the corruption in his own school, going on under his own nose.

'Have the police seen this evidence?' he asked. 'The book, and the . . . film?'

We looked at each other. 'No,' I said.

'Do you *want* to go to the police?'

Strangely, this had never really occurred to us. We'd been so busy trying to avoid their scrutiny over Henry's death ourselves, that we'd never thought to pursue the Medievals with the law.

'Leaving aside the historical actions of the Friars for the moment,' he said, 'let us turn to your contemporaries.' He picked up the paper he'd been scribbling on and read out what he'd written. 'Henry Cookson. Piers Holland. Charlotte Lachlan-Young. Lara Petrova. Esme Dawson.' It sounded like some sort of perverted register – a roll call of guilt. The Abbot waved the list. 'The actions of these five, they were undoubtedly cruel, but were they *murderous*?' He looked at Nel. 'Let's start with you, Miss Ashton.'

'Well,' Nel began, 'on the first day, the huntin' day, it was Henry who gave me his jacket, and set the hounds loose. The others . . . well, they didn't really do anything, until they sort of helped to look for me.'

'They helped to look for you?'

Nel squirmed a bit. 'Yes, but they *enjoyed* it, if you see what I mean. It was part of the hunt.'

'And you, Mr Jadeja?'

Shafeen, too, shifted uncomfortably. 'Well, on the shootin' day, it wasn't any of them that shot me. It was Henry.'

'Did they attempt to assist you once you'd been injured?'

'Yes,' said Shafeen in a small voice. 'They offered to help me back to the house.'

'I see,' said the Abbot gently. 'And what about you, Miss MacDonald?'

I thought about it. 'They didn't actually *do* anything. But that was exactly it – they didn't lift a finger to help me out of the water. But they didn't put me in there either; that was Henry.' I was beginning to understand – it would be my word against all of theirs.

The Abbot shook his head. 'From what you say, it sounds as though it would be hard to make a convincing case against them. At best they were accessories to attempted murder, but proving such a charge would be difficult, particularly if they all decide to tell the same story. All the same, I would be remiss in my duty not to advise you to go to the police, and to assure you that if you do so, you will have the full support of the school.'

I thought of the bother – questions, hassle, parents knowing, press knowing. The paparazzi were already at the gates – there would be a feeding frenzy. We looked at each other. I collected the expressions of the other two, and spoke for all of us. 'No. No police.'

'Very well,' said the Abbot. 'Here is my contention, for what it is worth, but I will be guided of course by you. Henry was undoubtedly guilty, but Henry is dead, and by his own hand. The Friars, it seems, are guilty too, but I do not know enough of the law to tell you with any certainty if they can still be prosecuted for crimes that took place almost fifty years ago, especially if you would rather not show this film to the police. In any case they can and will be dismissed – that is something I can do immediately *without* recourse to the law.' He patted the black morocco cover of the game book and his wedding ring gave a faint clunk. 'With your permission I will keep this game book in my possession, in order to show the Friars the evidence that exists against them and ensure that they leave quietly. I will replace them with the brightest and best teachers from the public sector. No ex-STAGS pupils will be considered for these posts.

'As for these young people –' he looked again at the list on his desk – 'I will speak to them, of course, and they will be stripped of their prefect status. They will be informed that evidence exists against Henry, with the assurance that we will pass it to the police if there are any further misdemeanours of this kind. I suggest, though, that instead of ruining five young lives – and condemning their characters as wholly evil when they may now improve without the malign influence of their ringleader – we let them complete the year and take their exams. I am afraid expulsion, considering their privileged backgrounds, would only harden their cruel tendencies, but a shock, and an opportunity to alter themselves, may well bear fruit.'

I saw the sense in this. Without Henry to impress, it was just possible that the Medievals *might* become halfway decent human beings.

'I cannot comment further on the alleged murders to which Henry alluded. I can only say that in both *known* cases of this deplorable practice – 1969 and this year – the ringleaders were de Warlencourts; and the entire sport – if so it may be called – was instituted by Conrad de Warlencourt on his return from the Crusades. Henry de Warlencourt is gone, and once the head of an organisation is removed, that organisation generally falls into chaos. The Friars and these prefects – Medievals, as you call them – were only followers. A fish stinks from the head, and only if malign leadership continues can evil prevail.'

I thought of Henry Cookson, and his transformation into the new Henry, but I didn't protest. It was such a relief to have someone – OK, OK, a *grown-up* – taking charge of this awful responsibility, that I let the Abbot continue.

'So, in an attempt to change the world order (if you will forgive the phrase) for the better, I hereby appoint you all the new prefects of St Aidan the Great School. Congratulations.'

He leaned across his desk and shook each of our hands in turn.

All thoughts of Cookson dropped out of my head. I couldn't quite believe it. Me, Greer MacDonald from Arkwright Road, a Medieval! I glanced at the other two and saw my own feeling reflected in their faces. They were pink with pleasure.

Then Shafeen said, respectfully, 'May I say something?'

The Abbot spread his hands benevolently. 'Certainly, Mr Jadeja. This school is now our joint concern.'

'If that's so,' said Shafeen hesitantly, 'I think you . . . *we* . . . should introduce a new admissions policy. I think we should admit more children of colour –'

'And more kids that aren't from aristocratic backgrounds,' Nel put in. 'Old money *and* new money –'

'And *no* money,' I added. 'We should offer more scholarships to state-school kids. One a year doesn't really cut it.' I had a flash of inspiration. 'We could call them the de Warlencourt Scholarships, in memory of Henry de Warlencourt.' It pleased me that clever kids from state schools would have access to STAGS and all its fantastic facilities because of Henry. 'He would hate it.'

Now, for the first time in the interview, the Santa Claus twinkle returned to the Abbot's eyes. 'He would indeed. But it seems to me a fine way to salvage some good from this tragic business.' He stood and smoothed his habit over his chest. 'If you trust me, we can transform STAGS into the school it can be. It will take some time, but as our motto says, *Festina Lente*. Will you help me?'

We looked at each other again, and started to smile.

Nel went to lock the Saros 7S away in her room, and I walked Shafeen back to Honorius. The moon was rising over Paulinus quad and I stopped by the well to see if I could see the moon in there. I still couldn't see the surface of the water. 'How deep is this thing?' I said.

Shafeen joined me, our heads close together, and we both looked down; down and down where I'd once thrown a coin and didn't hear it hit the water. Just as Henry had fallen and we didn't hear him land. Then I looked up, at the moon and the stars in the clear sky. Now, at last, I felt like I could say what I'd wanted to say to Shafeen for weeks.

'I'm sorry.'

'For what?'

'This could all have been stopped sooner. If I'd seen what was going on. If I'd not let Henry fool me. That very first night, when they all jumped on Nel's accent, I could see Henry enjoying it. No, it goes back further than that. In history, when they were picking on you. But I just didn't want to see it. And then, after Nel got hunted, he took me up to the top of the house. We went through this kind of door from the long gallery onto the roof, and he showed me his world.'

'Greer,' he said gently, 'you don't have to –'

'I'm trying to explain something to you,' I said desperately. 'The next day I couldn't find the door again. I couldn't tell you then, but I understand it now. I think I always believed Nel, deep down. But I was afraid that if I *said* I believed her, and I made a fuss, I'd never be able to get back into Narnia again.'

Shafeen was silent, looking at me.

I gave a half-shrug. 'It sounds so stupid.'

'No,' he said softly.

'I was obsessed with their world.'

He leaned against the edge of the well. 'Since we're admitting things, I was wrong too. I thought Henry was trying to hold back a world that was approaching. He wasn't. He was trying to bring back a world that was already gone.'

I put my hand on the cold stone. 'Well, if we're being fair, their world *did* have some good things about it.'

'Of course,' he said. 'And that's their great advantage. You weren't the only one who was seduced.'

I looked at him questioningly.

'My dad . . . me . . .'

'You?' I was surprised.

'Oh yes.'

I thought for a moment. 'I suppose, in an ideal world, you'd keep the best of the old stuff and adopt the best of the new. But can it be done?'

'Let's see.' He turned to face me. 'We've got a year left at STAGS after this one. *Festina Lente.*' He smiled his rare smile. 'Make haste slowly.'

And he put his hands in my hair and kissed me.

Epilogue – One Year Later

On the last day before Michaelmas half-term Shafeen, Nel and I had arranged where we would meet, so we could go to Justitium Mass together.

Paulinus quad was bathed in October sunshine and striped with long shadows. I was the first one there, so, shoving the ghosts of last year's Medievals aside, I went to lean on the well, where I'd first kissed Shafeen.

It had been a weird year at STAGS, watching the Friars all retiring, one by one, and the power of the Medievals ebbing away. The Abbot had been as good as his word. The new teachers, all whip-smart and highly dedicated, only cared about their subjects and their pupils and didn't give a crap about the jumped-up status of a bunch of over-privileged kids. I didn't know what the Abbot had said to them, but Cookson, Piers, Charlotte, Esme and Lara had all become good as gold and decided that there was nothing to be done but to knuckle down and concentrate on their exams. They'd all got their A*s in their A levels, despite the small detail of the death of their dearest friend. I pictured them now; all starting their new year at Oxford and Cambridge and Durham and Sandhurst, ancient foundation that weren't too different from Daddy's house.

The Friars had all gone by Christmas. For appearances' sake there was a big farewell assembly where they were all presented with these gold clocks engraved with the words '*Festina Lente*'. The whole school sang them that bizarre song about being Jolly Good Fellows. Shafeen, Nel and I were the only ones who didn't sing.

At Christmas Nel's dad, a cheerful northerner in a sharp suit and lots of jewellery, had come to pick Nel up in a gold Rolls, and had given me and Shafeen the brand-new Saros 8, for being good friends to his daughter. The phone was amazing: rose gold and as thin as a piece of card. But I'd put the lid back on the box. As Medievals, we'd relaxed the unwritten rules about the use of phones and screens, but I didn't forget Henry, who'd had so much distaste for the modern world that he couldn't live in it. I decided that sometimes I would leave the phone in my drawer: there was more fun to be had In Real Life.

I was thinking, of course, of Shafeen.

Reader, I'd started going out with him.

I'd met his dad too, over the summer, when I'd been to stay in Rajasthan, at the house in the Aravalli mountains above the hill station at Guru Shikhar. At first I couldn't quite reconcile Prince Aadhish Bharmal Kachwaha Jadeja, this distinguished white-haired Indian gentleman, with the terrified misfit teen I'd felt so deeply for in the Longcross library. But I tried my best with him. I was really hoping Aadhish would like me – not just because I'd risked my life for the boy he once was, but also because of what had happened between me and Shafeen.

It was OK though; it turned out that Aadhish *did* like me. He'd been really smiley and sort of courtly, and my stay in his palace had been amazing.

A whole summer with Shafeen, him in a white shirt, me in a floaty dress, wandering through the palace gardens with the white peacocks and the fountains and the tigers, looking like Jasmine and Aladdin in, well, *Aladdin*.

And now we were at the top of the school, a very different school to the one we'd enrolled in.

The Abbot had kept all the good things, like the traditions of the ancient foundation of St Aidan the Great, while doing away with all the bad ones, like running a murderous child-killing cult.

I hadn't been waiting long at the Paulinus well when I saw Shafeen and Nel crossing the quad, from different directions. You could see their stockings a mile off – now we were Medievals, we didn't have to wear the regulation red. I'd found silver ones dotted with little black-and-white film clapperboards. Nel had defiantly chosen shocking-pink Chanel stockings with the little double Cs of the logo picked out in gold. Shafeen had chosen tiger stripes, and I smiled whenever I saw them, remembering that he was the tiger's son.

We stood there, the three of us, breathing in the autumn air, the holiday weekend stretching ahead. Justitium began that evening, and we knew that, for the first time in hundreds of years, no one would be going to Longcross, or one of the other stately homes, to be hunted, shot and fished. All the kids would be going home to their parents, just as they should. I myself would be going home to Dad, to our new flat in Salford Quays, overlooking the BBC studios. It was right in the middle of a landscape of modern iron and glass. There would not be a hillside, a tree or a lake in sight.

The bell began to ring for Justitium Mass and students began to cross the quad in twos and threes towards the chapel. A figure waved at me, a new girl called Tyeesha. I knew her slightly as she was one of the first batch of the new de Warlencourt scholars the Abbot had started to admit to the school. I waved back automatically and Tyeesha started walking over. I couldn't help sighing. The three of us didn't need other company right now; things were so perfect. But I reminded myself that I couldn't exactly tell her to get lost. She was the only black girl in Lightfoot, and she'd been having it a bit tough at the beginning of term. I'd sort of taken her under my wing, hoping to be the friend *I'd* never had as a new girl. Blanking her now would make me no better than those blonde Medieval bitches. So instead I turned to her and gave her my best smile. 'Hi, Ty,' I said. 'How are things?'

'Great!' she said. I was a bit taken aback by her enthusiasm. '*Really* great,' she repeated.

'Oh yeah?' I said.

'Yeah,' she said in her strong London accent. 'I think I've turned a corner. Those kids that were bothering me – twins, they were – well, I think they like me now.' She looked like she was all lit up from the inside.

'Good,' I said. 'That's really good to hear.' I supposed it

would take a little time for the new scholarship kids to fully settle in to the school, but you had to give it to the Abbot, he had made a start. 'Going someplace nice for Justitium?'

'Oh *yes*,' she said, but she didn't volunteer any more information.

'Post some photos on Instagram,' I suggested.

She frowned a little. 'No,' she said. 'No – I don't think so. I think I'll send you a postcard instead.'

'Cool,' I said. 'Have fun.'

She smiled this huge, beaming smile. 'Thanks. I think I will.'

At that moment, the chapel bell started ringing double time as it always did for the five-minute warning. Tyeesha turned and hurried to catch up with the rest of the school as they filed into the chapel. I followed her, thoughtfully.

In the chapel everything had changed. Yet everything was the same. I thought about last year's Justitium Mass, the morning before I'd gone to Longcross. Last year on this day, the three of us had sat dotted around the chapel on our own. Now we were no longer lonely, even if the darkest of reasons had brought us together. We sat there, by some accident of fate, right under the same stained-glass window of St Aidan and the stag. The white deer stared me down throughout the service, just like Jeffrey had done.

Just like a year ago, we sat in our rows, in our black Tudor coats. The new Friars sat in their pews in their brown habits. Just like a year ago, the Abbot got to his feet in his black robes. For the hundredth time we were treated to the story of our founder, Aidan, and the stag. It was just like *Groundhog Day*. My mind wandered. I turned to look at the stained-glass window of the saint, but somehow my gaze never reached it. For just like a year ago, I found myself gazing at the back of a perfect blond head; the scroll of an ear, close-cropped hair glittering at the nape of a neck and disappearing into the black collar of a Tudor gown. My heart stopped.

It was Henry de Warlencourt.

Of course it wasn't him. I spoke to myself harshly: *Get a grip, Greer.* This kid wasn't Henry – yes, he looked like him from the back, but he was smaller, and he was sitting with the Six Ones, Tyeesha's year, the year below me. I moved my gaze to the girl next to him, my heart beginning to beat again. You might just as easily have said that she looked like Charlotte from the back. *You're seeing ghosts again*, I told myself. I gave myself a little shake, but I couldn't tear my gaze away. As if they could feel my gaze boring into the backs of their necks, the two blonds turned, and my blood turned to ice.

They had Henry's face.

Not just the boy, but the girl too.

They looked at me for a moment, with eerily similar stares. Then both of them gave me an identical, amused smile, just as Henry had done exactly a year ago.

Heart thumping again, I looked away, but the chapel, my friends, the Friars, all of them disappeared. I was far away at Longcross, and it was night. In the blue-white moonlight Henry and I were sliding down the Long Gallery in stockinged feet, the haughty de Warlencourt ancestors staring down from their portraits on the walls. And instead of the Abbot's voice reading the lesson, I heard Henry, calling down the gallery, *I used to do this with my cousins all the time. Twins, a boy and a girl, a bit younger than me. They'd go like lightning down here. It was so funny.*

Twins.

With Henry's face.

Could these twins be de Warlencourts?

I shifted on the pew, an uneasiness rising in my throat. I thought I was going to puke. Once again I had to calm myself down. Surely they couldn't be de Warlencourts – it would be too much of a coincidence. And if they were, it didn't mean they were the Devil's spawn like Henry was, even if they did look like something out of *The Shining*.

No, I told myself. STAGS was no longer a school where evil could flourish. *We* were Medievals now, all the Friars were great and I had to trust the Abbot. I raised my eyes to where he stood reading the lesson. He'd made all the changes he'd promised, even if the lesson he was reading was the same as ever. I watched as he pushed his glasses higher up his nose and read from *The Life of St Aidan* where it balanced on the eagle lectern. I determinedly didn't look at the freaky blond Henry-looky-likey twins. Instead I gave the Abbot my full attention, as he read the story of St Aidan's stag hiding in plain sight. His voice rang out, clear and true, and he didn't sound old any more. '*The blessed saint, when the hounds were running close, held up his hand to the stag and rendered him invisible. In such wise the hounds did pass him by, and their tooth did not touch him; whereupon Aidan restored the stag to the sight of men, and his pelt and antler could again be seen, and the stag did go upon his way in peace.*'

By the time he'd finished, my racing heart had slowed down

again, soothed by the familiar text. The Abbot reached out to close the volume and his hand rested for a moment on the leather cover of the book. At that moment, from above my head, the low winter sun hit the only bit of the window that was plain colourless glass – the panes that made up the invisible stag. A shaft of sunlight struck his flank and shone directly through onto a jewel on the Abbot's wedding finger, kindling it into fire. It was like that bit in *Raiders of the Lost Ark* when Indy finds the Well of Souls with a shaft of daylight. The jewel was a ruby, the colour of arterial blood, the colour of the stockings of the STAGS uniform. The ruby caught the rogue beam and shone like a lightsaber. The ring wasn't a plain wedding band after all. It had turned around on the Abbot's finger. It was a ring like the ones that popes wear, that kings wear. It was a ring that other people kiss, when they really want to kiss ass. It was a ring that meant you were the head of something. A religion. A kingdom.

A *cult*.

The organ thundered out and we stood for the final hymn. The shrill voices of the kids sang in my ears, and snippets of memory entered my head with the song.

St Aidan's stag was hiding in plain sight.

The Abbot didn't wear a signet ring, but he did wear a ring on his wedding finger.

We'd never seen a Mrs Abbot.

The game book had said: 'The Grand Master, Rollo de Warlencourt'.

Friar Skelton had said Hannibal didn't wage war with elephants. He waged war, with elephants.

Friar Skelton had said the placement of commas was crucial; they gave the same sentence two different meanings.

The Grand Master and Rollo de Warlencourt were two people, not one and the same.

I stared at the Abbot until my eyes watered, unable to quite believe what my crazed thoughts were telling me. Then I moved my blurring vision to the pews where Six One were sitting. And the cascade of revelation carried on.

There were new blond twins in Six One.

They were bootleg copies of Henry de Warlencourt.

Tyeesha had said twins had been bothering her, but they weren't any more.

Tyeesha was going somewhere nice for Justitium.

Henry's last words had been: 'The Order will go on, even without me.'

These fragments of bright nonsense gathered in my head, shard by coloured shard, to form a clear picture, like the stained glass of Aidan and the stag over my head. I could hardly wait for the final hymn to finish before I grabbed Shafeen and Nel by the arm, and, heart thumping, marched them out into the quad. It wasn't until I got to the Paulinus well, and there were four green lawns between us and any other living soul, that I told them. I told them that Henry de Warlencourt's last words had been absolutely, completely and one-hundred-per-cent true.

THE END?

Acknowledgements

I was always taught that it's polite to say thank you, so here goes.

Thanks to my son Conrad for translating teen-speak for me.

Thanks to my daughter Ruby for fascinating animal facts.

Thanks to my partner Sacha for his encyclopedic film knowledge.

Thanks to Conrad's friends Greer and Shafeen for lending me their names.

Thanks to ace cinematographer and all-round nice guy Nic Lawson.

Thanks to Teresa Chris, uber-agent and true friend.

Thanks to Emma Matthewson and Talya Baker at Bonnier for their eagle-eyed editing.

Thanks to Jeffrey, who started life as a deer ornament on our Christmas tree and ended up as a talking stag head on a wall.

If I'm thanking Christmas ornaments I really ought to stop.

I pillaged various huntin' shootin' and fishin' websites for information on sporting life. Any mistakes are mine, not theirs.

I referenced lots of films in this book, but the major influence was *The Shooting Party* (1985) directed by Alan Bridges, based on the novel by Isabel Colegate. If you're a Savage, watch the film. If you're a Medieval, why not read the book?

M. A. Bennett

M. A. Bennett is half Venetian and was born in Manchester, England, and raised in the Yorkshire Dales. She is a history graduate of Oxford University and the University of Venice, where she specialised in the study of Shakespeare's plays as a historical source. After university she studied art and has since worked as an illustrator, an actress and a film reviewer. She also designed tour visuals for rock bands, including U2 and the Rolling Stones. She was married on the Grand Canal in Venice and lives in north London with her husband, son, and daughter. Follow her at @MABennettAuthor on Twitter and at m.a.bennettauthor on Instagram.

Look out for . . .

SEVEN STUDENTS.

ONE PLANE CRASH.

NO RULES.

The ISLAND

M. A. BENNETT

Want to read
NEW BOOKS
before anyone else?

Like getting
FREE BOOKS?

Enjoy sharing your
OPINIONS?

Discover

READERS FIRST

Read. Love. Share.

Get your first free book just by signing up at
readersfirst.co.uk

HOT KEY BOOKS

Thank you for choosing a Hot Key book.

If you want to know more about our authors and what we publish, you can find us online.

You can start at our website

www.hotkeybooks.com

And you can also find us on:

We hope to see you soon!